THE ORPHAN'S
CORONATION

ROSIE DARLING

PROLOGUE

20th June 1837
Kensington Palace, London, England
A little after 5 am

"Find somebody then, man," the Archbishop of Canterbury barked in a most unholy manner.

"Yes, your grace," his coachman hurriedly said and scampered off.

They were waiting outside the gates of Kensington Palace, having ridden through the night, leaving Windsor Castle just before a quarter to three in the morning. Yet no one was here to grant them admittance.

"You would have thought they would be expecting a visit at any hour, given the circumstances?" the Lord Chamberlain, Francis Conyngham, said to the archbishop with a touch of frustration.

1

"Just another failing of that fool Conroy," William Howley, Archbishop of Canterbury, replied, shaking his head. "His Majesty, sorry, His late Majesty was right. We should be glad that we have avoided a Regency. Still, the palace will be swarming with people in a few hours. They will not have seen anything like it. The rider that was sent to the Prime Minister would undoubtedly have got to him before we got here. I would expect him to be present within the next hour or so."

Both men were dusty and thirsty after the long journey. But there was no time for a drink or a change of clothing. Their task could not wait.

"Lord Melbourne is indeed efficient," agreed Conyngham. "Messengers will be going to the privy council as we speak."

"If we wait here much longer, she will be the last to know."

"As soon as we are admitted, word will spread around the palace like wildfire," Conyngham said half under his breath. "You know how servants love to gossip. There can be no other reason for our presence at this ungodly hour."

The pair heard some hurried conversation from outside. It was the coachman chivvying someone along. "I have the Archbishop and the Lord Chamberlain inside. They have urgent business with the princess. Quicker if you will."

They heard a clinking of metal as the gates finally began to open. The carriage shook slightly as the coachman climbed back up to his seat. A few seconds later carriage moved forward into the grounds of the palace.

In less than two minutes, they were outside the front door, banging upon it with their silver-tipped canes.

"I've never known anything like it!" the archbishop shouted in exasperation. "Open up."

Finally, the door opened, and a footman sheepishly looked out. "Sirs?"

"Open the door, man. I am the Archbishop of Canterbury, I'm sure you recognise me. This is the Lord Chamberlain. We need to see the princess immediately." By this stage, the archbishop's face was as scarlet as the lining on his cape.

"Indeed. My apologies, your Grace," he stammered quickly in the direction of the archbishop. He opened the door wider, allowing them inside. "My Lord, my apologies," he nodded his head in the direction of the Lord Chamberlain. "Take a seat, I will be back shortly."

"Be swift, man," the Lord Chamberlain said softly. "We have urgent news."

The footman nodded his head as though he fully understood and quickly walked away.

The palace had been waiting for this visit for a

number of weeks. It was common knowledge that the king was seriously ill. Pneumonia had struck him, and he was already old and with a heart that pained him. However, for some reason, no one had been appointed to wait by the door in case news came in the early hours.

After a few minutes, Sir John Conroy, the duchess of Kent's comptroller and the man who all but ran Kensington Palace appeared, smoothing down his black suit as though he had just got dressed.

As soon as he saw him, the archbishop sighed. "I trust Lord Melbourne will advise her against this man," he whispered to his companion.

"Undoubtedly."

The visitors both rose as Conroy approached them.

"Sir John, we need an audience with the princess immediately, sir," the archbishop demanded.

It took all his effort to say the word 'princess'. Strictly speaking, it wasn't true and hadn't been for four hours.

But, despite the fact that the archbishop knew perfectly well that Conroy and the rest of the staff understood the reason for his and the Chamberlain's visit, he didn't want to spell it out in such blatant terms.

Princess Alexandrina Victoria deserved to be the first to hear the actual words.

"I understand, your Grace," Conroy said, immediately summoning a maid with a click of his fingers and a shout.

All around them, the palace was beginning to come to life. Butlers, footmen, and maids all appeared, scurrying about and preparing for the day. The word was spreading quickly that important visitors had arrived. They would not be the last of the day.

The maid to whom Conroy had spoken virtually ran upstairs.

Five minutes later, a regal but nervous-looking woman appeared. The Duchess of Kent; the princess's mother.

She spoke in hushed tones with John Conroy at the bottom of the stairs before approaching the two gentlemen.

They both bowed, "Good Morning, Your Highness."

"Your grace. Your Lordship. If you follow me, I will go and wake my daughter," she said in her heavily accented Germanic voice.

"Thank you, Your Highness," the archbishop replied with another small bow.

The Duchess of Kent was pretty much despised in royal circles. She had become enchanted with John Conroy after the death of her husband, the king's younger brother. Everyone knew that the pair sought to control the young princess.

With the Princess now just three weeks past her eighteenth birthday, the provisions that had been made for a Regency were no longer valid. His late Majesty, William IV would be most pleased. He in particular despised the duchess. Now his niece had come of age, she would be able to rule alone without hindrance or interference from her mother. At least, that was the hope.

The duchess led the archbishop and Lord Chamberlain up the grand staircase and through the dimly lit corridors of Kensington Palace.

"Please wait here, gentlemen," the duchess said with a wave of the hand. The men stopped walking and the duchess continued through a set of double doors, leaving them in the sitting room.

She continued through the maid's room and into the huge bedroom. She had insisted that her daughter sleep in the same bedroom as her, even though she had reached the age of eighteen. The princess had tolerated it only because she, like everyone else, knew that it couldn't possibly be for much longer.

The duchess walked quickly over to the little bed on her own and looked down at her daughter. She paused for a second, not wishing to wake her. It was such a burden for one so young. Why not let her sleep in ignorance for a little while longer? But mostly it was out of selfishness. The Duchess had a feeling that her and John's plans would come to nothing. Her daughter was headstrong like her dead husband, and she would soon have others the likes of Melbourne and Peel pouring advice into her head.

She lingered a moment longer and then bent down and kissed her daughter on her cheek.

The princess's eyes slowly began to open.

"The archbishop and Lord Chamberlain are here, mein Liebling," the duchess said softy.

There was just a second of hesitation in the eyes of the young woman and then she arose quickly from the bed and draped herself in a white dressing gown. She quickly checked her appearance in the mirror and ran a brush through her hair.

"Do you wish for me to accompany..." the duchess began.

"No, thank you, Mother," she interrupted. She knew that now was the moment to gain control of her life. There could be no better time. She gathered herself, offered her mother a slight smile and left the bedroom. She paused for just a moment in the maid's room, took a final deep breath and then entered her sitting room.

The early morning light was flooding in through the pair of huge windows that overlooked the palace gardens. The sunlight danced on the candle stick that was still on the piano in the corner of the room from the previous evening. The book she was currently reading, written by Sir Walter Scott, was left on the chair by the piano. Last night she had stayed up to read it while her maids took down her hair.

In the middle of the room, the two visitors were on their knees, awaiting their audience.

They didn't rise when she entered, instead, she approached them.

"Your Majesty," the Lord Chamberlain said, breaking the silence. With that greeting, everything she already knew was officially confirmed.

She was Queen.

"Your Majesty, we regret to inform you that your uncle, the king, breathed his last at 12 minutes past two this morning," the archbishop added. "As a consequence, you are now Queen."

"I thank you for travelling to bring me this grievous news," the Queen said in a pained voice. She had adored her uncle who she knew perfectly well had done his very best to protect her from her mother and Conroy.

She held out her hand and Archbishop and Lord Chamberlain both kissed it in turn. Conyngham handed her a folded sheet of paper. "The King's death certificate, Ma'am."

She simply nodded and turned to the archbishop. "I ask your Grace to pray for me."

"I shall, Ma'am," replied the archbishop, amazed at her maturity.

And with that, she turned and walked back to the maid's room.

The next few hours passed quickly for the new queen. She was dressed in a black mourning dress that had already been selected in anticipation of this moment. She wrote letters to her sister, her Uncle Leopold and her now-widowed aunt, Queen Adelaide. She then took breakfast alone.

She also sent instructions that her mother was to be moved from her chambers.

The news was now known to all of those in the palace and it was starting to spread across London. Proclamations were being prepared to be sent to Scotland, Wales, and Ireland.

The queen spent most of the rest of the morning huddled with her Prime Minster, Lord Melbourne. Melbourne explained the process for the rest of the day. She tried her best to recall everything. He assured her that he would respond to the occasion.

At a little before eleven-thirty, she walked alone down a flight of stairs to the Red Saloon. It was a steep flight and she smiled as she did so as it was the first time she had ever walked down them without holding the hand of a guardian. It had been one of Conroy's set of rules that he said were designed to ensure nothing tragic occurred. She believed they were nothing more than a means to control her.

She walked into the Red Saloon. She was a slight, small woman, standing little more than five feet. Those present, some two hundred, would say that she looked little more than fifteen years old on that morning.

The first eye she caught as she entered was that of the Duke of Wellington, then she saw Sir Robert Peel and Lord Palmerston. The room was full as far as the eye could see of the most important and imposing men in the land.

Some in attendance were waiting for the young queen to falter. But she was determined that she would not.

She took her seat on the throne and spoke in a clear, loud voice, "I ascend the throne with a deep sense of the responsibility which is imposed upon me; but I am supported by the consciousness of my own right intentions, and by my dependence upon the protection of Almighty God. It will be my care to strengthen our institutions, civil and ecclesiastical, by discreet improvement, wherever improvement is required, and to do all in my power to compose and allay animosity and discord. Acting upon the constitutional principles by which I have been educated, I shall on all occasions reserve my confidence for ministers possessed of the affection of the people and the esteem of the Houses of Parliament. It will be my care to promote the happiness, to maintain the just rights, and to advance the influence and honour of my kingdom."

There were loud murmurings of contentment and admiration among those present. "She doesn't just fill the chair, but the whole room," Wellington whispered to Sir Robert Peel who was standing next to him.

Her final act at the council was to take up the pen and sign her name.

Her heart pounded in her chest. She dipped the pen into the inkwell and wrote on the parchment. She formed each of the letters carefully with a steady hand. When it was done, she sat back and looked around the room with a strong and unwavering stare.

In a pen stroke, she had dropped the name Alexandrina and simply wrote Victoria.

The King was dead. Long live the Queen.

CHAPTER 1

ighteen Years Earlier
1819, Southwark.

"C OME ON," he hissed through his rotting front teeth.
He stopped, turned, and gave her a glare.

She hurried the best she could. The glare he had given her would usually have made her shiver but the wind from the river to her right was already doing that. Despite it being June, it was cutting through her like a knife. She guessed that even the June winds were cold before dawn. She held the tiny bundle in her hands closer to her chest.

He turned and continued walking. She followed, taking care not to slip and fall on the muddied cobbles underfoot.

She sensed the bulk of the Tower of London over on the far bank of the river. Its grey, imposing bulk cast a watchful eye over thousands of years of history. Terrible things had happened in that place. And terrible things were about to happen yet.

She had no desire to do what they were about to do but her father had given her no choice.

"I'm paying to feed you both," he spat viciously. "Either the child goes or you both go."

Cat decided that they would both go. If she had said the child, her father would have snatched it from her arms and brought it to the riverbank. She couldn't even begin to think about what he would do next. But she knew. That's why they both had to go; she couldn't let that happen. At least this way they would be together. They would both stand a chance, despite the horrors she had heard about this place.

She didn't feel well. The birth had been long and difficult. Had it not been for the skilled hands of the midwife that her younger sister Matilda had begged to come and help, she knew that right now she and her child would be dead.

Exhaustion filled every part of her body and mind. She knew that dragging herself along the streets was the last thing she should be doing a matter of hours after bringing a child into the world.

Her father was disgusted when she finally built up the courage to tell him that she was pregnant. She was just fifteen years of age. But what did he expect? He had been whoring her out on the Southwark streets since she turned fourteen. When a ship came in from the Indies, she might see six sailors a day. It was a miracle she lasted this long.

He gave her a concoction to get rid of the child. It didn't work and secretly Cat was glad. She wanted something to love and adore in this world that she could truly call her own. A baby. A daughter.

Her mother was stolen from her when she was just four years old, giving birth to her youngest sister Elizabeth. Since then, she, her two sisters, and three brothers had been living under the care of their father.

Not that you could call it care.

Her father was a born villain and brought up all his children to be the same. Each of them could silently pluck a silk handkerchief from a gentleman's pocket just as easily as they could count the fingers on their hands.

Her brothers had graduated from pickpocketing into the horrors of body snatching. They would wait until midnight and then dig up a recently deceased corpse and take it to one of the physicians who would gladly pay a handsome price for the fresh meat. Within hours they would be cutting up the cadaver to learn how the human body worked.

How no one in their family had their necks stretched, Cat had no idea.

As they turned into Mint Street, her father dropped back to walk alongside her. "You remember what I told you to say," he said.

Cat just nodded, turning her head away from the stink of his breath.

"You hear me, girl. You bring 'em to my door, you'll regret it," he repeated, more insistent than before.

"Yes. I know."

Then they came to a stop. A tall, foreboding brick building loomed above them. The bricks were dark and discoloured, savaged by the smoke from the factories and kilns. The stink was nauseating. Decay and dampness hung heavy in the early morning air. The building had few windows and those that were there were tiny and the glass was dirty and stained, hinting at the darkness that lay inside. The heavy wooden door was studded with iron and gave no cheerful welcome. The place seemed to ooze misery and hopelessness.

It was a place where no one wanted to end up.

A wooden sign proudly written in white lettering was neatly nailed to the door.

Established In the Year of Our Lord 1729
The Parish of St George-The Martyr
Southwark

Surrey

WORKHOUSE

For receiving and employing all the poor of the Parish.

Underneath were listed all the rules and bylaws relating to the operation of the house.

Few among the poor of the Parish would have been able to read them. Cat and her father certainly couldn't.

"Remember!" her father said, coming up close to his daughter and waving his finger in her frightened face. He took two paces backwards and then hammered heavily on the door. He walked quickly back to Cat and looked her up and down. His eyes paused for a moment on his grandchild. "Good luck," he offered.

Cat simply stared back at him with an air of defiance about her.

He didn't wait. He turned and disappeared into the darkness of the alleyways and side passages. Cat would never see him again.

A few minutes passed and finally, a grill was pulled down in the door. A pair of black searching eyes stared out. "Yes?" the rough voice demanded.

"I request admission for me and my newborn daughter," Cat said, uncovering the little bundle in her arms for just a second to give the man inside the workhouse sight of her.

"You are too early," he spat back, making moves to flick the grill back up.

"Please, Sir, my daughter is but a few hours old. I fear she won't last without help," Cat said. Such was her condition that there was no need for her to make herself look and sound pitiful.

The man paused. "Husband?"

"I'm a widow, Sir. My husband was an army man. Fighting for good King George. Brought back something nasty from India with him. He died six months past."

The man behind the grill let out a low guttural moan as though contemplating her answer. "Wait." The grill slammed down.

Cat slumped against the door, a sudden weakness overcoming her. Despite the cold wind, she sensed that her forehead was covered in perspiration. She felt pain in her lower stomach. She didn't want to go through the door, but she knew that she had no option. Not if she wanted her daughter to live.

None of her siblings had stood up for her that morning. Elizabeth was still asleep, but the others had watched their father push her and the child out of the door. She couldn't blame them. No one crossed their father. Her brothers had all been the victim of his fists at one time or another. They had seen what he could do to a fully grown sailor with just his fists. They would never argue with him no matter what terrible course of action he took.

A smaller door within the huge studded one opened. It was barely wide enough for a man to slip through. A tall thin woman with a beak-like nose stood sneering down at her. She was dressed in black from head to foot as though someone had died.

"You have nowhere else to go?" she demanded of Cat in a manner that suggested she already didn't believe the answer she would be given.

"No, Madam," Cat offered in return. "I need refuge for myself and my newborn daughter." Again she revealed the baby wrapped in its dirty shawl.

The woman nodded her head. "Come."

She disappeared inside the doorway and Cat summoned the courage to follow.

The inside of the workhouse was even bleaker than the exterior if that could be possible. The once-white paint flaked on the walls, and the smell of dampness was even more pronounced. Cat guessed it was because of the proximity to the river. Nothing escaped its force.

There was a little light; the thin woman with the beaklike nose held a small oil lamp in front of her as she walked away along the corridor. Cat struggled to keep up and her breathing became laboured.

Finally, the woman stopped and turned into a room on the right-hand side of the corridor.

She took a seat behind a simple, plain wooden desk and place the oil lamp upon it. Cat stood in front of the desk, having not been offered a seat.

"I am the matron, Mrs Bird," the woman said. "You will call me Matron or Ma'am at all times. Understand?"

With her beak-like nose, Cat couldn't help to think that her name was appropriate. "Yes, Matron. I understand."

"The Master will need to formally check you in after he has breakfasted and attended Chapel. Let me just take some basic details. Your name?" She pulled what seemed like a scrap piece of parchment in front of her. She carefully dipped a pen into the ink pot and eyed Cat suspiciously.

"Catherine Monday, Matron."

Cat had decided to keep things simple and retain her first name and then make up the second. She was mindful of the warning her father had given her. The last thing she wanted was for the overseers of the Workhouse to take her home to him.

The matron scratched the name down on her parchment. "Your age?"

"Eighteen, Matron."

The matron began to write the numerals down but then studied Cat. She took her in from head to toe. "Eighteen?" She half laughed as though it were preposterous. In truth, she had good reason. Cat did not look eighteen, she looked fifteen years and no older.

"Yes, Matron," she replied as she pulled herself up to her full height. She knew perfectly well from her time stealing on the streets of London for her father, once a lie had been told there was no way you could possibly go back. You simply had to ride with it and display confidence.

Matron narrowed her eyes in doubt and then wrote down the number. "The gatekeeper tells me you're a widow?"

"Yes. My beloved Martin died six months past. He was a soldier over in India. He brought some disease back with him. He would break into fevers and have such sweats, you have never seen anything like it. He'd talk of strange things. He would then recover and remember nothing of it. It got worse and worse. Until finally he just burnt up and I couldn't keep him cool."

It was something Cat had heard the sailors who had returned from the tropical climate of India gossip about in the taverns. People bought back all manner of strange diseases not seen before on the shores of England. Some survived. Many did not.

"And the child? How old is she?"

"What is the time now, Matron?"

Mrs Bird pulled out a small pocket watch and studied it over the end of her nose. "A quarter to five in the morning." She gave out a noise that suggested no one should have any business here at this ungodly hour.

"I recall hearing the clock of the church strike midnight just after she was born."

"So less than five hours. Has she fed?"

"I was unable to do so. She wouldn't take to the breast," Cat whispered, never feeling more like a failure in this world.

"You must continue to persevere. In the meantime, we will ensure she has milk."

"Thank you," Cat said as gratefully as possible.

"Her name?" Matron asked, her pen hovering over the parchment once again.

Cat hadn't given the matter any consideration. Unlike many young women, she hadn't spent hours deciding the names of all the children she would have. But one name entered her mind as she was asked the question. "Jane. Her name is Jane."

That had been her mother's name. It seemed a fitting choice.

"Where was the child born?" the matron asked.

"In the graveyard of the church," Cat lied smoothly. She had heard about such things happening in the past and it seemed as good a place as any.

"You have no home?"

"No. Not currently."

"And where did you live before then?"

"I was in the rookeries. I couldn't work the last month of my pregnancy; the pain was too much. So I had no money for the rent. Landlord threw me out. I thought I could cope. But…"

The Matron seemed satisfied with the answer because she rose from behind her desk. "The Master will likely ask you these questions again for the register. But for now, follow me."

They walked another thirty or so yards up the corridor. There were some large windows at the far end of the corridor and light was flooding in.

This time, the matron turned into a room on her left-hand side. It was covered from floor to roof with six-inch square white porcelain titles. Two tin baths stood in the middle. One had three inches of water in it. On the far wall, four plain white chairs were lined up along the length of the room. On one of them was a pile of garments, neatly folded. The whole place had a strange smell which Cat recognised but couldn't quite place.

Another woman was waiting there. Although dressed the same, she was considerably younger than Mrs Bird. She was far heavier set and had a bright red face that suggested she might like a glass or two of gin.

"Give Martha the child," the matron demanded.

Cat shrank back towards the corridor, clutching

her baby tighter to her chest. She couldn't help but glance at the tin bath with the small amount of water in the bottom. "Why?"

"Remember what I said back there, Mrs Monday? You will call me Matron or Ma'am at all times." The matron blew out heavily in frustration.

"Sorry, Matron. But I don't want to give up my baby," Cat objected.

"You aren't giving her up, Catherine," Matron responded slowly. "Martha here is going to bathe and feed your baby. You will be reunited after you have seen the Master."

Cat was still hesitant and glanced nervously at the matron.

"I promise," the matron said, softening her tone.

Reluctantly, Catherine did as she was bid. Martha simply nodded her head and walked out the door. It took all of Cat's strength not to chase after her and rip the child back.

The matron nodded her own approval. "Strip. Place your garments in the corner."

Cat looked back at her, horrified.

"You must bathe yourself. I shall cut your hair and then you will dress in the workhouse uniform. Your own clothing will be returned to you when you leave this establishment."

Cat couldn't believe how degrading this was going to be. Still, she stood.

"Strip," the Matron commanded again.

Slowly Cat started to obey, removing filth cover layer after filth cover layer. Her undergarments were the worst as she hadn't washed since the birth. Shame cut through her as she undressed under Mrs Bird's watchful glare.

"Good," Matron said when she finally stood naked on the cold tiles. "There is a bar of soap there." She pointed her thin finger to the side of the bath. "Wash your body and hair. I shall return in five minutes."

She turned and left leaving the door wide open.

Cat breathed a sigh of relief that at least she wouldn't be forced to go through the humiliation of being watched while she bathed.

She picked up the small brown bar of soap. She sniffed it. It was the same pungent smell as in the room. Cat knew it was carbolic soap, used for the prevention of spreading diseases. As she scrubbed, it was harsh on her skin, and it released more of its foul smell.

After a minute of scrubbing, she came over weak. She dropped the soap into the water and began to cry.

CHAPTER 2

our hours later, Cat was sitting outside the master's office on a hard wooden chair, waiting to be summoned inside.

She felt terrible. Her brow was covered in sweat, and she knew she was starting a fever.

The matron returned, as she had said she would, within five minutes with a large pair of blunt scissors, and she hacked at Cat's hair unceremoniously almost down to the very roots.

When she was done, she ordered Cat to put on the scratchy workhouse uniform.

The dress was shapeless and dark brown in colour. A thin white apron went over the top, which Matron tied so tight that Cat struggled to breathe. She was told that she would get used to it. A black shawl went over her shoulders. Cat was gland it was

June as the shawl was so thin she doubted it would offer much warmth and comfort. Finally, a simple white bonnet covered what remained of her hair.

She was now one of many. Stripped of her own identity. Cat would now conform to the rules.

She did however take some comfort in the fact that at least the uniform was clean.

Keeping clean had always been a difficulty for the poor. Cat and her sisters would attempt to wash their clothes, but clean water and soap were not that easy to find. Many would simply wash their items in the waters of the Thames. But Cat refused to allow her sisters to do that. She had seen what went into the river. She would rather their clothing remain dirty.

Cat was told she would have been made to sit outside the master's office until he was ready to formally admit her to the Workhouse but in light of the fact that she had just given birth, she was taken to a small bare room and given a piece of hard bread with the tiniest piece of cheese. She ate it ravenously.

Her labour had been long and arduous, lasting for the best part of two days. She hadn't eaten at all during it. The meal the previous night had just been a thin, watery vegetable stew with a small stale loaf to share amongst her siblings.

That was the standard fare at home, at least for the children. Her father would take most of the money and dine and drink in taverns at night. He didn't believe in feeding his children; they just needed enough food to keep them alive so that they could go out on the streets and thieve for him. At least, that was his belief.

Cat was briefly reunited with baby Jane. Jane had been cleaned and was wrapped in white swaddling clothes. Once again, she attempted to breastfeed and this time there was a little more success. It gave her a little hope.

Cat had to accept that she and the child had a better chance here within the workhouse.

When the time came to see the master, Martha again took the baby, reassuring Cat that they would be reunited once the formal admission process had been completed.

Cat reached up and wiped the sweat from her forehead. She knew that this fever wasn't a good sign. She prayed that it wasn't childbed fever. She knew that if that came, her survival would be in the hands of God.

She sat silently, unmoving until finally a voice boomed out from within the master's office, "Come."

She stood a little too quickly. She felt a moment of dizziness overcome her, and for a second, she thought she might faint. But she regained her composure. She knocked loudly on the door, and an exasperated "Come!" followed from inside.

She opened the door and entered the master's

office. As she walked, she felt the hard black shoes on her feet pinch her toes. She hoped that over time they would stretch and become more comfortable.

The master's office was lavishly furnished, the first room she had seen like it in the workhouse. Up until this point, everything had been sparse with just the very minimum in each room to ensure its functionality.

The master's office was a different story altogether. A huge black fireplace dominated the room, surrounded by titles with painted flowers upon them. Fortunately, as it was June, the fire wasn't lit. With her fever raging, she was glad of it.

A thick carpet lay on the floor in reds, yellows, and blues all dancing in a pattern that pleased the eye. The walls were painted a brilliant white, and there were various portraits hung upon them. She recognised King George back when he was a handsome young man. Not the old mad fool people said he had now become. The king hung over the master's desk as though watching everything he did. Then various smaller ones of unknown dignitaries clearly had some connection to the workhouse.

On one side of the room was a brilliantly polished brown dining table with six chairs around it. It was at this dining table that the master would eat the majority of his meals. Sometimes alone, other times with other overseers of the workhouse.

Then there was a huge oak partner's desk with a blue leather blotter, although there were no partners, it was only the master who used it.

He sat behind the desk now, a huge man with uncontrollable brilliant white hair and a matching moustache and beard. He was so fat he could barely fit in the chair behind the desk. The buttons on his jacket fought under the strain of his belly.

"You were admitted early by Matron, I understand?" the master boomed.

"Yes," Cat replied as confidently as possible.

"I'm told you are eighteen years old and a widow and that you've just given birth?" He studied the scrap sheet of parchment from the matron in front of him. "A girl, I understand?"

"Yes, sir."

The master studied Cat closely. She prepared herself to lie once more about her age, but the master didn't bother questioning her. Instead, he just led her through the same series of questions that the matron had asked earlier in the day. He carefully recorded her responses in a huge black ledger.

Finally, he asked her to sign the ledger.

"I can't write, sir," Cat said with a touch of embarrassment.

"I did not expect it," the master said. "Just make your mark."

He pushed the ledger towards her. She moved

31

forward, picked up the pen, and scratched a huge X where the Master pointed at the end of the ledger next to her name and that of her daughter.

"The rules must be obeyed at all times," the Master said in a slightly softer tone. Somehow the quietness of his voice made it sound sinister. "Otherwise, punishments will be doled out. They will be severe."

"I understand, sir," Cat said.

"Go," the Master said with a final nod of his head as a dismissal.

"Thank you, sir," Cat said, turned, and exited the office. The matron was waiting for her outside.

Once again, that feeling of faintness came over her and she staggered slightly.

"Hold yourself up, woman," the matron said sternly.

Cat gulped down the air and steadied herself. She didn't want to transgress the rules within minutes of her formal admission.

"You will be placed with the women with young children for now. You will receive three meals a day and you will work when you're not caring for your child."

"Yes, matron," Cat agreed.

As she was led down the cold and dimly lit corridor, Cat couldn't help but wonder what her future would hold.

Unfortunately, it would hold little.

And what little there was, was filled with misery and pain.

By the end of the day, her stomach pained her constantly and her breathing grew rapid. By morning, she was almost drowning in sweat, and they took her away to the infirmary. She couldn't even remember the last time she saw her daughter, beautiful little Jane. She knew she had been in the little cot next to the bed. But she knew they had come to remove her when Matron decided that she was ill.

The physician grunted and groaned as he examined her.

"Childbed fever, I fear," he said to the matron, confirming Cat's worst fears.

"Where is my daughter?" Cat tried to say but no words came out.

"Hush, there," the physician said to Cat with a smile. "I shall give her quinine and a poultice on the swelling on the abdomen."

"I see," Mrs Bird said. She cocked her head to one side and raised her eyebrows. The physician saw her gesture and knew what she was asking. He simply shrugged his shoulders in response.

He had no idea as to her chances.

She might survive.

She might not.

The matron nodded and left.

Over the next few days, the physician did his best.

Unlike many of the staff here, he did not consider its inmates a burden. He tried everything he knew to save the young mother.

He purged the body with laxatives to remove any toxins that might be inside. Quinine had reduced the fever for a while, but it came back worse than before. She became delirious. She ranted about her father and his lies. Now quinine failed to work.

The physician resorted to bloodletting, although he was not convinced that the old-fashioned treatment did much good. By this stage, there was little more to try.

A small wooden bowl collected the drops of blood from Cat's arm. It dripped monotonously in a slow steady stream.

And as it did so, Cat's life drained away with it.

Jane Monday was less than a week old.

She was in the workhouse. A burden to society. An unwanted and unloved orphan.

What possible future could she have?

CHAPTER 3

9 *years later.*

In the first nine years of Jane Monday's life, two defining moments would shape her character and forge her spirit forever.

The first occurred just a matter of days after her birth.

Her mother died, leaving her an orphan. A fragile, helpless soul at the mercy of the stern overseers of the workhouse who cared little if she lived or died.

The second significant event occurred two days after her ninth birthday. Not that she knew it was her ninth birthday, of course; such celebrations were a luxury, unheard of in the workhouse. It was two days after this unmarked occasion that Kate Larkin was admitted into the dismal Southwark workhouse.

Kate Larkin was already ten years of age, her eyes

possessing a mischievous gleam that said she had a knowledge of the world that few her age held. It was obvious to all who laid eyes on her that she would develop and flourish into a captivating beauty.

She had been admitted to the workhouse along with her father. He had, for a time, been a successful businessman, and Kate had grown up surrounded by all the trappings of wealth. But in recent years, he had fallen on hard times. Drink slowly began to consume him, before he finally lost everything.

Left with nowhere else to turn for himself and his daughter, he swallowed his pride and brought them both to the workhouse, seeking shelter in the one place he had never imagined he would rely upon.

Kate Larkin was petrified.

She had heard all the terrible tales about South-wark Workhouse that circulated in the outside world. They were whispered in hushed tones among the desperate and the destitute. They were told by the drunks in the taverns and housewives in church. All those terrible tales were completely true, each one a testament to the harsh reality of life within those cold, damp walls.

In fact, the overseers helped to circulate the stories. It was a scheme that prevented people from attempting to gain admission unless they truly had no options. The tales of misery ensured It was only the truly desperate that came knocking at the huge, studded workhouse door.

Kate Larkin had been separated from her father immediately after signing the black ledger in the master's office, her elegant handwriting evidence of the education she had enjoyed in her early years while funds were plentiful and society embraced the Larkins.

She was then subjected to the same humiliating ritual as Jane's mother Cat had been subjected to nine years previously. Times had not changed in the workhouse; if anything, they had only grown crueller and more unforgiving.

When she was finally brought into the girls' dormitory, her heart was pounding with fear and her eyes were wide. The first person she saw was Jane Monday.

Jane saw Kate's frightened face and moved by compassion, walked over with a huge, welcoming smile that lit up her pale, tired features.

"Hello, my name is Jane. What's yours?" Jane asked quietly, her voice gentle and soothing, in a kind attempt to make the girl feel welcome and safe.

Kate stood and stared at her for a moment, her eyes darting around the room as she assessed her surroundings. Then, in a swift and unexpected move, she punched Jane squarely in the nose.

Jane's nose broke with a loud crack, and blood

spilt down the front of her once brilliant white apron, staining it a deep crimson.

There were tears.

But strangely, the tears didn't come from Jane. They came from Kate.

The other girls gathered around the scene, their eyes wide with excitement and curiosity, hoping to see a full-on fight. Mrs Bird, the matron, who had changed little in the last nine years apart from the deepening lines on her face and slightly laboured walk, hurried over to break up the commotion, her stern expression betraying her irritation.

"Jane Monday? What on earth is happening here?" she demanded, her voice sharp and accusatory.

Jane was just about to speak, her eyes still filled with shock and confusion when Kate interrupted her.

"That girl hit me, Matron. Pulled my hair, pinched me, and told me that I was good for nothing. She said I'd be better off killing myself," she continued, her fake tears flowing like a river.

Matron believed Kate Larkin's story in an instant. She was quite the little actress. Even though Jane Monday had never harmed a soul in her nine years in the workhouse or transgressed a single rule, Matron immediately took Kate Larkin's side, her expression hardening with every word Kate spoke.

"Come, to the master's office with you," she

grabbed Jane by the ear, her grip like a vice, and dragged her outside, ignoring all her protests.

She was marched before the master, her feet stumbling on the cold stone floor. It wasn't the same man who had admitted her mother all those years ago. Not that Jane would have known, of course. The previous master had died of a heart attack, his life snuffed out as he was patting his stomach after enjoying his fill of beef, blood, and gravy. They found him lifeless on the floor when they came to serve him ginger pudding and custard. His replacement looked no different, except perhaps his hair was not as white, there were still flecks of grey and black in his mane. However, his belly was certainly just as big, straining the buttons of his gold-coloured waistcoat.

A new king hung behind the desk, not that Jane would have remembered the old one. Jane studied it and thought that King George IV looked very similar indeed to the master.

Matron had explained what had happened. At least, Kate Larkin's version.

She hadn't been given a single opportunity to open her mouth in her own defence. Matron had ensured that, her iron grip never faltered as she told the pack of lies that she had been fed.

The master recorded his punishment in a blue ledger. Before issuing it, he told Jane that she was the wickedest girl that he had ever had the misfortune to cast his eyes upon. That hurt more than the unexpected blow from the new girl.

She would receive twelve strokes of the cane in front of the rest of the girls in the morning. It was a harsh and humiliating punishment designed to break the nature of the children that transgressed the workhouse rules. The usual punishment was eight strokes, but due to the nature of her attack, she would get four extra strokes.

She knew better than to speak when she didn't have permission. So instead of protesting about the unjustness of it all, she stood with her eyes cast to the floor.

And tonight, she would have no dinner. Hunger was always there, gnawing around the edges of her stomach. But tonight, it would consume her and she was told it was all her own fault.

Kate Larkin slept soundly in her bed that night, albeit with three others. A sly smile played on her lips as she drifted off. Jane Monday did not. Usually, she managed to ignore the elbows or knees of the other girls, but tonight she could not. Her stomach ached with emptiness, and she had a throbbing nose that still continued to bleed. Tomorrow, all she had to look forward to was twelve harsh strokes of the cane.

As expected, the blows administered by the matron the next morning were unyielding and merciless. Jane tried her best not to cry, but she knew from watching other girls receive the punishment over the years that very few managed to hold out. She did well, only finally sobbing on blow number seven, her tears hot and bitter as they traced lines down her cheeks.

The pain she could deal with. The tears she knew would dry. But all the while, there in her eye line, Kate Larkin stood and watched smugly, her eyes gleaming with cruel satisfaction.

All Jane had been trying to do was be welcoming, to extend a hand of friendship in a place where kindness was rare. Who was this horrible girl who had turned her world upside down? She had no idea, but she knew perfectly well that in the future, she would stay as far away from Kate Larkin as possible.

That proved to be impossible.

Kate Larkin went out of her way to make Jane's life as miserable as possible. For what reason, Jane had no idea.

Kate swiftly managed to turn the rest of the girls in the dormitory against the timid Jane.

Many of the girls had actually witnessed the chilling incident that had transpired when Kate first arrived that day. The memory of Kate's fierce and unprovoked punch haunted them, and they became willing to obey her every command in order to avoid her wrath.

Even Jane's former best friend in the girl's dormitory, Mary Spencer, found herself drawn into the newly formed, influential inner circle of the manipulative Kate Larkin. Together, they bullied everyone mercilessly, their taunts echoing through the corridors. But their cruelty was particularly aimed at Jane, who became their primary target.

If it hadn't been for Robin Buckley, Jane might have become insane.

Robin, with his tousled brown hair and bright blue eyes, was the same age as her. Although the strict rules of the workhouse kept them apart in boy and girl dormitories for meals and sleeping, they met each day during their school lessons and the minimal recreation they were grudgingly permitted.

Robin would lighten Jane's heart with his endearing antics. As they exercised in the bleak, stone-paved yard, he would perform comical impressions of the stern matron or the fat master, causing Jane to nearly double up with laughter, momentarily forgetting her troubles.

Robin, too, was an orphan. He had been admitted to the workhouse alongside his weary parents. Over subsequent harsh winters, both caught illnesses and eventually succumbed to their ailments. Now he was stuck here, just like Jane.

With a hopeful glint in his eyes, Robin assured Jane that there was a vast, vibrant world outside the imposing walls of the Southwark workhouse and that one day, they would both get to enjoy the freedom and beauty of life beyond.

But not all talk was so joyful. He explained that the world outside these walls was a very divided place.

Robin explained to Jane how so many people in the city of London lived in poverty. They did what they could to keep themselves out of places like this. For some, that meant turning to criminal ways. Robin said he didn't blame them. There was a lack of opportunity out there for many people.

He talked about the slums and the rookeries, places of despair.

Robin was hopeful, though. Having been raised in the workhouse meant something important. They'd had an education, something that many living in the London slums did not enjoy. They could read. They could write. The vast majority of people outside the workhouse walls could not.

That's why he was always full of hope.

He said that one day he would get a clerical job in a bank or a similar institution. He wouldn't live in the slums; he would live in one of the small, terraced houses where clerks and assistants always lived. He would have a beautiful wife and five happy, healthy children.

Jane laughed as Robin told her about his future. Jane could hardly see further than the end of the week. She knew nothing outside these walls and therefore could not dream anything up.

On some of his more flamboyant days, Robin would talk about the grand housing that existed in London, in which the wealthy lived. They were almost like palaces where the king would reside. Huge houses with white fronts and big iron gates at the front to keep out undesirables. These houses would have so many large windows that Robin would be unable to count them all. They would have servants: cooks, cleaners, maids, houseboys, and butlers attending to their every need. They were so rich, they wanted for nothing.

His dreams of a little terraced house with a beautiful wife and five children were just a stepping stone. One day, Robin dreamed that he would live in a grand house like that.

Jane struggled to imagine life outside the workhouse. After all, it was all she'd ever known. A strictly regimented existence with bland meals served at the same time each day and the same monotonous food served on each day of the week.

Jane's days were filled with repetitive chapel services, tedious school lessons, and bullying. No day would be complete without Kate and her friends doling out some form of abuse on her.

Except for Sundays. Sundays were by far the best

day of Jane's week. Something to actually look forward to.

After the morning chapel, the children were permitted to rest for the remainder of the day. It was, after all, written in the Bible, and Jane knew that the sacred words of the Bible must outrank the oppressive rules of the Southwark workhouse.

Jane and Robin would spend their cherished Sundays together, playing in the yard, or just talking quietly together. Robin worked for a few hours each day in addition to his school lessons. He had a job in the kitchens. A general dogsbody someone had called him. He might be taking the rubbish out one minute or peeling vegetables the next. He was good at work. And so, he also helped those preparing the food for the master and overseers.

It gave him opportunities.

Opportunities to steal.

Most weeks he would manage to snatch some form of delightful morsel. A slice of beef or mutton. A piece of gingerbread or treacle tart. He would always hide these and bring them to share in secret with Jane on a Sunday.

It was their special secret. The first time he pulled out a breast of chicken. But before he did so, he made Jane swear to never tell anyone. He told her that it was important to keep secrets. "Secrets are important," he said. "If someone trusts you with a secret, you must always keep it."

She agreed and promised with all her heart.

Jane never knew such delights could be found. She was used to her bland diet of porridge for breakfast. Meat and potatoes for lunch and dinner. What the meat was, she didn't know. But rumours went around the workhouse. She shivered just thinking about it. But she ate the food because she was always hungry.

One Sunday, Jane was in tears. She had had yet another disheartening encounter with the notorious Kate Larkin and her menacing gang of bullies. She didn't even want to enjoy the piece of Parkin cake he had managed to steal this week.

"You have to stand up to these people at some point," Robin said firmly, his eyes narrowed with determination as he looked at Jane. He knew the harm these horrible girls did to his friend.

"I can't," Jane replied, her voice shaking. "They have the entire dormitory on their side."

"They don't, Jane. The entire dormitory is just frightened of them, like a flock of sheep controlled by a snarling dog. If you put them in their place, they would soon change. At some point, we all have to stop being meek and stand up to those who are doing us wrong," Robin said thoughtfully, his gaze unwavering.

Jane stared back at him, her eyes wide with a mixture of fear and admiration. It seemed to her to be the wisest thing that anyone had ever said to her, but it also seemed dangerously foolhardy. How could she, a timid girl, stand up to those who were causing her so much harm? It might be one thing to take issue with Kate, but she couldn't possibly stand up to the stern matron or the master who sat behind his desk in his fine clothes.

"Stand up and fight," he said, nodding his head.

His words lingered in her mind, giving her something to think about. She played with those thoughts for a very long time.

Then, one bleak Monday morning, Robin simply wasn't there. She didn't see him in chapel. He wasn't in the school lessons. She couldn't see if he was at the meals as she wasn't allowed to turn her head.

Jane worried that he might be sick.

The same was true the next day. There was no sign of his bright smile in the chapel pews and again, he wasn't at lessons.

Jane finally summoned up the courage to ask Matron where he was. "Matron? Can I ask where Robin Buckley is? He hasn't been to class in two days. Is he sick?"

Mrs Bird looked at Jane with irritation. "The boy has been apprenticed, I believe."

It happened all the time. Orphan boys and girls

from the workhouse were apprenticed out to all manner of trades. Blacksmiths. Carpenters. Glovers. Undertakers. Dressmakers. There seemed to be no limit. They would pay the workhouse a small fee and then they would get a new apprentice.

The idea was that the young orphan be taught the trade. In practice, the apprentice was nothing more than free labour. They would be paid nothing, just given a bed and a half-empty plate at mealtimes. The workhouse overseers did not care as it was one less burden on them.

"Where at, Matron?" Jane asked, trying her best to stop her bottom lip from quivering.

"Well, I truly don't think that is any of your business, is it, Jane Monday?" Mrs Bird said in a dismissive tone. "He is gone and that is all you need to know, girl." She turned and marched away.

In short, she would never see him again.

Her only light in the darkness had gone.

That night Jane cried herself to sleep. She doubted her tears would ever stop.

CHAPTER 4

ne year later

*O*ne year later
The next twelve months were pure hell for Jane Monday.

Her only friend was gone. Now she didn't even have Sundays to look forward to.

She just lived day-to-day, praying that one day she too would be apprenticed so she could escape the misery of her life inside the workhouse. She hung onto the hope that there was a vast, vibrant world outside the tall walls, just as Robin had told her.

Each day, she tried her best to keep out of the way of Kate Larkin and her gang of bullies. There hardly seemed a week that went by without Kate doing something to humiliate or hurt her.

However, it wasn't just Jane now who was picked on by Kate and her equally cruel friends. Anyone who arrived in the dormitory who showed a moment's weakness was also singled out for abuse. It seemed that Kate never tired of inflicting misery and pain on others.

Those who were not members of Kate Larkin's circle of friends did their very best to avoid getting on her wrong side. Often, this meant pointing out faults or problems that some of the weaker girls had so that Kate could mercilessly exploit them. Jane could not really blame them. If Kate was picking on someone else, she wouldn't be picking on them.

The winter after Robin had been apprenticed, the workhouse was hit by a horrendous outbreak of typhus fever. It came through the front door without mercy and inflicted its own pain and misery. Unlike Kate Larkin, it didn't just prey on the weak. It took anyone who stood in its unrelenting path. Man, woman or child. None were spared from its terrible grasp. In three short weeks, the population of the workhouse had been reduced by almost a third.

One of those taken was Kate Larkin's father.

She too was now an orphan. She didn't know how to grieve in the workhouse, but to be fair, few did. She took her pain and hurt out on one particular person: Jane Monday.

Kate sought her out just to hurl abuse at her. She would call her names, pinch her skin, or pull her hair. She would tell lies about her to the other girls or even advise the matron that Jane had transgressed the rules. Jane had suffered three more canings because of Kate's lies.

One evening, just before bedtime, all the girls in the dormitory had changed into their nightdresses.

One of the female staff members rushed into the dormitory. "Matron, you must come quick, we have a problem."

Mrs Bird glanced around the dormitory for a moment and then nodded her head. "I will be back shortly, girls. When I return, you will all be in bed. There will be no problems while I am gone. Understand?"

Jane Monday was almost sure that Mrs Bird was singling her out as she spoke those words.

Unsupervised and with an audience to play to, Jane knew immediately what was going to happen. Kate Larkin wandered over, her little gang of friends behind her.

"Why are you so ugly?" Kate demanded of Jane.

"Go away. You heard the matron," Jane tried to argue while half turning away from her.

"I bet your mother was ugly too. That's probably where you got it from. You didn't know your mother, did you? I heard she was a nasty piece of work. The way I understood it, she'd rather die than look after you. That's what she did, isn't it? She took one look at you and decided to die. No one could blame her. I'd do the same myself."

For months, Jane had been thinking about what Robin had told her in the yard that Sunday.

"You have to stand up to these people at some point."

She knew his words rang true, but up until this moment, she hadn't had the courage to act on them.

But something inside her snapped as the unwarranted insults against her mother flew out of this vile girl's mouth. As quick as a flash, she punched Kate twice in the stomach, doubling her over in pain and making her gasp for air. Then she grabbed her blonde hair and pulled it backwards, causing Kate's neck to jolt and her eyes to look up at the dirty ceiling.

"Shut up, you vile piece of work!" Jane said in a sinister hiss that she didn't even know she had inside her. She was conscious of not making a noise to attract the Matron or any other member of staff.

Kate's bully friends were too shocked to do anything to help their leader. This was the first time anybody had ever fought back. They had no idea how to react.

But Jane wasn't finished yet. She pushed Kate to the floor and put her knees on her shoulders so that she was pinned down. She pointed her finger squarely at Kate's nose. "Now you listen here, Kate Larkin. You've picked on me and the others here for the very last time. If you ever speak to me again, I will do far worse. I'll beat you so hard that you'll never be able to spread your vile lies again."

Jane had absolutely no idea where these words were coming from. She had never hit anybody in her life, and now she was threatening the worst bully in the entire workhouse.

"And when I get off you, you're going to go over to your little bed and you're going to climb inside and not speak a word of this to anyone. Do you understand?" she jabbed Kate's forehead with her finger as she spoke the final words.

Jane stared down into the frightened eyes of her rival and waited for a response.

None came.

Jane grasped Kate's head on either side of her temples, pulled it towards her, and then banged it down on the floor. She didn't hit as hard as she could; she just wanted to frighten and hurt the girl, not knock her out.

"Do you understand, Kate Larkin?"

Kate could hardly believe the change in the girl who was now in full control of her. Usually, Jane had been like a timid little mouse, hiding in the corners and shadows, trying not to be seen as she went about her daily business. But now, at this moment, she was like a lion.

"I understand," Kate finally spat out as she tried to regain control of her breathing.

Jane looked up and glanced around the dormitory. Dozens of amazed eyes stared back at her. "Nobody here saw anything. Do you understand? None of you saw a thing. Nothing happened. Not unless you want this to happen to you."

She watched the girls shake their heads, agreeing with her that they had seen nothing.

"We had better get in bed before the matron comes back. Do you all agree?" Jane said.

This time, all the girl's heads nodded in agreement, and they all fled to their beds, three or four children in each. Each seemed desperate to get underneath the covers in case they offended Jane Monday.

Slowly, Jane got off Kate. Kate just lay on the floor, shocked at the series of events that had just taken place.

"Go," Jane commanded. "Never ever speak to me again."

Kate did exactly as she was told.

Jane was the last to slip under the covers that evening. Just as she did, she heard the rap of the matron's steps in the corridor outside. If the matron had seen what had just occurred, Jane couldn't begin to comprehend the punishment she would have had to endure.

But she didn't.

Finally, Jane had stood up to the bullies.

Finally, she had taken action on what Robin had said she ought to do.

She didn't sleep a wink that night. Something flowed through her, preventing sleep. It was as if she knew something huge had changed.

The next few weeks were like a different world for Jane. For the first few hours and days, she was frightened that someone would tell Matron what had happened. But the girls in the dormitory treated her like a new person. They all lived in fear of her. They offered her the occasional smile, but most just kept out of her way.

This suited Jane just fine.

Kate was also changed.

She lost her unofficial top-dog status in the dormitory. She was no longer the bully tormenting everybody. Everyone knew that all you had to do was stand up to her and she would crumble. When Kate saw Jane Monday coming along the corridor, it was now her who turned away, hiding her head.

"Bullies are all cowards. When you take them down a peg or two, you'll find they've got no fight in them," Robin had once said after she had been upset by another incident.

He had been right.

She wished she could tell him about it all.

Three months after that fateful night in the dormitory, an unexpected occurrence took place during Jane's lessons on a rainy Tuesday morning.

A female staff member whom Jane had never laid eyes upon before, appeared at the door of the schoolroom. She handed a note to the teacher with an air of importance.

"Kate Larkin and Jane Monday are to report to the master's office forthwith," the teacher announced in a prim and proper voice, her enunciation crisp and clear.

The master's office, thought Jane, her heart skipping a beat.

Why on earth would she and Kate Larkin be required to report to the master's office?

Someone must have finally divulged her actions that night to the matron, and now the master was calling them both to his office to get to the heart of the matter. Kate would say that she had been attacked. She would turn on the tears and say she was too frightened to speak out and then Jane's punishment would follow. The master would see how many times Jane had already been punished from the records in his ledger. This time, his sentence would be harsher than ever.

That was the only explanation that came to her mind. She had never been to the master's office for anything other than a matter of discipline.

"Jane Monday, did you not hear me?" The teacher repeated in a harsh tone. Jane glanced up and saw that Kate Larkin was already standing by the door, waiting impatiently.

With haste, Jane stood up and joined her.

"Follow me," the unfamiliar female staff member instructed.

Jane was grateful for the presence of this stranger. Walking side-by-side with Kate Larkin was awkward enough. Without a third person present, it would have been utterly unbearable.

At least this way, neither had to attempt any sort of interaction.

As they approached the master's office, Jane grew increasingly nervous, her hands clammy with dread as she imagined the punishment that awaited her.

"Wait here," the staff member instructed. She knocked on the door.

Master's voice boomed from within, "Come in."

Jane listened to a few moments of hushed conversation inside before both girls were ushered into the master's office.

They both stood demurely in front of the master's huge partner's desk. Everything appeared just as it had the last time Jane had been here. King George IV still hung behind the master. He wasn't dead yet although the rumour around the workhouse was that it wouldn't be long. She had heard people say that he was getting fatter by the day and was now almost as mad as his father had been before him. She couldn't repeat some of the other things that were said about him, they were so rude.

The master was grinning, proudly patting his substantial stomach as he did so. "Here they are. Both fine girls, wouldn't you agree, sir?"

It was only then that Jane noticed the slender man seated at the dining table. He appeared to be in his early thirties. He was dressed in a fine brown suit with a red shirt and a bright yellow tie. He was striking in his appearance. The type of man who would make single women of marriageable age blush. He rose from his seat and sauntered over to inspect them both.

"This is Mr Briley. He works at the Theatre Royal in Drury Lane. The theatre manager, Mr Richard Sheridan, is in need of a girl apprentice. You two have been selected as potential candidates. Stand up straight, both of you."

They did just that. Kate Larkin seemed to gather herself and flashed a warm, radiant smile at Mr Briley.

"They can both read and write?" he inquired, studying Kate intently.

"Indeed. Both are veritable scholars," the master responded. This was a bit of a stretch; while Jane performed well in her lessons, Kate Larkin consistently ranked towards the bottom of the class.

"They both appear thin and nimble," Briley observed.

"Of course. As you know, there isn't much money to spend on luxuries like food," the Master replied, his voice tinged with bitterness.

Briley made an indistinct noise in the back of his throat and glanced at the Master for a brief moment. "Of course."

Jane was certain she could detect a hint of sarcasm in his tone.

"Which are you?" Briley queried, focusing his attention on Jane.

"Jane Monday, sir," she responded with as much confidence as she could muster.

This was her opportunity. This was her chance to finally escape the oppressive workhouse walls. She knew that theatres were enchanting places where actors and actresses performed mesmerising shows that enraptured audiences, who would cheer and applaud at the finale.

It sounded like a truly magical way of life.

"Have you ever been to the theatre, girl?" Briley inquired.

"No, sir. I've spent my entire life within the confines of the workhouse. I came here just hours after I was born, Sir."

Once again, that peculiar noise emanated from the back of Briley's throat as he contemplated her response.

"I need someone who can fit into small spaces. We need people to operate trapdoors, blow smoke through the floor, drag scenery around - that sort of thing. Would you have any difficulties performing those tasks, girl?"

Jane pondered for a moment. She loathed being in tight, dark places. It stirred a peculiar feeling of unease within her. She much preferred the wide-open dormitories and halls to being trapped in a cramped space.

"I'm not certain, sir."

She noticed the master's face contort into a scowl. "The girl will manage just fine," he interjected.

Yet again, that strange noise returned to the back of Briley's throat. He took a step towards Kate Larkin.

"And you are?" he demanded.

"Kate Larkin, sir. At your service." Her face blossomed into a captivating smile and she offered him a graceful curtsy.

"Have you ever been to the theatre, girl?"

"Oh, yes. My father used to take me quite regularly before we fell on hard times and had to seek refuge in the safety and sanctuary of this splendid institution."

Jane could see the master's face brighten as Kate deployed her charm. Even at her tender age, she could effortlessly captivate people.

"Which ones?"

"Your very own, Theatre Royal in Drury Lane, sir. It's my absolute favourite," she replied, her voice dripping with sincerity. "I've been to the Haymarket and the Sans Pareil. They are nothing compared to yours in Drury Lane."

"Would you have any issue with navigating small spaces beneath the stage? Or climbing up the rigging to shine lights down on the actors?"

"Oh, no, sir. Not in the least, sir. It sounds positively thrilling."

Briley was silent for a moment. He flicked his eyes back to Jane Monday but held them there for only an instant. He turned back to the master. "I don't believe there's much of a contest here, is there? I'll take this one. Miss Larkin."

Kate turned to Jane Monday and flashed her the most wicked, self-satisfied smirk she could muster.

"An excellent choice, Mr Briley. An excellent choice, indeed, sir. You, girl, wait here," the master said, directing his comment at Kate. "You, the other girl, return to your lessons forthwith."

"Yes, sir," Jane replied, her voice tinged with despondency.

Jane sensed that Kate was itching to cast her one

final smug glance. She refused to give her the satisfaction. Instead, she turned and marched out of the master's office with her head held high.

Kate Larkin was to become an apprentice at the theatre while poor Jane was doomed to remain within the dreadful workhouse walls.

Why wasn't life fair?

Why wasn't she granted even one break in life? Just one opportunity? That was all she needed.

CHAPTER 5

*I*t was tremendously difficult for Jane to resist sinking into despair during the initial week after being spurned in favour of Kate Larkin. The bitter sting of rejection lingered, and Jane felt as if she were shrouded in a cloud of gloom.

However, as the weeks passed and the hurt gradually subsided, her spirits began to lift anew.

The girls' dormitory appeared to be an entirely transformed space. No longer was the loathed figure of Kate Larkin present, casting a dark shadow over the room. The past few months since Jane's public humiliation of her tormentor had been disquieting for all. A palpable tension hung in the air as if everyone held their breath, anticipating Kate's eventual retaliation against Jane.

Yet, that moment never arrived. And now Kate was gone.

Jane exchanged warm smiles with some of the other girls and they reciprocated her friendly gestures. She even struck up conversations with one or two of them, gradually coming to regard them as friends.

Perhaps life in the workhouse wasn't as terrible as she had once thought. She was still receiving an education, which her dear friend Robin had always emphasised as being crucial for a future beyond the confines of the workhouse - at least someday. She was provided with three meals a day, even if they were invariably bland, monotonous, and unimaginative. Nonetheless, at least it was sustenance.

When new girls were brought into the workhouse, Jane would occasionally overhear whispers about dreadful tales. Families who had gone without food for days or even weeks at a time. At least within these walls, she was assured of three square meals each day.

Then, nearly three months after Kate departed from the workhouse, all the girls were assembled. At the commencement of their embroidery lesson, they were informed of something new.

In addition to the standard curriculum of reading, writing, and arithmetic, all the children in the workhouse would acquire skills that would prove valuable in the real world. For the girls, that meant learning needlework, sewing, and embroidery.

Jane had always derived enjoyment from these particular sessions. There was a sense of satisfaction in mending a tattered workhouse uniform and darning it as if she was giving it a new lease on life.

But today's task was a departure from the usual. They were each given a small piece of fabric and an assortment of brightly coloured threads and were instructed to create something decorative and eye-catching.

Three hours were allotted for the task. As usual, there was to be no talking. That suited Jane just fine; she could lose herself in the work. This was a refreshing change and a break from the mundane routine that had dominated their lives thus far.

Jane took to it with enthusiasm.

She crafted an elaborate design of interlocking daisies, the petals appearing almost lifelike in their intricate detail.

As she completed the final stitch, the teacher announced that time was up.

Jane would have cherished the opportunity to keep her creation; she felt immensely proud of it. However, at the end of the session, the teacher collected all the pieces. When a courageous girl inquired about the fate of their handiwork, she was curtly informed that it was not her concern.

Almost a week later, Jane had all but forgotten about the task when the staff member who had previously summoned her and Kate to the master's office reappeared during their lessons.

The staff member whispered a word to the teacher and handed her something. The teacher nodded her head as though she understood.

She held up the embroidery that Jane had completed the previous week. "To whom does this piece of work belong?"

Timidly, Jane raised her hand. "It's mine, Miss."

The teacher handed it back to the staff member.

"Jane Monday, report to the master's office immediately."

Jane leapt from her chair and trailed the female staff member down the long corridors towards the master's office.

This time, fear did not grip her. She was acutely aware that she had done nothing amiss. There had been no rules broken. There was no way she was heading to see the master for punishment. Instead of the fear, she felt something else – excitement.

She surmised that someone awaited her in the master's office. Someone seeking an apprentice.

It had to be a dressmaker, she reasoned. What other explanation could there be? The dressmaker must have set this task for the girls and for some reason, Jane had been selected.

A nervous flutter stirred within her stomach. She longed for an apprenticeship, yearned to escape the confines of the workhouse and discover what life was like in the real world.

She couldn't help but recall her humiliating experience a few months prior. The man from the theatre had so clearly preferred Kate over her. The memory still pained her.

As instructed, she waited outside the master's office, collecting her thoughts as she did so. She reflected on that earlier encounter and the cunning tricks Kate Larkin had employed. Jane decided there was no harm in learning from that experience.

"Come inside," the female staff member said.

Jane dutifully followed and stood before the master's desk. "Good morning, sir," she greeted with a warm smile.

Again, nothing had changed. The King still sternly watched everything that unfolded in the office. Jane couldn't help but wonder if everything they said about him was true. If so, why was he king? He seemed a most unsuitable person. But as quickly as the thoughts entered her head, she removed them. There were more important matters at hand.

She noticed a man and a woman seated at the master's dining table; they appeared to be in their early forties. Both were elegantly attired. The gentleman was strikingly handsome and the woman, whom Jane instantly assumed to be his wife, exuded warmth and amiability. She beamed when Jane entered the room.

"Here she is. Here she is. Mr and Mrs May, this is the girl. Jane Monday," the master boomed in his usual style.

"Isn't she just splendid?" Mrs May exclaimed delightedly, clapping her hands.

"Carol, remember the reason we are here," the gentleman admonished gently.

The smile vanished from the woman's face and she nodded her head obediently.

"Mr May is a goldsmith and a jeweller in the city. He is seeking an apprentice, someone to perform intricate work. He was rather impressed by the sample you produced," the master informed Jane.

A goldsmith and a jeweller. Jane wasn't sure what those were but they sounded far more interesting than a dressmaker.

The master inquired loudly, "Mr May, what are your thoughts on the girl?"

Mr May rose from the dining table and scrutinised Jane. He appraised her as though he was evaluating a horse for purchase. "Show me your fingers, girl."

"Certainly, sir," Jane replied, grateful she had remembered to thoroughly clean her hands that particular morning. She extended her hands; her fingers were long, slender, and delicate.

"Come and look, wife," Mr May invited.

His wife promptly joined him, smiling warmly at Jane. There was something about the woman that Jane instantly found endearing.

An undercurrent of tension seemed to permeate the couple's interactions. Jane couldn't quite put her finger on it, but it felt as if they each desired a different outcome.

"Those are precisely the fingers we are looking for," Mrs May told her husband. "You'll never find those in a boy. It's pointless to take one on; boys soon mature into men with large, clumsy fingers. I'll wager this girl's fingers will remain as they are as she grows older."

Mr May grunted in agreement. "Why is she here in the workhouse? Any thievery in the family? I won't tolerate any thievery, especially not in my line of work."

"The girl was practically born here, sir. She was but hours old when she arrived with her mother, a widow, according to the records. The wife of a soldier. Absolutely no thievery in her background," the master confirmed. "The mother died of childbed fever."

Jane listened with interest as the master spoke of her mother. She knew that her mother had died of childbed fever. She had asked what had become of her and the matron had, for once, answered. But this was the first she had heard about her father. A soldier. She didn't feel anything when she heard the words from the master. Her parents had never been a part of her life and she didn't know what feelings she should have for their memory.

"She can read and write?" Mr May demanded.

"Of course," the master agreed.

"Behaviour? Is she unruly?" Mr May asked.

Jane felt a heavy weight press on her shoulders. This was it. This was where the master would be forced to list all of her punishments and then Mr May would think that she was a terrible girl, and he would refuse to apprentice her.

But the Master calmly shook his head, "Impeccable behaviour, Sir. No records against her. You won't find better."

Jane took a deep breath, shocked at the master's lie.

Mr May stood for a moment in silence, staring at Jane's fingers that were still held out in front of her.

"What do you think?" Mrs May inquired of her husband, gently touching his arm. "I like her."

Her husband shot her a cautionary glance. "We are seeking an apprentice, remember?"

"With those fingers, she will undoubtedly make a fine apprentice. Just what you need."

Mr May studied his wife for a second as though trying to work out her true feelings. Finally, he said, "We'll take her."

Mrs May nodded her head in agreement and Jane look up at her and smiled. Jane could just tell that the woman was resisting the urge to smile back.

Jane took a deep breath and fought back the tears. She had been apprenticed. In a matter of minutes, she would be taking her first steps outside of the workhouse.

Suddenly fear gripped her. Jane had no idea what life was truly like outside the walls. She had heard stories from Robin and other children but stories were just that. She had no idea how she would cope.

But she glanced up at Mrs May once more, who gave her a reassuring nod of the head as though she understood the concerns that Jane had and that she would help her. And in that moment, Jane thought she understood the tension between husband and wife.

Mr May was seeking an apprentice but Mrs May was seeking a daughter.

"Excellent, excellent," the master said, patting his stomach in excitement. He stared at the goldsmith for a moment before adding, "There is just the small matter of the fee."

Mr May hesitated for a brief moment before his wife nodded her head in agreement. "Of course."

He reached inside his jacket but the master interrupted him, "You, the girl, please go and wait outside. I believe Matron will be there. She will give you further instruction and you will wait for Mr and Mrs May there."

"Yes, sir," Jane said quickly. She was slightly disappointed not to see how much money the fee entailed. However, she rather thought this was the reason for her dismissal. She took one final look around the master's office and seemed to think the king was now looking down at the master with a certain degree of contempt. She wondered how much of the fee would actually go towards the upkeep of the poor inmates of the workhouse and how much would go into the fat master's pocket. Again, she had heard rumours around the workhouse that the master, the matron, and the overseers would take money off the top of everything for their own use. She could believe it. The master didn't get that fat on just a usual wage, surely.

"Thank you, sir, thank you, madam. I look forward to seeing you outside," Jane said humbly.

She remembered the way Kate Larkin had behaved. If these two people were to be in charge of her, she wanted to endear herself to them. She felt that gaining the favour of Mrs May wouldn't be hard at all. Mr May, however, had a certain stiffness about him, and there was something she couldn't quite put her finger on. Something was lurking under the surface there. She would be careful around him.

Mrs May smiled back warmly, "We won't be long, Jane."

Jane attempted a small curtsy just like she'd seen Kate do, and then she turned, leaving the master's office for the final time.

The matron, Mrs Bird, was indeed waiting outside. "Well, girl, are you to be apprenticed?"

"Yes, Matron," Jane said with enthusiasm.

"Good," the matron said with half of her mind on the transaction that was probably being undertaken at this very moment within the master's office. Jane wondered how much the matron would receive of the fee. "You must be on your very best behaviour, Jane Monday. You must not let down the reputation of this institution. Do you hear me?"

"Yes, Matron."

"Listen to all you are instructed. You know nothing but life in this workhouse, girl. I understand that. That will put you at a disadvantage in the outside world because you know nothing about it. Life has a quicker pace by far out there. Do as you're told and nothing more, and you will get along just fine. You have been chosen for your skill, Jane Monday. Make sure that you work hard."

"Yes, Matron. I will."

With that, the door of the master's office opened

and Mr and Mrs May emerged. Mrs May looked pleased with the transaction they had just conducted, Mr May, slightly less so.

"Right, girl. You have no other clothing, I assume?" Mr May asked, realising that the girl was still dressed in a workhouse uniform.

"No, sir. On account of the fact she was just hours old when she arrived at this very institution, sir," the matron answered on Jane's behalf. "If you would be so kind, sir, to return the uniform after you provide her with suitable clothing."

Mr May took a deep breath as though he was about to argue but his wife put a gentle hand against his leg to hush him. "Of course. We will send that on immediately," she said. "Right, Jane, follow us, please."

"Goodbye, Jane Monday, and good luck," the Matron said, perhaps the kindest words Jane had ever heard from her.

"Goodbye, Matron," Jane said.

And with that, the Mays set off along the corridor. Jane followed just a few steps behind.

Now that the matter was done, a real sense of tension filled her body. She had no idea where she was going, what she was about to do, or where she would sleep at night. Would there be other girls there? Or would she be alone? She had too many questions and not enough answers.

But she was excited to see what the world was like

beyond the walls of the workhouse. She remembered Robin's words, that it was a vast and vibrant place.

She hoped it was. She wondered what had become of Robin. Maybe one day she might run into him again. She wondered if he would recognise her.

They opened the doors and entered the courtyard to a beautiful sunny day. The sort of day when life itself felt hopeful.

They headed straight for the large wooden gate and the gatekeeper opened the small, narrow door. On occasion, Jane had managed to catch a glimpse outside, but now for the very first time, she stepped through the door and into a new world.

A carriage was waiting for the Mays. Mr May opened the door for his wife, and she climbed up. "Up you go, girl," Mr May instructed firmly.

Jane did as she was told. Mrs May patted the black leather seat next to her, and Jane obediently sat down.

Mr May followed and shut the door. He reached up through the window and knocked on the roof. The carriage jolted forward, and Jane gasped.

Mrs May gently patted Jane's knee. "Nothing to be afraid of, young Jane. I suppose you have never been in a carriage before?"

Jane had only seen a horse about five times in her entire life when one brought deliveries into the yard, and it just so happened to coincide with a recreation period. A carriage being pulled by two horses was something she had not even considered, let alone travelled in.

"No, madam," Jane said. "I have not."

"Just relax, look out of the window."

Jane did just that. Well, at least she looked out the window; they seemed to be going at a rather frightening speed to her. Relaxing was not really an option, especially as they seemed to hit a huge bump every few yards and they would almost fly up into the air. It didn't seem to bother the Mays, so Jane assumed that this was normal.

She wondered if this was how the Mays travelled all the time. When Robin talked of the outside world, he said that carriages were just for the rich. She wondered if the Mays were rich. But then she realised that they probably weren't, otherwise, Mr May would no longer be a goldsmith.

She tried to put the questions out of her mind. This was her first view of life outside the workhouse. She knew that she should savour all of it.

Jane almost gasped as she watched the city go by. There just seemed to be so many people. They were all rushing and bustling about, going about their daily business. They were all dressed differently which, after life in the workhouse, seemed very strange to Jane. There were gigantic red brick factories which spewed thick smoke into the air, painting the sky with their sooty residue. There were so many shops, each with painted signs, selling all manner of goods. She wondered how they could all make money, there were so many.

Then they came to a bridge and Jane got her first glimpse of the River Thames. It shimmered in the sunlight, but there was something dark and mysterious about it. Jane was shocked at the size of it; when people talked about the river, she had in mind something more akin to a modest stream. She knew that wasn't the correct image because she had heard of the ships that used to sail up and down it. Now she could see them all. The masts stood proud in the sky, like sentinels guarding the waterway. Smaller vessels pumping out steam and even smaller wherries rowed by oarsmen fought for space amongst the tall ships. Jane never expected it to be as busy as it was.

The landscape changed as they crossed the river. She saw imposing, dark stone buildings, and churches with majestic spires and crosses upon them. Then she saw a huge dome, perched atop a mound of light grey stone. It was the most breathtaking building she had ever seen in her life.

"That's St Paul's Cathedral," Mrs May said kindly. "We attend the services there regularly."

"We do, not the staff," corrected Mr May from the opposite side of the carriage.

Jane caught the couple exchanging stern glances.

It was obvious that this issue would have to be resolved between the two adults. Mr May only wanted Jane as an apprentice, a member of staff from whom to profit. It was not the same feeling she got from Mrs May who certainly wanted something more.

The carriage continued through wide avenues; the houses changed, and there were some exceedingly grand buildings. These must have been the houses to which Robin had referred. She wondered if he had managed to move into one as he had always sworn he would.

It wasn't just the view out of the window that amazed Jane; it was the noise of the city as well. Everyone seemed to be shouting, carts clanked, and whistles blew. It was all very overwhelming for a girl who had lived in a workhouse all her life under strict, regimented control. Despite the number of people that would sit in the dining hall three times a day, there was silence. People were not permitted to talk at mealtimes.

Jane had just assumed this was how life was but now she could see that wasn't the case. Noise was something that she was going to have to adapt to rather quickly.

They turned a corner and went up a gentle incline. There was a park on one side of them with verdant grass and tall, lush trees. Other than in a book, this was the first time she had seen trees. She stared at them in wonder; they were so beautiful.

Then, on the opposite side of the road, the grandest house she had ever seen in her life came into view. Jane couldn't help but shake her head in wonder as they rode by.

"The old Queen's house. It's now called, Buckingham Palace. One of the King's many houses," Mrs May declared.

Jane thought back to the portrait of the king that hung over the master's desk. Did he truly look like that, she wondered. She wondered if one day she would ever get to see him in the flesh so that she could know for herself for sure.

However, she remembered the rumours around the workhouse that he was a terrible man who would spend money hand over fist while so many in his kingdom had nothing. She also recalled that people said he wasn't long for this world and that he was as mad as his father.

She was about to ask about these things but decided she would save it for another day. She didn't want to annoy her new masters.

"Here we are," Mr May said after a few minutes of silence. "Cockspur Street."

"Is that where you live, sir?"

"It's where we all live now," Mrs May interrupted.

"It is where I live and carry out my work. It is

where you will work as well, girl. When you alight this carriage, you'll go straight inside. I have no intention of allowing my clients to know that I've apprenticed a girl from the workhouse. Do you understand?"

"Yes, sir," Jane said.

"Carol, you get off first and take the girl straight in."

Carol did not respond to her husband. She simply nodded her head.

The coachman opened the door and helped Mrs May down. She then turned and held out her hand for Jane to grasp. Very carefully, the young girl climbed down the steps of the carriage and, for the first time, stood in the City of London.

Now the smells hit her: horses, smoke, food, sweat, and other things that she didn't even want to consider.

People rushed by on each side, completely ignoring Mrs May and Jane as they stood there.

"Come on," Mrs May said, grasping the girl's hand tighter. She moved forward and walked into a shop with a sign emblazoned with the name Russell May across the top, followed by 'Goldsmith'. A huge man with no hair, dressed in a tight black suit, nodded his head and opened the door for them.

"Thank you, Grimes," Mrs May said.

He didn't reply, just nodded his head and looked

Jane up and down. She shrank away closer into Mrs May's skirts. Grimes seemed frightening. What did he do here? She hoped he would have nothing to do with her.

As she stepped inside, Jane knew that this was it. This was her new life. She was determined to grasp it with both hands, to learn and grow in this unfamiliar world that had suddenly opened up before her. The bustling streets, the grand buildings, and the endless possibilities of the City of London now awaited her.

What would she make of it all?

CHAPTER 6

"Mrs Johnson is the cook. Miss Dawson is the maid. My wife takes care of all matters relating to the home. Virgil and Gideon Harrington work with me. And Grimes keeps out the vagabonds and criminals. Understand?" Mr May demanded.

They had entered the shop front and gone upstairs. Mr May wanted to hold this conversation in the workshop, but Mrs May had insisted it take place upstairs in their own lodgings. They sat around the dining room table.

"Yes, Sir," Jane said, knowing perfectly well that she wouldn't be able to remember all of the names.

"You will sleep in the attic room that my wife had prepared for you. For an apprentice, it is lavish. But that is my wife, generous to a fault. You will always go straight up to your room. In other words, never come to this floor. You will take three meals a day in the kitchen with Mrs Johnson or Miss Dawson. Mrs Johnson has been instructed on the amount to feed you. Any stealing of food will not be tolerated..."

"Russell!" Carol interrupted. "The girl is not a thief. And she needs to fill out a little."

Russell May glared at his wife. "Not at my expense, she doesn't."

"Remember, girl, you are here to work. And work you shall. It will take you time to learn, but you had better do it quickly, or..."

A heavy sigh from Carol interrupted him again. "Shall I show her to the room? Get her changed and then send her down to the workshop?"

Russell May looked as though he might want to argue, but he nodded his head. "Quickly then."

"I'll introduce her to Mrs Johnson as well."

"Yes fine. Just get her to the workshop so she can start to earn her keep."

"Of course," Mrs May agreed with a pacifying smile.

Russell disappeared, chuntering under his breath.

"Right then, Jane," said Mrs May with a warm smile. "Let's go and see your room, shall we?"

"Yes, Madam," agreed Jane. She couldn't imagine what having a room would be like.

"Now when you come upstairs, Mr May insists

that you go straight up to the attic. This is the floor on which he and I live. You are not to come here unless one of us invites you. Do you understand?" she said, repeating a point that her husband made a few minutes before.

Jane nodded her head obediently. She liked Mrs May and was eager to please her.

"Good girl," said Carol. "I know this is probably all very overwhelming, but you will get used to it."

"It's a little, madam. I've lived my entire life in the workhouse with only stories of what life was like beyond those dreadful walls, and now suddenly I'm here. I do hope that you and Mr May will find me a suitable apprentice. Even though I have no notion of the work which I will be undertaking."

"My husband will teach you the work. You have been selected because it is quite intricate, and a good steady hand is required. No doubt he will explain more. He does have a tendency to be a tad gruff, but he is a splendid man. Do you understand?"

"Yes, madam," agreed Jane, even though she wasn't entirely certain that she did.

"Was life genuinely terrible at the workhouse?" Mrs May asked in a gentler tone.

Jane contemplated for a moment. "I suppose I have nothing to compare it to. I would hear tales of what life was like in the city and it certainly sounds far better out here. I would often go to bed famished.

In fact, I can never recall a time when I wasn't hungry. Some of the girls could be frightful bullies as well." She was just about to tell Mrs May that the matron would thrash them with a cane but then she remembered the master had lied and said her behaviour was impeccable. She decided she would keep that to herself.

"Well, I promise that you will never be hungry here. Come on, let's go up to the attic room, show you that, and get you out of that workhouse uniform and into something more suitable."

"You have clothes for me?" Jane asked in amazement.

"Yes, of course. They're likely to need a few minor adjustments, but I can do that myself over the next few days."

Jane shook her head. She could scarcely believe her good fortune. She stood up and followed Mrs May out of the door into the base of another flight of stairs.

This flight was narrower, and she could feel that the steps were a lot thinner beneath her feet.

When she emerged at the top of the stairs, she saw rows and rows of boxes stored impeccably in long lines. There a small skylight allowing in a modest amount of natural light.

"Don't worry. This isn't your room. This is where

my husband stores various items. This way," Mrs May directed.

She moved over towards the left and through a small door and Jane followed, taking care of her footing in the semi-darkness.

Jane gasped. It was a small room, but it was enchanting. It had a larger skylight which made the room feel light and airy.

A delicate pale blue rug lay on the floor. A slim, narrow wooden bed was made up with a crisp white sheet and a single pillow. An aged wardrobe stood in the corner. There was a small chest of drawers next to it. In the far corner was a blue and white chamber pot and a matching basin in which to wash. A tiny mirror hung on the wall.

Jane cast her eyes around and instantly burst into tears.

"My dear, what on earth is wrong?" Mrs May asked, rushing over to comfort the girl.

The older woman sat on the bed and hugged Jane close. It was the first time in Jane's life she'd ever had such intimate contact. It felt immediately reassuring and comforting.

She wanted to stay there forever.

"No. Everything is splendid, madam. It's all so beautiful. I'm so grateful."

Mrs May laughed. "You silly girl. Come on. Let me show you these clothes."

Jane felt that Mrs May was almost as reluctant to break the embrace as she was.

The older woman opened the wardrobe door and pulled out four sets of different clothing which she laid on the bed.

A simple black dress. A more elaborate black dress. And two grey dresses.

"They're beautiful," Jane said, on the verge of tears once more.

"Well, I think functional is a more fitting word, my dear. You will wear one of the two grey dresses while at work in the workshop. If you happen to be in the shop or be asked to run any errands outside, you will change into the simple black dress," Mrs May said, pointing to each one in turn. "If you happen to attend any events with us, for example, a service at the cathedral, then you will wear this more elaborate black dress." Mrs May's voice dropped to a whisper, and she nervously looked over towards the doorway. "Strictly speaking, my husband doesn't know about this particular dress. So I doubt there will be any events in the near future. But who knows what might happen?"

To Jane, it all seemed a tad odd. She suddenly mustered up the courage to ask a question that she had in the back of her mind for a few hours. "Do you and Mr May have any children of your own, madam?"

Jane saw a shadow of sadness fall over Mrs May's face. "We did once. A girl. She did not live to see six months."

"I'm sorry to hear that," Jane said in a manner that suggested she was far older than her years.

In her mind, it did confirm a little of her suspicions. Mr May was certainly after an apprentice. Someone on whom he wouldn't have to lavish a great deal of expense yet could see him make a good return. Mrs May wanted somebody that she could love and look after. Jane wanted that as well, and she wondered whether, in time, Mr May might soften his stance.

She remembered Kate Larkin and the way she managed to act and twist everyone around her little finger. Although she didn't wish to be so manipulative, Jane knew that she would have to behave a little like that and try to charm her new employer.

"Let's get this workhouse uniform off and get you into one of these grey dresses. Then I'll take you downstairs, and you can meet Mrs Johnson and then go and start work."

In less than three minutes, she discarded her workhouse uniform for the final time. She felt no shame in undressing under the watchful eyes of Mrs May. She had been changing clothes in front of women all her life. There were also four new sets of undergarments to accompany the dresses. She pulled one on and marvelled at the fact that it didn't chafe her skin.

She slipped the grey dress over her head and was ready.

"You look marvellous, dear," said Mrs May, nodding her approval. "To be honest, I don't think we need to make any adjustments to that whatsoever. You will fill out a little over the next few weeks."

The thought of more food almost made Jane's mouth water. She hadn't eaten since breakfast and had missed the mid-day meal. She didn't dare say anything because that would appear impolite.

However, there seemed to be conflicting messages coming to her. Mr May seemed intent on ensuring that she only had a certain amount of food whereas his wife seemed keen on fattening her up.

She wondered if this would result in disputes over the next few weeks and months.

She put it to the back of her mind and smiled warmly back at Mrs May. "It's wonderful, thank you ever so much."

Mrs May waved away her thanks. "Come on. Fold the workhouse uniform and bring it for the maid to wash and send back to the workhouse."

Five minutes later Jane was seated at the small wooden kitchen table eating a crust of bread and butter with a piece of red cheese.

Mrs Johnson was a stout woman of approximately sixty years with snowy white hair, rosy cheeks, and an ample girth that filled her apron. She looked like a typical cook. Mrs Johnson had agreed with her mistress that the girl needed feeding and that they would keep it between themselves. It was then that Jane finally had the courage to say that she hadn't eaten since her breakfast of thin workhouse porridge.

As quick as a flash the bread was placed in front of her.

"Eat it quickly, my dear," said Mrs May. "My husband will be waiting."

"Yes, Madam," she said her mouth full of food. It tasted divine. Butter didn't taste like this in the workhouse and the red cheese filled her mouth with flavour.

A striking young woman sauntered into the kitchen, capturing the attention of everyone present. Her chestnut brown hair was neatly tied up in a bun atop her head, and she was impeccably dressed in the traditional maid's uniform. Her eyes sparkled and danced, and Jane's first impression was that she had some kind of magnetic charm that commanded attention. Jane found it hard to guess her age but thought she was probably about twenty.

"Ah, this is Miss Dawson, our maid," Mrs May directed at Jane. The young girl smiled warmly. "Jennifer, this is Mr May's new apprentice Jane."

"A girl?" Jennifer Dawson said in surprise. "For some reason, I was expecting a boy." She didn't acknowledge Jane, just offered a non-committal stare.

Jane felt the maid's eyes bore into her and for some reason, a shiver went down her spine. Jane's eyes widened and she knew that there was something she didn't like about Jennifer Dawson. She didn't know what, but it was almost as if she were waiting for the maid to punch her in the face, just like Kate Larkin did at their first meeting.

"Yes, we thought with the nature of the work, a girl would be more suited," Mrs May said warmly. She pointed to the pile of clothing that Jane had brought downstairs. "Jennifer, could you launder that uniform and arrange for it to be returned to South-wark Workhouse?"

"Of course, Madam," confirmed Jennifer who set about removing the clothing. She didn't speak a single word to Jane.

"Right then, dear. You had better go and see my husband to start work," Mrs May said as Jane polished off the rest of the bread.

"Yes, Madam," Jane said nervously as she stood up.

Mrs May smiled warmly and pointed down the corridor. "Just listen carefully to everything he tells you. It will be alright."

CHAPTER 7

*M*rs May was indeed right.

After overcoming her initial hesitancy, Jane found herself surprisingly enjoying the task that her new master had set for her in the dimly lit workshop.

When she entered the workshop, Mr May had given her some very clear instructions, his voice stern yet precise. At no point was she ever allowed in the foundry at the rear of the property, with its glowing embers and scorching heat.

It was far too dangerous.

Mr May emphasised that he wasn't particularly concerned about her getting hurt, but rather, the potential for her inadvertently setting fire to the entire property. The only people granted access to that area were himself and his two assistants, the enigmatic Harrington twins.

When she was introduced to the pair, she almost jumped out of her skin. They were somewhere between fifty and sixty years old, and they were strikingly identical with weathered faces and a somewhat eerie air about them. They grunted a brief greeting, their voices deep and gravelly, before they left to resume their work. Mr May explained, with a hint of nostalgia, that the men had been his father's original apprentices and he had kept them on. They had never married and lived together in a modest house on the other side of the river where they employed an old woman with one arm to cook and clean for them.

They looked as strange as their story sounded.

They had bald heads, shining under the workshop's flickering light, and eyebrows that were almost invisible, making their expressions difficult to read. She noticed over the course of the next few hours that they hardly ever seemed to talk, adding to their mysterious nature. Instead, they would merely glance at each other and make a few subtle gestures here and there with their calloused hands. That appeared to be enough to allow them to communicate with one another as if they shared a secret language born from years of living side by side.

Surprisingly, she found Mr May to be rather

patient with her, even when she asked what seemed to her to be foolish questions, like what the foundry was.

Mr May patiently explained that the foundry was the place where they melted down gold so it could be shaped into various forms. He also elaborated that his thriving business focused on producing ornate pieces like grand candlesticks and impressive plates for affluent households. They still did similar work and crafted huge chalices for churches, but that work was becoming less frequent in nature. The craftsmanship was truly breathtaking, with intricate patterns and ornate designs adorning each item.

But now, he aspired to delve into the world of intricate jewellery. The wealthy of London liked to make a statement and there was no better way than a set of shiny jewels around a merchant's wife's neck.

And this was where Jane fitted into his plans.

It was her remarkable dexterity that he sought.

He led her to a well-organized workbench, every tool meticulously placed, and presented her with a woman's brooch. The brooch was shaped like an elegant bird, a bird he named as a peacock. Jane was uncertain if such a creature existed but if it did, it must be unimaginably beautiful, judging by the stunning craftsmanship of the brooch.

Over the coming hours, Mr May demonstrated to Jane how to insert an array of coloured gems into the delicate framework he had crafted. Diamonds that sparkled brilliantly like stars in the night sky, emeralds as green as the lush grass outside, sapphires as blue as the heavens above, and rubies that resembled tiny droplets of crimson blood. The gems glistened and gleamed under the light, their colours dancing together in a mesmerizing display of opulence.

Jane watched Mr May's every movement, absorbing his techniques and replicating them immediately afterwards. Her fingers moved deftly, with a natural grace that belied her inexperience.

By the end of the working day, he even managed to offer her a rare smile.

"Excellent. You will improve and get quicker, I have no doubt. Your work there is outstanding. I believe we have made the right choice," he said, his voice warm with approval.

"Thank you, sir."

But then the sternness returned to his face. "These gems are worth a small fortune, girl. Each day I will know precisely how many I have given you and precisely how many need to go in the piece. If you thieve any, I will take you to the police and they will lock you up forever or hang you from a noose. Do you understand?"

A shiver went down her spine at the threat. "Yes, sir. I'm no thief, sir."

"Good. You will have one last task every day and

that will be to clean the workshop. That can only be done once the twins and I have left. If we are busy, that might be quite late at night."

"Yes, sir."

"After that, you may go and eat with the cook. Remember, despite what my wife says, I do not have the money to lavish on food. The cook knows precisely what to give you and no more. Children can be very greedy at times. But not in my household. Again, do you understand?"

"Yes, sir," Jane repeated for what seemed to her to be the hundredth time that day.

"After you eat, you go and sleep. And then we work again."

"I understand. I'm very happy to be here, sir. I enjoyed the task."

Mr May simply grunted. "Right, It's time for cleaning up. Let me show you."

Less than half an hour later, she was savouring a thin sliver of chicken pie with potatoes and carrots.

The flavours burst in her mouth. Mrs Johnson was kind throughout the meal and inquired about her life in the workhouse and how she had come to end up there.

Jane answered as respectfully and quickly as she could while trying to cram the delicious chicken pie into her mouth. She looked around, hopeful that there might be more. But it seemed that at this meal, Mr May's rules applied.

After she'd finished eating, Mrs Johnson told her to get to bed. "Remember, do not linger on that middle floor. Straight up to your room."

"Yes, Mrs Johnson."

Just as she was leaving the kitchen, the maid walked in. Jane could see now that she was actually younger than she'd originally thought. She might not be much older than sixteen. That was obviously why she was unmarried. It was her body that made her seem older; she had an ample bosom and sensuous hips. She was pretty, but unlike Mrs Johnson, had no smile or warmth or welcoming aura.

She simply sneered at Jane and sauntered past.

That night, Jane said her prayers before getting into bed. It would be the first night she had ever slept in a bed alone. At the workhouse, there were three to a bed. She considered herself incredibly fortunate at having been apprenticed.

The work she was set to do seemed to be engaging and enjoyable.

Her new mistress had evidently taken a great liking to her, and her new master was pleased with her work. The twins were somewhat peculiar, but she doubted she would have much to do with them. The imposing man at the door was intimidating, but again, she doubted she would have much to do with him. In fact, she had already forgotten his name The cook, Mrs Johnson was congenial, and she was confident that over time she would manage to endear herself to her.

The only thorn in her side seemed to be the maid, Jennifer. Jane's presence seemed to offend her in some way, but she had no idea why.

There was something about her that reminded Jane of Kate Larkin. She wouldn't turn her back on Jennifer. And even when standing in front of her, she would remain cautious, in case fists suddenly started to fly.

CHAPTER 8

*O*ne year later.

    About three weeks after Russell May had shown Jane how to incorporate what he called special stones into the exquisite pieces she crafted, King George IV died.

"The king is dead," Gideon said immediately after the twins' arrival one morning.

He said it in a matter-of-fact sort of way as though he were talking about the weather.

It was only four words, but it was one of the longest sentences Jane had heard him utter in the time she had been apprenticed to Mr May.

She gasped in shock and put her hand over her mouth. "The poor man."

Mr May walked into the workshop. "What was that, Gideon?"

"The King is dead. The city is awash with news of it."

"Is he indeed?" Mr May said thoughtfully. "Can't say I cared for the man much. The money he lavished, and none of it in our direction. The size of him as well. No control. Let's hope his brother will be better. The man is over sixty himself, isn't he? He can't last long, can he?"

The twins shook their bald heads perfectly in time with each other. It was almost comical to watch.

"Then who is it? Isn't it some girl? Princess Alexandrina? The daughter of the Duke of Kent?" Mr May continued.

"I believe so, Sir," Virgil, the other brother, said.

"Interesting though. Interesting," Mr May muttered, his mind clearly preoccupied with something.

"Well, to work. I'm sure the new king wouldn't want us idle."

The twins offered him a grin that suggested the new king couldn't care less, but they headed out to the foundry at the back. Jane put her head down and continued on the piece she was working on.

It was a bracelet. More than sixty diamonds and twenty rubies were to be inlaid into this intricate piece. In addition, there were four of the special stones that Mr May had recently instructed Jane to include in some pieces. To her, they appeared identical to diamonds and weren't special at all. Mr May offered no explanation for them. He did not wish to know where the stones were set in each piece; he simply gave instruction that they should not be on the outer edges where possible.

He also mysteriously instructed her never to breathe a word of this to anyone. Not the twins. Not the cook or maid. And certainly not his wife. If she did then bad things would happen.

It was the harshest he'd spoken to her in six months.

Over the past twelve months, Jane had flourished. She had taken to the work quickly, and as Mr May predicted, she'd got quicker and her skills improved month on month. She could now produce the most intricate pieces, which Mr May could only dream of producing. Her small, delicate fingers were nimble and moved skilfully around the gold frames he produced.

The bracelet she was working on at present was for Lady Wells, the wife of Baron Wells. He was minor aristocracy, the latest Baron Wells in a line that went back over six hundred years.

Mr May was thrilled to get the commission.

"We're going up in the world for sure," he declared to Jane as he explained the piece. "Another member of the House of Lords purchasing pieces from me."

"Excellent news, sir," Jane said with a smile.

It was then Mr May pulled out the four special stones. "Make sure to include these," he said softly, placing them in a small pile next to the diamonds.

If there was an accident and the two piles got mixed up, Jane would never be able to tell the two apart. Jane rather felt that that was the idea, but she didn't understand the reasons.

She settled down to work but couldn't help but think about the portrait of the dead king that hung over the master's office in the Southwark Workhouse. No doubt that would soon be replaced by a new portrait: the king's younger brother, William. As Mr May had said, the man was already old, and the rumour around London was that he too was in poor health. Maybe they would be changing the portrait in the workhouse twice in rapid succession.

After about an hour's work, Mr May got up and declared that he was going out.

Jane simply nodded her head in agreement and continued making the bracelet. All the special stones had been skilfully inserted. She simply had a handful of diamonds and about ten rubies left to insert. She was hoping she would have it done by lunchtime so she could start something new in the afternoon.

Jane was not a girl who was afraid of work.

As the morning progressed, she continued to meticulously insert the remaining diamonds and rubies into the bracelet, her nimble fingers working with precision. The final result was a breath-taking piece that sparkled with an array of colours, the special stones hidden among the more conventional gems.

As she ran the final piece through her fingers, she could no longer tell which were the diamonds and which were the special stones. For a moment she wondered about the special stones and why her master insisted that they be kept a secret. Then it was gone as Mr May returned.

"I've finished, sir," Jane ventured.

"What?" he replied, his mind still clearly elsewhere.

"The bracelet, sir. It's done."

"Ah, yes." Mr May walked over, still dressed in his black overcoat and top hat. He picked it up and ran it through his hands. He paused occasionally, studying it. "Excellent." He glanced down at the workbench and could see that there were no more stones. "I shall count the stones later. You will begin a new piece shortly. Go to the cook and eat."

"Yes, sir," Jane said. That was the level of praise she got. A simple word. *Excellent.* For a piece that her master would sell for hundreds and hundreds of pounds.

Jane didn't care, of course; her life was immeasurably better now that she had left the workhouse.

For the most part, her work was enjoyable. Sometimes, Mr May hurried her to finish a particular piece so that she could start to work on another. But apart from that, she suffered little in the way of hardship. Even cleaning the workshop at night took little effort. The nature of the work meant the surfaces had to be clean during the day, so there was little extra to do at night. She also took the newspapers that Mr May had purchased each day to her room at night. She found she loved reading and was strangely grateful for the education that the workhouse had provided. As she read, she learnt more and more about the city, the country, and the world in general.

It seemed that over time, Mrs May's ideas on her food consumption began to best those of her husband. The cook gradually started to increase the girl's portion sizes as Mrs May insisted she fill out a little more. She would even give her the occasional treat. About a month ago, Mr May ventured into the kitchen while Jane was eating a thick slice of chocolate cake, and he didn't even bat an eyelid.

Mrs Johnson told her quietly that the truth was how Mrs May had told her husband he would get a bad reputation at Goldsmith's Hall because Jane was so thin. She also said that Mr May knew perfectly well that Jane produced such fine jewellery, and he would be hard-pressed to replace her. He wasn't for a moment going to risk that for the cost of three decent meals each day. That afforded Jane a huge sense of pride.

Jane enjoyed spending time with Mrs May. However, this only happened when Mr May was out at any one of his many clubs in the evening. He was out of the house alone on at least three occasions each week, and more often than not Mrs May would invite Jane to spend an hour or so with her. They would play games and talk and Mrs May taught her how to sew for pleasure as a lady was expected to do as opposed to a seamstress. Her mistress produced treats in the form of bullseyes, pear drops, and sticky black toffee. Jane told her how she loved to read, and most weeks Mrs May would produce a new book for her to enjoy. Jane found she loved escaping into the stories she read. She also enjoyed factual books and reading the history behind the Kings and Queens of England. So much of the history she read was almost more unbelievable than the books of fiction. A king who murdered his nephews in the Tower of London to take the throne. A king with six wives. A queen who never married but ruled England with an iron rod. Mrs May insisted, however, that her husband hear nothing of their meetings or the gifts she gave Jane. It was to be their secret.

Jane promised faithfully that she would never breathe a word of it to Mr May just as she promised

Mr May that she wouldn't breathe a word of the special stones to his wife.

It seemed that Jane was to be trusted with numerous secrets around the house. She remembered Robin's words on that day he pulled the stolen chicken breast from the kitchen, *"Secrets are important. If someone trusts you with a secret, you must always keep it."* She would do just that.

Jane was pretty certain that the maid Jennifer Dawson had secrets of her own to hide. Jane would often see her sneaking about late at night. One night when Jane couldn't sleep, she watched from her little attic window as the maid disappeared out of the back of the building past the foundry and into the city beyond. She didn't say anything, of course; it wasn't her business.

Jennifer had not become any friendlier towards her, nor had she bullied her or hit her. It was clear that she considered Jane a threat in some way and that was why she ignored her for the most part.

But Jane couldn't quite understand why.

She was fairly sure that her master, Mr May, had trusted the maid with a secret as well. She'd seen Jennifer emerging from Mr May's office where he kept his papers on more than one occasion when his wife was out for the afternoon with her friends. Mr May would have been at work in there with the door firmly shut. They were always in there for a while.

Again, whatever secrets were being shared were none of her business.

Jane had just finished eating when Mr May entered the kitchen.

"Right, I hope you've finished? Let's get you back to work," he said to Jane.

Immediately, she leapt from her chair. "Yes, sir."

"I went to Goldsmiths' Hall this morning. The consensus is that the coronation will be held before long. That means there will be a good many very wealthy lords and ladies requiring items to show off their wealth for the coronation service and the subsequent festivities. I think we're going to be very busy over the next few months. We'd better get back to it straight away."

CHAPTER 9

1 *3 months later*

"The Half-Crown Coronation, they're calling it," Mr May sneered.

It had now been over a year since the king's death, but still the coronation hadn't taken place. There were still a few months to go until the event in Westminster Abbey.

After the outlandish excess of his brother, the new king decided he didn't want to lavish public funds on his own celebrations. As a result, only a fraction was spent when compared to the coronation of his older brother.

This disappointed Mr May. He had hoped to receive a commission from the government to produce an extensive array of gold, jewellery and banqueting plate that would be required at the coronation.

Regrettably, due to the budgets involved, he had only been awarded the making of twenty-five coronets for baronets. Even then, he had to reduce his bid for the work considerably. He smarted with resentment at the situation.

Mr May was reading from The Globe newspaper, which he had picked up after they had attended service at St. Paul's Cathedral that morning.

About three months earlier, Jane had started accompanying the Mays on Sunday mornings when they attended services. Mrs May had ardently fought for this arrangement with her husband, ultimately triumphing. She made certain that before their first visit to the cathedral, Jane received a brand-new dress. The original one, provided when she first arrived at the May's residence, had become far too snug. That particular dress had only been worn on a handful of occasions, such as Christmas Day.

Mr May looked Jane up and down, obviously calculating the cost of the garment when he saw it that Sunday morning. But he said nothing.

Three months later, Jane was now sitting around the dinner table with the Mays on Sundays.

Yet again, Mrs May waged a battle with her husband regarding this, and once more, she prevailed.

Little by little, Jane was becoming less of an apprentice and more of a member of the family.

She still slept in her attic room, but she was perfectly happy there, surrounded by her books gifted by Mrs May. She still worked diligently in the workshop, with her skills advancing consistently over time.

"John Bridge was crowing down at Goldsmith's Hall on Friday that the work on St Edward's Crown had been done," Mr May said to neither his wife nor Jane in particular. The distaste in his voice was obvious. "His finest work ever, he said." Mr May let out a snort that sounded like an elephant. "What did he have to do? Resize the thing slightly? Why do they have to keep giving the work to them, is what I want to know. Philip Rundell is dead, he was the genius."

"They do have the Royal Warrant, Russell," said Mrs May softly. "They could hardly go elsewhere, could they?"

Again, Mr May let out a huge snort. "There are plenty that think they should. Especially now Rundell is dead. Apparently, they have also made a new Sovereign's Ring for the occasion. A huge lumbering thing by all reports. Ugly and crude. No flair."

He lowered his paper slightly and peered over the top at Jane who was sitting upright in her chair behaving impeccably, listening attentively in case she was asked anything by Mr May. She had been told by Mrs May to be on her very best behaviour during these meals so that her husband would have nothing to complain about, apart from the additional cost.

"Of course, barring a miracle, the next monarch will be a woman. Princess Alexandrina is a child, and they say very small for her age." He paused for a moment as he studied Jane. "And we produce the finest pieces for women in the country." He broke out into a smile, "The Princess won't be able to wear St Edward's Crown. It's far too heavy. Changes will have to be made."

Mrs May looked at her husband studying Jane. She knew perfectly well what he was thinking. He could see a route to obtaining a royal warrant when this king died. That route was through his apprentice's skill. She smiled to herself, knowing that her husband would be far more amenable to her plans.

Despite Mr May's upset at the lack of official business from the coronation, he had been right about one thing.

London's aristocrats and wealthy patrons flocked to his shop to commission new pieces in anticipation of the coronation festivities. Russell May Goldsmiths' clientele now featured duchesses and countesses; the very pinnacle of British nobility.

The special stones, as Mr May still called them, were used and inserted into the vast majority of pieces. Although the pieces commissioned by the duchesses and countesses very rarely did. Jane had become skilled at studying the stones through a loupe and being able to detect which were diamonds and which were the special stones. She wasn't sure if Mr May was aware of her skill in this matter and she didn't dare mention it.

She started to have suspicions about these special stones. Jane speculated that they might be a means of avoiding the use of real diamonds in the pieces on which she worked. She couldn't fathom why Mr May would do this, and she certainly had no intention of interrogating him about it. She resolved to keep following orders, day in and day out.

Particularly now, as Mrs May was making progress with her husband on making Jane feel more a part of the family.

During their evenings together, Mrs May had often spoken of this. Mrs May had often discussed this during their evening conversations. She had recently confided in Jane that she thought of her as a daughter. Both women had found themselves tearfully embracing that night. Jane, who had never known her mother, had secretly yearned for one throughout her life. At last, she felt she had found one, even if they had to conceal the truth from Mr May.

Mrs May explained that Mr May's reluctance to

accept Jane into the family was due to the hurt and pain he felt when their own daughter died. His wife was convinced that Mr May would never love another child again, just to protect his own heart.

On more than one occasion, Jane had thought of sharing the secrets she knew about Mr May with her new mother. She wanted to talk about the special stones. She was worried about them. She feared that Mr May might be engaging in some nefarious activities and could potentially find himself in hot water, which would undoubtedly distress Mrs May.

Under no circumstances did she want that to happen. But she had remembered Robin's words in the workhouse that day. Secrets were something that should never be shared.

She decided to keep quiet.

Two weeks later, Jane witnessed something strange.

She was well aware that Mr May and the maid, Jennifer, would slip away to his office when Mrs May was out in the afternoon. Sometimes they would spend a mere fifteen minutes there, while other times they lingered for an hour. More often than not, Jennifer would emerge from the office looking dishevelled and flustered. As she thought in the past, Mr May had some form of secret that he clearly shared with the maid.

But now they were arguing outside.

Jane was in the privy on the other side of the foundry and it was clear that neither the master nor the maid was aware of her presence. They never raised their voices because it was obvious that neither wanted to be overheard.

"I tell you, it is not mine," Mr May said insistently.

"Russell, it is," Jennifer replied, her voice breaking with emotion.

Jane was a little surprised; she hadn't heard anyone else in the household call him Russell other than Mrs May. She certainly never heard Jennifer calling him by his first name when anybody else was within earshot. For the first time, Jane realised that there was a sense of intimacy between the two.

It sent a shiver down her spine. She suddenly realised that something was going on that her new mother would be hurt by. But she didn't know what.

"Don't you think that I know about your illicit nighttime activities? I see you disappear into the shadows. God knows how many men you have around the city," Mr May spat at her.

It seemed that Mr May knew about Jennifer's secrets. Jane tried to make sense of the conversation, but her lack of worldly ways made it almost impossible. What was this about Jennifer having men in the city? What did it mean?

She sat in the privy, quiet as a mouse, knowing perfectly well that she was not meant to hear this conversation. She knew that if they found out she'd overheard, things would not go well for her.

"You promised to make me your wife," Jennifer said.

Mr May gave his customary snort of derision. "Make you my wife? Imagine what they would say at Goldsmiths Hall, girl. You were a pastime, nothing more."

"You made that workhouse girl your daughter, haven't you?"

There was a moment of silence, and then a whack. Jennifer gasped and started to sob. Jane realised that Mr May had slapped her.

"Despite what my wife thinks, that girl is not my daughter. She is an apprentice, just like you are a maid and a pastime. Nothing more. I tell you, it is not mine." Mr May's voice was getting strained now.

"It is, Russell, despite your objections. And I will let the world know about it."

"I'll deny it all. Who will the world believe? Me, a respected man of the community, or you, girl? A mere maid who's is nothing more than a whore who disappears out of my house at night to visit all and sundry?"

"But..."

"But nothing," he interrupted, not allowing her to speak. "That is the way it is. You'll get rid of it. I know a woman who will do it. I'll pay but you won't mention me."

Jane peered through a small crack in a door, she could see Jennifer move her hand from holding her face to her stomach.

"No, Russell. I will not. I'm going to tell the mistress everything." She turned and took two steps towards the door.

Mr May's heavy hand reached out to her shoulder and stopped her. He swung her around, so she faced them. "You breathe a word of this, and it will be the last thing you do. I will say diamonds have gone missing and they will be found in your room. They will think you make these claims because of that, and you'll swing for sure. You hear me?"

The maid's eyes grew wide as she took it all in.

"I don't want to get rid of it," she sobbed.

"Fine. I'll pay you to go. You will write a letter that some young scoundrel has got you in a delicate condition, which, let's face it, is the truth. And you'll disappear tonight. We will never see you again."

"But what about us, Russell? This is our chance together."

"There is no us. I'm not leaving my wife. She is a woman of breeding. Ideal for a Goldsmith's wife. You and I had relations. I enjoyed you. That is all. It will go no further. Now, you have one final chance. You can be well paid to go quietly."

Jennifer looked at him and Jane could see that the tears were streaming down her face. "How much?"

"Thirty pounds."

"Fifty," she countered after a moment.

Again Mr May snorted. "That's almost two years' pay. You think I'm a fool."

"And I have your child for the rest of my life," Jennifer said.

"It's not mine, remember?" Mr May said slowly, but Jane heard the doubt in his voice. "Forty."

"No. Fifty," Jennifer insisted after pulling herself upright. Her tears had dried and suddenly she seemed ready to fight for her future. "That's a pittance, considering what you had promised me."

Mr May scratched his chin. "Forty-five pounds and you go tonight. If I hear from you again or if my wife hears rumours, I will say you stole from the business. I will say you took gold, rubies and diamonds and then you fled into the night like the ungrateful wretch you are. They will come looking for you and you know perfectly well they will find you." He stopped speaking for a moment before adding, "You know what will happen then."

Through the small crack in the door, Jane could see Jennifer, her eyes glassy with fear, swallowing slowly, as though she could almost envisage a noose tightening around her delicate neck. The setting sun cast eerie shadows on their faces, further high-lighting the grim atmosphere.

"Agreed," Jennifer muttered, her voice barely audible.

"You'll be gone by morning," Mr May said menac-ingly, his eyes narrowing as he cast the most sinister glance Jane had ever seen. His usual handsome face was cold and cruel. "In fact, there need be no letter. My wife is too compassionate. She'll end up doing something stupid. You'll disappear into the night."

Silently, Jennifer nodded, her face ashen.

He nodded in return, a twisted smile playing on his lips, and he walked off, his footsteps echoing as he left.

Jennifer took a few moments to compose herself, her chest heaving as she took several deep breaths to steady her trembling hands. Gathering her courage, she walked over to the old wooden privy and opened the door with a creak.

There was a moment of shock on her face, her eyes widening in surprise when she saw Jane sitting there.

Jennifer studied her for a moment, her gaze searching, and then said softly, "I guess you heard all that?"

Jane simply stared at her dumbfounded for a few seconds, her mind reeling. In all the time she had lived with the Mays, other than a few grunts and forced words, this was the first time Jennifer had addressed her directly.

"I did," Jane replied with a nod, her voice wavering. Suddenly, an impending sense of doom washed over her like a cold shiver. Jennifer was obviously looking for somebody to take out her frustrations on. As Jane sat there on the privy, she slowly clenched her hands into fists, her knuckles white with determination. She would not let another Kate Larkin situation happen today.

But instead, Jennifer slumped her shoulders and let out a huge sigh, her eyes filled with sadness. "Be careful, little one. He'll be inviting you into the office in a few years. Don't believe a word he says. It's false promises and lies, all sugar-coated like poison." She patted her stomach, a rueful smile flickering across her lips.

With that, she turned and disappeared into the shadows of the foundry, her footsteps fading away.

Jane didn't see her again.

wo years later

"Thank you, Miss Jane," Mrs Wilson said with a hint of a smile after Jane had praised her for the impeccable cleaning of her room that day.

Mrs Wilson was the new maid. She was a widow with a sombre air, almost sixty years of age and she had been in service all her life. Her hands bore the marks of years of hard work, and her eyes held a quiet wisdom that said she had seen and heard it all before.

Mrs May had begun the interview process for a new maid almost a week after Jennifer had mysteriously left in the middle of the night. The sudden departure had left Mrs May quite shocked. Mr May, ever so rational, put forward the theory that Jennifer must have had a secret suitor somewhere and had run off to marry him. With no better explanation, Mrs May was forced to reluctantly agree.

Jane, of course, kept silent. It was a secret she knew intimately and, as with all secrets, she knew she could never tell.

Intriguingly, Mrs May undertook the interviews for the new maid alone. Now that she was a little older, Jane found it curious that Mrs May had chosen an older woman like Mrs Wilson as opposed to a young girl who would have more energy. Jane couldn't help but wonder if Mrs May had known all along about the unspoken truth between her husband and Jennifer. Again, it was a discussion she knew she could never have with her new mother.

Jane was now present at the Mays' dinner table every single night. It was another battle Mrs May fought with her husband from which she emerged victorious. In private, Jane would lovingly call Mrs May 'Mother'. However, she knew perfectly well that in front of Mr May, that word could never be used.

Everyone in the household understood the complex dynamics that had formed between them all. This was why the new maid, Mrs Wilson, with her understanding eyes and quiet demeanour, respectfully referred to Jane as Miss Jane.

Russell May Goldsmith's continued to attract new business, especially ladies looking for exclusive pieces. Mr May took on a new man to help the twins.

Hans Biesenbach was a German and his lack of English meant he fitted in well with the strange way in which the twins communicated.

After a significant amount of persuasion and a great deal of discussion, Mrs May finally agreed to take on another apprentice. Mr May believed that with two apprentices possessing the skill level of Jane, he could double the output of his workshop. Mrs May, on the other hand, was rather reluctant. She cherished the relationship she had built with Jane and was hesitant to let anyone else come between them. But in the end, she conceded to her husband's persistent demands.

However, she made a mistake. She allowed Mr May to select the new apprentice himself, without her guidance.

He returned triumphantly with an older girl named Mary, who was nearly sixteen years of age. She had long blonde hair, piercing blue eyes, and a captivating beauty that turned men's heads whenever she passed. Jane saw her mother's face drop, a mixture of surprise and displeasure very apparent when Mr May walked into the room with Mary in tow.

Determined to be welcoming, Jane offered warm smiles to the new girl. She remembered all too well the trepidation she had felt on her first day, coming from the workhouse. Mary had been pleasant enough without being overtly friendly. Jane discerned that she had only been in the workhouse for eighteen months, arriving there with her elderly grandmother who had since passed away. She had no fears of the outside world that Jane had. Mary had been given a small, simple, but functional room alongside those of the cook and the maid.

That night when Jane lay in bed, she could hear the muffled sounds of Mr and Mrs May arguing downstairs.

"Do you think I'm stupid, Russell?" Mrs May shouted, her voice tense with anger. "Why did you choose her, I wonder."

Jane strained to hear Mr May's reply, but his voice was too soft.

"You just want to continue to humiliate me."

The heated exchange went on for what seemed like an age until there was a sudden, deafening silence.

If her mother didn't like the new girl, then Jane knew there would be a good reason. She thought she probably understood her concerns. She wondered how long it would be before Mr May started inviting her to his office when his wife was out for the afternoon.

However, all their concerns turned out to be for nought. Mary did not respond well to the tasks Mr May had set her. She was clumsy and slow. She lasted just two days and then, when they awoke in the morning, they discovered that she had fled into the London night.

Apparently, it was a common practice for apprentices to abscond.

"Don't you get any ideas, girl," Mr May barked in anger that morning. He was obviously thinking of the lost fee he had just paid to the Workhouse master. And probably the lost pleasures he was already planning. "Your apprenticeship is lodged down at Goldsmiths Hall. You are mine to do with as I say until you're 21 years of age."

"Why would I want to leave?" Jane replied kindly, attempting to placate him.

Mr May gave his typical snort of derision and marched out of the workshop, his face red with fury.

Moments later, she saw him leaving via the shop entrance, speaking quickly to Grimes before he left.

Jane returned to the intricate piece on which she was working. So far, it had taken almost a week's work. It contained 432 shimmering diamonds and 121 sparkling sapphires. There were no special stones involved in this case. It was almost complete. The piece was to be a necklace for the elegant Countess Stanhope, the young wife of the Earl.

Mr May would charge the rather extravagant sum of £1,000 for it.

It was almost complete, but it had to be perfect.

And it had to be delivered tomorrow. Jane would ensure that was the case.

Mr May returned mid-afternoon, he was soaking wet and the weather outside was foul. He was also reeking of alcohol. This was highly unusual for him. He generally enjoyed a few drinks when he visited his gentlemen's clubs in the evening, but he never drank during the day, and never to the degree that anyone would notice he was inebriated.

"I have brilliant news. Jane, go fetch the twins and Hans from the foundry." He took off his top hat and draped his coat over one of the workbenches. Jane got up and did precisely as she was told. She wouldn't enter the foundry, of course, simply calling the twins and Hans from outside. To this day, she had never been inside. What lay within its confines was a mystery to her. She had no idea what this brilliant news was, but the fact that Mr May's mood had brightened was a relief to her.

When she returned, Carol May was also in the workshop while Grimes hovered in the doorway between it and the shop.

"John Bridge is dead," Mr May announced with undisguised glee. "Apparently, his nephew, also called John Bridge, is taking over the running of the firm. He's nothing more than a boy. So you know what that means?"

Jane sensed a feeling of unease in her stomach.

She understood perfectly well what this could mean for Russell May's business but to openly celebrate a rival's death seemed somewhat unbecoming.

No one replied to him for a moment. Not even his wife. Jane could sense that her mother shared the same feeling of revulsion as she did.

Finally, Mr May's stare fixated on Jane. She felt compelled to offer a reply. "There's a chance to become the Royal Goldsmiths, sir."

"A chance we will take with both hands."

"I must write a letter of condolence to John Bridge's wife," Mrs May finally said, acknowledging the situation.

"Excellent idea. We will, of course, attend the funeral."

There was a silence for a moment before Mr May clapped his hands sharply. "Right. To work."

By dinner time, Mr May had sobered up. Mrs Johnson had prepared a roast chicken, one of Jane's favourites.

She attacked it with enthusiasm.

Jane noted that there was still an air of tension between husband and wife. Her mother, she only thought of her as this now, and it took quite the effort not to say the word in front of Mr May, was still angry at his choice of a new apprentice. However, since the girl had fled, there seemed to be an unspoken peace. Jane knew perfectly well that her mother would not agree to another apprentice so easily.

Jane wished that Mr May would not do things that hurt her mother. She didn't want to see her sad. Now she was older, she understood more about the strange conversation she had overheard between her master and Jennifer. She knew that if her mother ever found out, she would be devastated. She worried a lot about the special stones. More and more she believed that something was amiss. What would happen if this practice was discovered? What would happen to Mr May? And how would it affect her mother?

There was something else alongside the worry and sadness. There was growing anger.

Anger that Mr May would treat her mother in this way. She didn't deserve any of it. Jane hoped one day he would stop. If not, Jane would have to step in herself.

She was no longer required to sit perfectly quietly at mealtimes. She could speak and ask questions. She rarely addressed Mr May directly, but when she did, she knew just how to do it.

Today, she had a genuine question.

"Do you think it feasible that you can win the Royal Warrant, Sir?" Jane asked after she neatly laid down her knife and fork after the meal. Despite her horror at the way Mr May had reacted to the news of his rival's death, she couldn't help but feel excitement at the possibility of working on pieces that the royal family might wear.

Mr May beamed. "I do. The key moment will be the death of this king. When his niece ascends the throne, everything must change. St Edward's Crown, which is traditionally used at the moment of coronation, weighs over 5 pounds. There is no way Princess Alexandrina will be able to wear that. Changes will need to be made. It's my belief that a completely new crown will need to be crafted, one suitable for a young woman. It is my intention to put forward designs when the time comes."

Jane had read a book about the Crown Jewels of England which Mrs May had found at a market stall. As she worked on magnificent pieces every day, it was natural that she took an interest. The gems housed at the Tower of London were not the original jewels, of course. The hapless King John had somehow managed to lose the first set in the wash while travelling from King's Lynn to his untimely death as a result of dysentery in Newark Castle. For years, treasure hunters had searched through the fens in a vain attempt to retrieve them. Nobody had ever succeeded, and they lay there to this day.

Of course, one precious item not lost to the waters of the fens was Saint Edward's Crown. The reason being, it was regarded as a holy relic and as such was always securely kept within the hallowed walls of Westminster Abbey.

Over the ensuing centuries, the Plantagenets and later the Tudors diligently worked to restore the Crown Jewels to their former glory. They succeeded and surpassed the collection lost by King John. The formidable Henry VIII, ever the extravagant monarch, commissioned the Tudor Crown. According to the tattered, leather-bound book Jane had been engrossed in, Henry's regal headpiece weighed in at a truly staggering 7 pounds.

The tumultuous era of the English Civil War resulted in Charles I losing his head, severed from his body with a single gruesome stroke outside the Banqueting House.

Oliver Cromwell then took centre stage and proceeded to ruthlessly destroy the Crown Jewels, remorselessly melting down both the sacred Saint Edward's Crown and the magnificent Tudor Crown.

Bizarrely, and rather miraculously, certain items managed to survive this brutal onslaught. Loyal Royalists, risking their very lives, covertly smuggled out specific gems and priceless artefacts and kept them hidden.

Upon the eventual restoration of the monarchy, these precious items were ceremoniously presented to Charles II. He immediately embarked upon the daunting and somewhat expensive task of restoring the Crown Jewels to their former dazzling glory. One of the very first pieces he created was a brand-new Saint Edward's Crown, meticulously crafted based on detailed drawings of the original.

It was this resplendent crown that had been reverently used at each moment of coronation since that fateful point in history. If Mr May was right, when the young princess became Queen, that would not be possible.

Jane imagined what a new crown might look like. She had seen drawings of the present ones in her book, and she had ideas of her own.

She could only imagine working on such an item for a new queen.

CHAPTER 11

*T*he next morning, Mrs May rushed into the workshop with an air of urgency. It was early, with the sun barely rising. The twins had just arrived and had disappeared into the foundry. Hans would be coming through the front door shortly.

Russell May Goldsmith's was coming to life for the working day.

"Jane, I need to speak with you a moment," Mrs May said, her worried expression deepening the lines on her face.

Jane stood up from the workbench, her hands covered in the fine dust of metal filings and followed her to the foot of the stairs.

"What is it, Mother?" Jane asked, full of concern, her heart beating faster in her chest.

"It's Russell, my dear. He's taken ill. I fear his getting drenched in the downpour yesterday has given him a chill. I'm going to send Mrs Wilson to fetch Dr Jenkins."

"Do you think it's serious?" Jane inquired, her eyes wide with anxiety.

"I pray not, but you know how quickly these things can develop," her mother said nervously, wringing her hands.

"But he wants to see you, Jane. He's fretting about this necklace for the countess. Do try to persuade him to put it from his mind. I feel that worry will do him no good in his condition. I've heard of men his age dropping down with bad hearts that have been caused by worry."

"Of course," Jane said, giving her mother a reas-suring hug. "He'll be fine. He's as strong as an ox."

In the back of her mind, Jane found it endearing how much her mother cared for her husband. She wondered if the situation were reversed, would Mr May act in the same worried manner?

Jane followed her mother upstairs, the floor-boards creaking beneath their feet, and into the Mays' bedroom. Despite her integration into the family, she had never been in this room before. The walls were adorned with various family portraits, and the room smelled of lavender and old books.

Mr May certainly did not look well. His skin was

ashen and clammy, and at the same time, a layer of sweat glistened upon his brow.

"Don't go too close," Mrs May whispered in Jane's ear. "Just in case it's something contagious."

"Jane, is the necklace for the countess finished?" Despite his sickly appearance, his voice was quite strong, albeit strained.

"Yes, sir."

"Is it perfect?"

"It is, sir."

Mr May paused for a moment, seemingly gathering his strength.

"I don't have the energy to check it. But I trust you, Jane. If you say it is perfect, I'm sure it is."

"I promise. It looks magnificent."

"I saw it myself, Russell. It is a spectacular piece," Mrs May chimed in, trying to reassure her husband.

"But I have another problem. The necklace is due for delivery today. Obviously, I was planning on taking it myself. That isn't going to be possible now. I cannot have my wife take it; it would be unseemly. The twins are simply not suitable for such a task. They would create an unfavourable impression, shall we say." At this point, Mr May was almost talking to himself, as though he were going over the problem in his mind, trying to find a solution.

"I could take it, sir," Jane piped up, her voice confident.

"Russell, Jane can't possibly take it. The piece is worth so much money. What might happen to her?"

Mr May seemed to ignore his wife. "That was my thought, Jane. I think you would represent our company well if you put on your best dress and behave immaculately. The countess almost certainly would not come herself to receive the piece. You will simply need to deliver it to her butler, who you will then ask to sign a piece of paper to say it has been received."

"Russell, the girl can't go out on her own on the streets with the item."

"She won't be going on her own. We'll make Grimes go with her. And he can actually carry the piece until they reach Mahon House."

Mrs May hesitated for a moment, her eyes flitting between her husband and her daughter, before finally nodding in agreement. "Very well, but only if Grimes accompanies her, and they take every precaution."

"Make sure it is signed for. There is a document on my desk for the task. Carol, you get it for her," Russell managed to say before he exploded into a fit of coughs.

Jane felt a flutter of excitement in her chest as she prepared herself for the task. She donned her best dress and took extra care in pinning up her hair in a neat chignon.

When she was ready, Grimes met her at the door.

He was an imposing figure, his broad shoulders and muscular arms well-suited for the task of protecting the precious necklace. The exquisite piece of jewellery was carefully tucked away in an unassuming wooden box, which Grimes held securely in his calloused hands.

Together, they set off for Mahon House, making their way through the bustling streets of London. She was no longer afraid of the city. She visited St Paul's most Sundays. She went shopping three or four times a year with her mother. And she had taken to walking up and down Cockspur Street after lunch on most days to stretch her legs. But today, Jane's heart raced with every step, a mix of excitement and trepidation. She was well aware of the responsibility that had been entrusted to her and was determined to make her mother proud.

As they approached the grand residence of the Earl and the Countess, Jane straightened her posture and took a deep breath. She knew that the success of this delivery would not only prove her capabilities but also solidify the reputation of her firm. Maybe that Royal Warrant could be gained? Maybe she might be working on the crown for the next Queen of England.

Grimes knocked firmly on the door and handed the wooden box to Jane. He took a step backwards.

The door was opened by a young footman with a sneering expression. "Yes?"

Jane handed the young man an embossed business card. "A delivery for the countess from Russell May Goldsmith."

The footman took a moment to glance at the card and ushered Jane inside. Grimes said he would wait outside. He wasn't a man for fine houses. Jane simply nodded her head.

Jane stepped into a grand, spacious entrance hall, its floor adorned with polished white and black tiles which formed an intricate pattern. The walls were lined with colossal portraits of stern-faced men in immaculate military uniforms, their eyes seeming to follow Jane's every movement, and stunning women dressed in flowing ballgowns, their beauty frozen with the strokes of the artist's brush.

The footman gestured towards an ornate wooden chair with a high back and carved legs "Sit."

Jane obeyed without hesitation. She would be careful not to bring any shame upon the company she represented.

Approximately five minutes passed before the young footman returned, his demeanour noticeably warmer. "The countess will see you now."

Jane's heart fluttered in her chest, an unexpected sensation. The countess?

"Am I not to just leave the piece?"

"No. Lady Stanhope wishes to view the piece in your presence before she signs for it," the footman explained.

Taking a deep breath, Jane rose from the chair, grateful that her legs didn't betray her weakness. She could hardly imagine that Mr May had anticipated this turn of events. Had he known, she was certain he would never have allowed her to come.

"Your name?" the footman enquired.

Jane regarded him with a puzzled expression.

"I am to announce you, madam," the footman said, a hint of exasperation tingeing his voice.

"Jane. Jane Monday."

With purpose, the footman strode along the elegant corridor and into an opulent drawing room. The walls were bathed in a soft shade of blue, with luxurious furniture upholstered in matching fabric.

"Jane Monday from Russell May Goldsmiths, your ladyship."

With a swift pivot, the footman vanished from sight.

A refined woman, exuding grace and kindness, rose from a plush blue sofa and approached Jane. She appeared to be in her late thirties or early forties, her flawless beauty accentuated by a stunning white satin dress.

"Where is Mr May?" the countess asked, her voice the epitome of the British aristocracy.

"I'm afraid he is unwell, your ladyship. The doctor is attending to him as we speak. He does send his apologies."

"I am sorry to hear it. Who are you?" the countess inquired.

"I am the jeweller who worked on the piece, your ladyship."

"I see," the countess said, a spark of interest igniting in her eyes. "I did not realise that Russell May employed young women."

"Only the one, your ladyship. I have been in his employment for several years. I am able to produce intricate pieces that perhaps men could not." Jane held out her hands to show her long thin fingers.

The countess nodded her head sagely.

Jane had made the conscious choice not to reveal herself as Russell May's apprentice. For some reason, she felt the countess might not take kindly to anyone less than a fully trained jeweller working on her commissioned piece. She thought that Mr May would understand.

"So, Jane, may I see it?" the countess asked, her voice tinged with excitement.

"Of course, your ladyship. Shall we go to the table?"

"Indeed."

Jane followed the countess over to the table, her heart pounding in her chest. With great care, she opened the simple box and withdrew a piece of black velvet, laying it delicately upon the finely polished mahogany surface. She gently placed the unassuming box upon it, then extracted another, far more elaborate box from within. Jane knew from Mr May's incessant grumbling that he had paid the handsome sum of sixty pounds to have this exquisite container crafted especially for this treasure. However, walking through the bustling streets of London, her bodyguard, Grimes, had deemed it prudent to conceal the precious cargo within a nondescript outer box.

With trembling hands, Jane placed the ornate jewellery box on the black velvet and dramatically opened it, unveiling the hidden masterpiece within.

The countess gasped in astonishment, her eyes wide with admiration. "It's exquisite," she whispered, her voice barely audible.

The piece of jewellery that lay before them was a breathtaking work of art. Intricate filigree formed a delicate framework of gold, while an array of precious gemstones adorned the surface, their vibrant colours dancing in the light that filtered through the drawing room's tall windows. Each detail had been meticulously crafted, the result of hours of labour and an unyielding dedication to perfection.

Jane's heart swelled with pride as she watched the countess's awestruck reaction. She had poured her heart and soul into creating this piece, and seeing the delight on the countess's face validated her every effort.

"Jane, this is truly remarkable," the countess murmured, her gaze never leaving the jewelled masterpiece. "You possess a rare gift, one that I hope you continue to nurture and develop."

Jane's cheeks flushed with warmth as she accepted the countess's praise. "Thank you, your ladyship. I am honoured by your kind words."

The countess finally looked up, her eyes meeting Jane's with genuine admiration. "Please extend my deepest gratitude to Mr May for sending you in his stead, and assure him that I am absolutely delighted with the piece."

"I will, your ladyship," Jane replied, her voice steady and confident. She paused for a moment. "Mr May was insistent I get a signature of delivery?" Jane pulled out two pieces of paper.

"Of course," agreed the countess, running her eye over the piece of paper.

"And I have the invoice as well," Jane also added a little shyly. It was a huge amount of money. It would not be paid now of course. Usually, clients such as the countess would pay within thirty days.

The countess took the delivery note over to a small desk in the corner of the room and signed and dated the paper with a flourish.

"There we go. Mr May has his signature," she smiled warmly as she handed it to Jane.

"Thank you, your ladyship," Jane said with a small curtsey.

"Now I will summon the footman and he will take you to my comptroller. You leave the invoice there with him. If he is not there in his office, his assistant will be. Again, you can leave it with him."

After another flurry of thanks and praise from the countess, she found herself following the footman down a corridor into the bowels of the great house.

Finally, they came to a large wooden door. The footman knocked, and a voice from within shouted "Enter."

He did so and Jane followed. It was a large office with one huge desk and one much smaller one pushed up against the wall. At the rear of the office was a set of small drawers, each clearly labelled. A man in a dark suit was fiddling with papers in one. He didn't turn around.

"Her ladyship says this lady is to present her invoice to Mr Taylor. As he isn't here, can you deal with her?"

"Of course," the man said without turning around. The slight squeak to his voice suggested to Jane that he was young, perhaps no more than a boy.

"Will you show him to the door afterwards, please? I have to get back to her Ladyship."

"Indeed," the man agreed.

The footman turned in his customary manner.

Jane stood in silence.

"One moment," the man said. "I don't want these papers out of order."

Jane cocked her head to one side. There was something about that voice. Something that she recalled.

The man shut the drawer with a bang and turned around.

It was Robin Buckley.

CHAPTER 12

The two just stood, staring at each other for what seemed an eternity.

Finally, Robin spoke. "Jane? What are you doing here?"

"I could ask you the same," she said before breaking out into a huge grin and running into her old friend's arms.

They embraced before Robin looked nervously towards the door and took a step back.

"The Comptroller, my boss, he might be back at any moment."

Jane nodded her head and took a respectful step backwards as well.

They hurriedly exchanged news on how they both ended up in their respective positions.

"Goldsmith? That's a most unusual trade for a

workhouse girl," Robin said after letting out a short whistle.

"I love it," Jane said. "I created the piece I just delivered for the countess. My master was ill, so I came instead. "

"It sounds like you're really going places, Jane. I'm so pleased for you," Robin said softly.

"What about you? You always told me you'd end up working in one of these fine houses."

Robin laughed. "I'd rather envisaged owning one. But this will do for starters, for sure."

They both stood in place, staring at each other. After so long apart, and such a sudden reunion, they both began to feel awkward.

Finally, Jane said, "I missed you, you know. I cried for days after you left."

"I missed you," Robin replied. "I begged the matron to allow me to come and say goodbye before I left the workhouse. But you know what she was like."

Jane nodded her head, recalling the stern face of Mrs Bird in her mind. She was thankful that her new mistress, her new mother, was nothing like that.

"I finally stood up for myself, you know. I put Kate Larkin in her place. I did it thinking about the words you said," she said.

Robin smiled revealing his brilliant white teeth. "I always knew that you would." Robin's eyes flashed to the door as they heard heavy footsteps along the corridor. "My boss," he murmured without a sound.

"Let's not lose contact, Robin," Jane almost begged. "You know where to find me now." She handed him the invoice for the necklace, with Russell Mays' crest and logo emblazoned upon the top and the address printed boldly underneath.

"You also know where to find me. If I move on, I will tell you."

"I will do the same."

The door swung open, and a thin man in his early 60s appeared. He scrutinised Jane closely.

"Thank you for this," Robin said formally to Jane. "It will be paid in due course."

Jane took her cue from Robin, and after one last, long, lingering glance, she managed to say, "Thank you, sir. My master will be most appreciative." She nodded her head, smiled, and turned to leave, nodding her head at Robin's boss as she left with her head held high.

The footman was waiting at the end of the corridor, ready to escort her to the front door. Moments later, she stood next to Grimes, who had a concerned expression on his face. "What happened to you? I thought you were just dropping the necklace off?"

"So did I," she said, somewhat absent-mindedly. "The countess demanded to see me. Fortunately, it all went well."

They walked back through the streets of London in near silence. Her mind was preoccupied with other thoughts.

Jane could hardly believe it. Robin Buckley. She truly believed she would never see him again in her life. She wished she could have stayed longer, but it was not possible for either of them. Service and etiquette demanded that they part once more.

However, now she knew where he lived. She was determined not to lose him again.

Upon returning to the workshop, she went upstairs to report back to Mr May. He was shocked to discover that the countess had seen her personally. But she assured him that all had been well. He eyed her suspiciously as though she were holding something back.

She had already made the decision not to mention anything about Robin to either Mr May or her mother. She didn't know why, but she felt it was a secret she wanted to keep to herself. She worried that her mother, in particular, might express concern about her having a friend who used to be in the workhouse and a friend who was a boy. And she worried that Mr May wouldn't like her having a friend at all.

That night, before she went to bed, she thanked God that the countess had liked the piece she had created. She prayed that Robin would keep himself safe and that she would see him again very soon. She soon fell into a deep and blissful sleep.

Jane awoke to the house in turmoil.

She could hear wailing from downstairs, and through the fog of sleep, she determined it was her mother. Fear gripped her as she threw off her blanket and rose quickly. She splashed freezing cold water on her face, her skin tingling from the shock, and hastily pulled her plain grey dress over her head, smoothing down the fabric.

Her heart racing, she ran through the attic room piled high with boxes and down the first flight of stairs, her footsteps echoing as she made no effort to tread quietly. She just managed to catch a glimpse of the physician, Dr Jenkins, his face grim and serious, disappearing into Mr May's bedroom.

Moments later, Mrs Wilson appeared from downstairs carrying a pile of freshly laundered towels. She was followed by Mrs Johnson, her cheeks flushed, who carried a huge pot of steaming hot water. Jane watched with an open mouth, her chest tightening with concern. Both women disappeared into Mr May's bedroom and then, moments later, came back out minus the burdens they had been carrying, their brows furrowed.

"What is it?" Jane asked softly, her voice barely a whisper, fearing the very worst.

"The master's fever has grown worse, my dear,"

Mrs Johnson replied, her voice heavy with concern. "He's delirious. The mistress ordered Grimes to go and fetch the doctor an hour before dawn."

Jane, looking nervously towards the bedroom door, wasn't sure if she should enter or not. Her hand hovered over the doorknob, indecision gnawing at her.

"Best leave it, dear," Mrs Johnson said gently. "They will give us a shout if they need us."

She hesitated a moment longer. This was a situation which left her confused. What was she? Apprentice or family? Would her mother expect her to be present in such a case? She thought for a moment and decided that Mr May would not want her at his sickbed.

Jane followed the cook and the maid downstairs, her footsteps slow and heavy. They all sat in the kitchen with mugs of steaming tea in front of them, the scent of the brew filling the air. Grimes even joined them, although he sat without speaking a word, his face drawn and sombre.

Jane sensed that this was a momentous moment for everyone in the household. The twins and Hans had yet to arrive, they knew nothing of the drama unfolding upstairs.

A thousand thoughts went around her head. If Mr May were to die, what would happen to everyone in this room? It was he who held the licence from Goldsmiths' Hall. The twins would not be able to work as goldsmiths without him. Nor would Hans.

And nor would Jane.

"What are his chances?" Jane eventually asked, her voice choked with emotion, a single tear sliding down her cheek. She wasn't crying for him but for her mother. She could imagine her fretting by the bedside, bathing his forehead, just begging for the fever to break.

"I've seen it go both ways," Mrs Wilson said with brutal honesty.

"Time will tell, dear. Time will tell," agreed Mrs Johnson.

Finally, after an hour of sitting around the kitchen table, Jane decided to get on with her work. She was working on a pair of earrings made with amber and red garnets for a banker in the city. Jane assumed they were to be a gift for his wife, but you never could tell. She had seen Mr May discuss business with many wealthy gentlemen with knowing looks and raised eyebrows. They could just as well be for an actress or a singer on the stage.

It was an interesting mix of materials and Jane soon lost herself in the work. So much so that she didn't rise for five hours, not even to use the facilities. She leapt when she felt a soft hand on her shoulder.

She turned to see her mother offer her a gentle, loving smile. She had clearly been crying.

Jane opened her mouth to ask, but her mother offered a slight shake of the head and said, "Come."

For a few terrible moments, Jane feared the worst. She followed her mother up the stairs and into the sitting room.

"I just wanted you to sit with me for a while. I need a break from that fetid atmosphere in his bedroom," Mrs May said despondently.

"How is he doing, Mother?" Jane asked, edging closer to her on the sofa so she could take her hand.

Her mother took it willingly and squeezed. "He's sleeping. Dr Jenkins says the next day or so are critical."

"He'll be fine. He's strong," Jane offered, not knowing if it was the right thing to say or not.

"He has been such a wonderful husband, you know," her mother said. Jane instinctively knew that she didn't require an answer, so she kept silent and waited for her to speak again. "My mother didn't want me to marry him, of course. She considered a goldsmith a serious drop in social class, despite the company's standing. My father is a knight of the realm, you see. By default, my mother was Lady Carol Porter. We had estates in the country, in Here-fordshire and Shropshire, as well as a townhouse here in the city. But of course, I was the second daughter. Like my sister, I would get nothing in terms of inheritance from my parents. That would go to my older brother. My sister had the pick of the best men. By that, I mean those with the greatest standing. I decided to marry for love. It was my father who managed to persuade my mother that this was the right course of action. He knew that Russell would do anything for me. And so it has been proved."

Jane's body naturally tensed. Her mother showed such love and devotion; if only she knew about the conversation she'd overheard between him and Jennifer Dawson. It was a secret, and she knew that revealing it would cause her mother pain. But did she know already? Had she simply blanked it out?

Mrs May continued, "I was so thrilled when I fell pregnant. He doted on our daughter. And then one morning, I just walked into her nursery, and there she was, lifeless."

Jane listened in horror as her mother recounted the story of her own deceased child. "It must have been horrific."

"Nothing can prepare you for the loss of a child. No parent expects to outlive their children. We all know it can happen, of course. It is a fact of life. But you don't expect it, not when you're in the fortunate position that we are, being able to afford doctors and the like. The thing is, she wasn't even ill. But he was understanding even then. He was kind and gentle with me. However, he's never properly recovered from the loss. That's why he insisted we have no more children ourselves. He wouldn't be able to cope. That's why I wanted you, Jane. I needed somebody to love and care for as well as my husband. There are so many different types of love in this world; we need to cherish and value them all."

Jane snuggled in closer. "If anything were to happen to Russell, I don't know what I would do," her mother said. Then the emotions of the last few hours erupted, and she collapsed in a flood of tears.

Jane did her best to comfort her, but she felt that she was failing.

CHAPTER 13

A daunting twenty-four hours followed. It extended into an unnerving forty-eight, which then agonisingly elongated into a tense seventy-two. Everyone in the household was left on tenterhooks, their nerves fraught and tense.

Miraculously, however, Russell May clung to life.

The wave of joy that engulfed Mrs May was near to delirium. Overwhelmed with relief, she, alongside Jane, sought sanctuary in the hallowed halls of St Paul's Cathedral that same night. The doctor had confirmed that Russell was no longer in danger and they both gave heartfelt thanks to God for this deliverance.

Despite this, it was still a fortnight before Russell May summoned the strength to leave his bed chamber. By a twist of fate, this very day coincided with the arrival of a new commission from the esteemed Countess of Stanhope. The task at hand was the creation of a new brooch, a delicate work of art.

The countess had personally requested that Jane, with her burgeoning talent, be entrusted with this precious assignment, to be fulfilled by month's end. It was also noted that the countess should like Jane to deliver the piece personally.

Mr May had grown frightfully thin, his frame shedding considerable weight during his debilitating illness. Mrs May made persistent pleas for him to consume more, but Jane observed, with a disquieting sense of concern, that he ate scarcely anything at the dinner table that evening.

Over the subdued clatter of cutlery, Mr May interrogated Jane about her dealings with the countess. Jane responded in a quiet, respectful manner, narrating a story that held no space for embellishments. Mr May listened with rapt attention, inserting intermittent grunts of acknowledgement, and finally proclaimed that Jane had executed her task well. Deftly, Jane steered clear of mentioning her unexpected encounter with an old acquaintance from the workhouse.

All the while, as Jane recounted her tale, Mr May seemed to be conducting silent calculations in his head.

Finally, after listlessly pushing his spoon away

after consuming two meagre mouthfuls of the treacle sponge that Mrs Johnson had painstakingly prepared, he revealed what had been preoccupying his thoughts.

"Young lady, you might be the route to my Royal Warrant," Mr May began, pointing a bony finger in Jane's direction. "I've been musing. Lying at death's door brings a man to his senses. I've been playing small for far too many years. Been far too easy going on my competitors. This new young John Bridge, he shouldn't have the Royal Warrant. It's nothing short of a travesty," Mr May's voice surged, and he became far more animated than at any other point during the day.

"But with the next monarch being a young girl, this is our chance. I'll do anything - anything, I tell you - to secure that Warrant. My father desired it, you know? But the opportunity never presented for him. Not with Rundell still breathing. But now, with both him and Bridge gone, Goldsmiths' Hall cannot justify the Royal Warrant remaining as it is. They must advise the royal household to go elsewhere. Surely?"

He sought confirmation from his wife. "I'm sure you are correct, dearest," Mrs May said softly in an effort to agree. Jane could sense that she was becoming worried. She clearly wanted Mr May to remain calm and composed. He had only been out of bed a matter of hours, yet here he was, working himself into a frenzy over the Royal Warrant.

"I am happy to do anything you wish of me, sir?" Jane said dutifully.

"Of course, you are my girl. You are my apprentice, are you not?"

That comment earned Mr May a scowl from his wife. Usually, she would have objected to such a statement. Mrs May considered Jane her daughter. A daughter who worked for the company. But a daughter all the same. If Mr May noticed his wife's scowl, he simply ignored it.

"Well, you seem to have charmed this Countess," he had picked up the letter commissioning the new piece. "I believe you should meet other clients to see if you can work your magic on them too."

"Russell," Mrs May objected. "Jane is a mere 14 years of age."

"Old enough. She knows her trade, the girl does," Mr May retorted. He scrutinised Jane closely. "Moreover, she appears older than 14. We'll procure some new attire so you can meet with clients alongside me. When women are present and involved, of course."

A tremor of excitement pulsed through Jane's body. Meeting more clients? Although she was apprehensive while meeting the countess, she had to admit she rather relished the experience of showcasing her work. She was keen to see the reactions when she presented other clients with the pieces she had crafted.

Mrs May pondered for a moment. "I shall see to the dresses then, Russell." It was evident to Jane that Mrs May wasn't going to let this opportunity to acquire her a wardrobe of clothing pass by.

To be honest, Jane couldn't see what objections a mother might have regarding this role. After all, she would only be conversing with respectable members of the community. It wasn't as though Mr May had suggested she pick pockets on the streets.

"Good, that is settled then," Mr May said with what finally looked to be a smile.

Mrs May looked apprehensive, but Jane couldn't hide her delight.

"Who would I say I am if asked, Sir? The countess asked, I know I am your apprentice…" Jane paused for a moment considering if she should speak. Finally, she decided to tell the truth. "But it seemed to me that a countess might not appreciate an apprentice working on her piece. So I said I was your jeweller."

Jane felt her mother stiffen as she spoke the words, as though she were worried about her husband's reaction.

Mr May rubbed his now pointier chin as he thought. "You did well. I confess that was good thinking."

"So how will you introduce her to clients, Russell?" Mrs May asked.

He considered for a moment longer and then he looked quickly between his wife and Jane. "Well, there is an obvious solution. I shall introduce her as my daughter."

Jane gasped in shock.

Her mother just stared at her husband, the blood draining from her face. "Russell?"

"Yes, I shall call her daughter," he said. "But now I must retire. I am feeling tired."

He stood up and walked out of the room, gently squeezing his wife's shoulder as he passed behind her.

Jane and her mother remained seated, just staring at each other. Neither could believe what had just been said.

Jane couldn't wait to go to bed that evening.

It had been an exciting day. A new commission from Countess Stanhope, a fresh role in the company, and Mr May had finally called her 'daughter'.

Yet, these weren't the only notable events at Russell May Goldsmiths that day.

A letter had also arrived for Jane.

It came along with the countess's commission, delivered by hand by an unseen individual. This mysterious person pressed both documents into the large hand of Grimes and then vanished.

The return address on the rear of the envelope told Jane precisely who it was from: Robin Buckley.

She had saved opening the letter almost the entire day, planning to read it that night in bed.

She had spent an hour with her mother, talking about the strange events of the evening meal. Finally, Jane had said she was tired, and her mother told her to get an early night. After saying her customary evening prayers, she climbed between the crisp, white sheets and closed her eyes for a moment as the events of the day played out in her mind.

Then she opened them once more and slid her hand under the pillow. She found what she had placed there earlier that day. She had never received a letter in her life and her fingers trembled in anticipation as she tore open the envelope.

Grimes probably thought nothing of the letter and simply handed it to Jane in the workshop with a grunt. Jane doubted whether either Mr May or her mother knew anything about it. For Grimes, it would just have been business. For some inexplicable reason, she wanted to keep Robin's letter secret. She had no idea why.

The letter was written in a graceful script, one any privately educated young man would've been proud of. But this one was penned by a former work-

house boy who had become an assistant to a comptroller for a countess. It was almost a fairy tale.

Dearest Jane,

*I am sorry I haven't written sooner. My work here for
the countess, well her comptroller at least, has kept me
busy.*

In truth, I've struggled to find the right words.

*Not a day has gone by since I left the workhouse in
Southwark that I haven't thought about you.*

*I've always wondered what became of you. Now, I
delight in finding you safe, well, and the most beautiful
young woman I've ever seen.*

*I'm glad you find your work fulfilling. The countess
wore the piece you created for her to a ball at the palace
recently. The servants were sharing stories of the countess
receiving nothing but compliments. I thought you would
like to know.*

*I shall write to you as often as I am able. I look
forward to your response, or better yet, seeing your face
once more when you visit the countess with your latest
impressive creation.*

Yours forever,

Your friend, Robin.

As she read the words, she couldn't help but
blush. To think her necklace had been discussed at
the palace itself. Perhaps the King had seen it? Her
mind wandered back to the master's office, where
she knew the portrait of the King would be hanging.

Maybe the Queen had asked the countess who had created it? It was a captivating thought.

However, the lines that appealed most to her were the personal ones written by Robin. She had never considered herself beautiful, yet now a young man was telling her just that.

It stirred feelings within her that she had never known existed.

CHAPTER 14

*J*ane began work on the commission from the countess the very next day.

However, she found it difficult to concentrate, her mind consumed by the letter from Robin. She knew she should write him a reply, but having never written a letter before, as he'd said in his own message, she was lost for words. She resolved to withhold a response, hoping to see him when she delivered the countess's piece by the end of the month.

Mr May had provided a single, solitary special stone to include in the piece, but its position remained undecided.

Her deliberations were interrupted by her mother who announced a trip to the dressmaker. Her new attire, suitable for her new role within the company, needed to be made. As Mr May's daughter, she was obliged to look the part. Mrs May wasted no time in arranging the appointment. She would not waste this opportunity to spend money on Jane without rebuke from her husband.

It had been an enjoyable yet tiring afternoon. Jane was somewhat shocked at the number of items Mrs May ordered. Twice Jane expressed concern, and twice her mother had told her the countess's latest commission would make the company more than ten times what they were spending. Her mother had assured her that her husband had approved the investment.

By the time they returned to the workshop, the twins and Hans had departed for the day and dinner was almost ready. Jane planned to return to the countess's piece in the morning when she had a fresh mind.

Before joining her parents for dinner, Jane tidied up the workshop. She pondered whether it was now appropriate to call them both her parents. Should she refer to Mr May as 'Father'? Ever since his emergence from his bed chamber after his illness, Jane had been concerned by his erratic behaviour. She'd witnessed his explosive anger that morning when Hans made a minor mistake on the chalice he was crafting. It was so insignificant, even the client wouldn't have noticed. Nevertheless, Mr May berated him, warning that any more errors of this nature would see him out on the streets, searching for new employment.

She picked up the newspaper to take upstairs for bedtime reading, but a headline caught her eye:

'Goldsmith Imprisoned for Selling Fake Diamonds.'

She quickly skimmed the article, then slumped into a chair to read it again in more detail.

Mr James Callaway, a goldsmith she'd never heard of, had been imprisoned for a total of nine years for what the judge described as a 'despicable act'. He'd apparently been incorporating fake diamonds in his creations and passing them off as genuine. He said he knew nothing of it and believed all the diamonds in his work to be real and sourced from the finest mines.

The issue had come to light when one of his clients had taken a piece to a rival firm for repairs. They had identified the counterfeit stones. The piece in question was entirely made up of fake diamonds.

A shiver coursed down her spine as she digested the article. Her worst fears were being realised. She knew instantly that the special stones Mr May had given her to incorporate into many of the pieces were the same fake diamonds.

She wondered if Mr May had seen the newspaper. Due to his recent illness, he hadn't been visiting Goldsmiths' Hall and so wouldn't have heard the news from his fellow members. It had said in the article that Callaway had only been arrested last week. He had been tried and imprisoned.

What if the very fate that had brought down the goldsmith in the scandal-ridden article were to befall Russell May? Her mother's world would crumble into fragments of despair and Jane along with it. This cataclysm, she decided, must be averted at all costs. Russell May needed to be informed about the article.

It seemed as though fortune favoured Jane this evening. As she climbed the staircase, each step heavy with apprehension, her mother met her on the landing. With an unusually pallid face, she expressed her intention of retiring early, a headache wreaking havoc on her usually strong constitution.

"Likely a result of the strain from the past tumultuous days," Jane observed, offering a comforting explanation.

Her mother agreed. "I'm certain I'll feel refreshed and myself again by morning. Will you dine with my husband, as you usually do?"

Jane nodded in dutiful affirmation. She headed to the dining room.

"How progresses the new piece for the Countess of Stanhope?" inquired Mr May, breaking the silence.

"Quite well, sir," Jane replied, her tone neutral. Inside, however, she felt a sting of disappointment at the lack of progress, a result of the distracting visit to the dressmakers in the afternoon.

She took her place at the ornate dining table, beginning to pick at her meal only once Mr May had started. Strangely, her usual hearty appetite seemed absent, a fact that didn't escape Mr May's notice. "You've barely touched your food, Jane. Is something troubling you?"

Taking a moment to draw a deep breath, Jane reached under the folds of her dress for the newspaper she had hidden there. Pushing it across the polished mahogany table towards Mr May, she asked, "Have you had a chance to read today's paper, sir?"

She laid her silverware to one side and watched him as he began to read. His face transformed from curiosity to shock, each line of the story casting a shadow over his features.

Finally, he set the paper down, his gaze heavy on Jane. She felt his scrutinising stare as if he were piecing together a puzzle, deducing just how much she had concluded from the newsprint.

"Well?" he managed, his voice a strained whisper.

Jane sensed the moment had arrived to voice her suspicions. "These fake stones are the ones you've been giving me to use in specific jewellery pieces, aren't they, sir? What do we call the special stones? The ones I must keep secret?"

He contemplated this for a moment, before responding. "What if they are?"

"I don't want the same to happen to you, sir," Jane said, the sincerity in her voice clear as she nodded her head towards the newspaper.

Despite her feelings towards Mr May being far from the affection she harboured for her mother, she understood the harsh reality of their predicament. If Russell were to be arrested, their world would spiral into chaos, and her mother would bear the brunt of the fallout.

"Have you already used the special stone I gave you in the countess's piece?" he queried.

"Not yet."

Mr May looked thoughtful, stroking his chin as he pondered their next move. After what seemed an eternity, he broke the silence. "Well, don't. We need to rid ourselves of these stones."

"We should act quickly, sir. What if the magistrates come knocking at our door tomorrow morning? What will you say about the stones? People will read that article and wonder if all goldsmiths are the same as that man." Jane's anxiety was evident.

Russell May fell silent again. It was clear that Jane was sharper than he had previously acknowledged. He had underestimated her intelligence for too long. It was probably the fact that she was a young woman. He was glad he had recognised that it was time he began to appreciate her acumen and involve her more in client discussions.

"Jane," he began, his voice firm but low, "If you recall what I said yesterday. You're my daughter. Remember that. Your loyalty," he paused, choosing his next words carefully, "should be to me first and foremost."

"Of course, sir. That is precisely why I brought this matter to your attention." She halted and then lowered her voice. "As you instructed, I have never breathed a word of this to anyone else."

Jane couldn't help to think back to the other matter she had never spoken of to anyone else. She wondered if he knew that she had overheard his conversation with Jennifer on that day. She doubted it. Jennifer wouldn't have said a word.

His gaze was drawn back to the newspaper, eyes skimming over the damning lines once more. When he had finished, he returned his attention to Jane. "Our situation, I believe, is not as dire as the one described here. We have used our special stones sparingly. The majority of the diamonds in our work are genuine. Many pieces had no special stones at all. The chance of someone unearthing our secret is slim. This poor wretch made an entire piece out of fakes."

Jane nodded, "I thought similarly. You would be unlucky if they identified a fake in a piece of two hundred gems." Although it did worry her how he referred to the secret as "ours." She had rather thought she was keeping a secret on his behalf.

"There are no records of the stones anywhere. I myself can't even recall which items had them and which did not." He nodded his head as though the path ahead of him had become clear. "Then all that remains," he said, a sudden resolve entering his tone, "is for us to get rid of any damning evidence."

As she watched him, Jane felt a mix of relief and apprehension. They were treading a thin line between respectability and ruin, but for now, they had a plan. One they must put into action before dawn broke.

Jane made her way down the stairs and collected the fake stone that lay on her workshop bench. It was nestled next to a cluster of genuine stones intended to be set in Countess Stanhope's new brooch. She checked it through the loupe. The last thing she wanted was to throw away a real diamond.

By the time she returned upstairs to the dining room, Mr May had been to the office and retrieved a black velvet bag from his safe, containing the other stones.

His breathing was laboured at this point. Even this minor exertion seemed to sap his energy.

"I'll take them and throw them into the Thames," he wheezed. He took the final stone, plucked from Jane's fingers, and added it to the bag.

His complexion seemed to turn a sickly grey colour. In an instant, Jane knew perfectly well that she couldn't allow him outside. Night was beginning to fall and with it came a chill. It could well kill him.

"You can't go in your condition. I'll handle it. I'll be there and back before you realise I'm gone." She realized that she sounded like a woman of many summers, not a girl of just fourteen.

He studied her carefully, deliberating whether this was a good idea or not. Ever since they had taken her from the workhouse, she had yet to venture out alone onto the streets of London. And was nightfall, clutching a velvet bag brimming with counterfeit diamonds, really the best time for her to be venturing out? He had serious doubts. However, he was acutely aware that these stones needed to be removed from the premises. The risk of keeping them there was too significant. He thought about his wife, tucked up in bed with a headache, oblivious to the drama unfolding. He was determined to ensure it stayed that way.

What would she think if he let Jane go out to the Thames at this time of the night? Mr May knew perfectly well what her reaction would be. She would be appalled, and he would never hear the end of it.

As if Jane could read his mind, she reassured him, "I won't tell her. It can be our secret."

Or rather, another secret, she thought.

Mr May pondered for just a moment longer, then

agreed. "Take them to Westminster Bridge and toss them over the side."

Jane nodded, seized the velvet bag, and headed for the dining room door. "Jane," Mr May called out in a soft tone.

"Yes, sir?" She halted and half turned to look back at him.

"Be careful. She would never forgive me if something happened to you."

"I understand," Jane affirmed.

"Slip out the back," Mr May instructed. "There's a slimmer chance you'll be spotted that way."

Jane doubted there was much likelihood of anyone keeping watch on the goldsmiths at this late hour, to see if there were counterfeit diamonds being smuggled in and out. Nevertheless, she didn't protest.

Pulling on her coat, she did as she was told.

She sprinted down Cockspur Street, her hand clutching the bag that needed to be disposed of. Within five minutes, she found herself standing on the banks of the Thames. Temptation urged her to stand there and fling it with all her might, yet she understood that if it wasn't cast into the very heart of the mighty river, there was a risk it could wash up along the shore.

She doubted anything could link the special stones to Russell May Goldsmiths, but she was determined to see the river engulf them.

She dashed along the banks of the river towards the green iron edifice known as Westminster Bridge.

Remarkably, no one called out or suggested it was unusual for a young woman to be darting along the streets of London. No one placed a hand on her shoulder to ask if she should be safely at home. She weaved around people immersed in their own affairs and quickly understood that they were as indifferent to her as she was to them. She was merely one amongst thousands in this vast city.

Reaching the bridge, she slowed her pace and sauntered casually to the middle. A mist began to gather above the river; the sun had finally set, leaving a faint blush in the sky.

She glanced about her to see only a couple starting to make their way across. A carriage or two passed her at great speed. But no one was close. She weighed the fake gemstones in her hand, and with a powerful exertion, she hurled them into the river. She watched as they made a splash before disappearing beneath the dark surface.

The incriminating evidence that could imprison Mr May was gone.

She had protected him and his secrets once again.

CHAPTER 15

*T*wo years later

"Was she thrilled?" Robin enquired.

"The same as always," Jane May chuckled.

She had just delivered the latest commission to Countess Stanhope of a matching necklace and earring set adorned with brilliant green emeralds and diamond clusters.

With an air of casual elegance, the countess had reassuringly confided in Jane that she intended to don the dazzling set at the forthcoming King's Ball. Such an event promised to hold a distinct element of intrigue, as Jane was privy to the knowledge that the equally distinguished Duchess of Devonshire would be proudly wearing a unique brooch of her creation, and the Countess of Arundel too, had requested a bespoke piece of pearls. Indeed, these were merely the latest additions to Jane's ever-growing portfolio. She estimated that probably at least ten ladies of the court would be wearing her exquisitely crafted jewellery on the occasion of the King's Ball.

She and Robin were seated on the banks of the Thames, watching ships drift back and forth, munching on thick slices of freshly baked white bread and creamy cheese. In many ways, it reminded her of her first meal with the Mays after she'd been rescued from the workhouse. Mrs Johnson had placed that tantalising slice of bread before her, and it tasted divine. The bread and cheese remained the same, but much had changed since that first day of liberation from the workhouse.

Since Jane had disposed of the counterfeit diamonds that Mr May had insisted she include in many of their commission pieces, the topic was never broached again. Jane was relieved that the underhand practice never resurfaced.

Instead, Jane found herself now granted the privilege to interact directly with clients alongside the esteemed Russell May. She now referred to him as father. Whenever he encountered a new wealthy woman or a lady of the royal court, he would proudly introduce his daughter who crafted pieces for the finest women in the country.

And the clients were always charmed by Jane. They were thrilled that the experienced goldsmith was bringing his daughter into the business. It was highly unusual for a woman to be working on pieces of jewellery. For some unexplained reason, the high-born women of the country found this scenario entirely fascinating. They flocked in droves to Russell May Goldsmiths to commission their own pieces of finery, all hoping to have them meticulously crafted by the young and talented Jane.

Many of the patrons expressly requested personal delivery from Jane, a task she relished. Countess Stanhope had been one such patron. On such occasions, the loyal Grimes would typically accompany her to ensure no harm befell her, only to tactfully depart soon after, leaving Jane to make her own journey home.

Today had been one such day.

Jane had managed to time her visit so that Robin could join her for lunch on the banks of the Thames. Jane knew with absolute certainty that she was profoundly in love with him. However, this powerful emotion remained unspoken between them. She prayed that he felt the same. Jane nurtured a hope, a dream that she would one day become Robin Buckley's wife. However, until they had completed their apprenticeships and had reached twenty-one years of age, that could not be possible unless their respective masters released them.

Despite her newfound relationship with Mr May,

Jane knew he would never release her from her apprenticeship. He would risk too much. If she became another man's wife, her loyalties would change, and Russell May was single-minded in his ambition to obtain the Royal warrant when the crown next changed hands.

The city's newspapers were consistently abuzz with whispered rumours and speculations about the King's declining health. Jane knew that any day now, the ominous news could break that the King had drawn his last breath, leading to a new, young Queen ascending the throne. Jane found it strangely intriguing that the heir presumptive, Princess Alexandria Victoria, was exactly her age. She wondered if a princess, despite her elevated status, experienced the same worries, uncertainties, and mundane concerns about life as she did. Was the princess in love with a friend from her childhood? She found it unfathomable to envision waking up one morning and realising she was now the queen.

Jane and Robin exchanged a steady stream of letters when they weren't able to meet. Jane had confessed to her mother that she had found her old friend from the workhouse. She somewhat suspected that her mother believed there was more to the relationship than mere friendship. However, if she did, she kept her thoughts to herself.

Sometimes they would rendezvous on Sundays

after Jane had attended church at the cathedral with her parents. Their meetings were usually brief stolen moments in between their busy schedules, but each one was precious. Each meeting, each shared glance, and each whispered conversation left an indelible imprint on Jane's heart, marking the chapters of her blossoming love story with Robin.

The pair exchanged news while they ate. Eventually, they fell into a comfortable silence, with the sun casting a gentle glow on their faces.

"You always said it would be a better world out here," Jane murmured.

"It couldn't be much worse than inside the workhouse, could it?"

"Possibly..." Jane replied thoughtfully. Despite her fortunate circumstances, interacting with some of the highest echelons of English society, she knew from her daily perusal of the newspaper, and her frequent excursions outside of the Goldsmiths, not everyone in England shared her luck. Crime was rampant, and people struggled to survive. Her problems were precious stones like sapphires and emeralds and where to place them in her creations. But she understood the hardship of many young women her age who were already burdened with children and the pressing need to feed them.

"I'm just glad it's all worked out for the best for us."

Robin gently reached out, his hand brushing hers. She shuddered with quiet excitement. "I always said it would."

After another bout of silence, Robin stood. "I have to get back. You know how my boss is."

Jane knew all too well what Robin's boss, the comptroller, was like. He was a strict taskmaster with an unyielding emphasis on punctuality and manners.

"You're right?" Jane questioned, almost pleading.

"Of course. Are you comfortable walking back alone?"

Jane nodded, always saddened by their partings.

Robin disappeared, returning to his work. She knew that one day he would end up a prosperous young man. His skills were invaluable, and he might even succeed his boss as the new comptroller of the Earl and Countess of Stanhope. If not, numerous other positions awaited him. He just needed to reach the mature age of twenty-one, granting him full freedom.

She lingered, watching the ships traverse the river. Where were they going? India? The United States? She contemplated the vastness of the world, and if she would ever get the chance to explore it.

Eventually, she reluctantly rose and began her walk back to the Goldsmiths. Work awaited her there, tasks that would occupy her for hours. Often, her fingers ached from the labour, and she savoured the occasions when she could visit clients to present her creations.

A bright thought suddenly dawned on her: tonight, she would accompany her parents to the theatre.

This was a rare treat. She had attended three shows the previous year and thoroughly enjoyed the captivating performances and changing scenery. The Mays were regular attendees, but Mrs May was particular about what she allowed Jane to watch.

Grimes greeted her with a smile as she entered through the front door. These days, she found his presence comforting, doubting any thieves or vagabonds would dare confront him.

Swiftly, she ascended to her attic room and changed into her work dress.

She then dedicated another three hours to a commission for the wife of a particularly wealthy banker. A gentle hand on her shoulder interrupted her, and she looked up to see the warm gaze of her mother.

"Come on, it's time to get changed. We're dining slightly early this evening because the carriage is arriving at seven."

"Of course," Jane replied obediently. "I'm looking forward to it. Are you?"

"I am indeed." Her mother always cherished their

family outings, and the opportunity to introduce Jane as her daughter.

That evening, they dined on roast beef, carrots, potatoes, and cabbage. Mr May seemed to enjoy his meal, but Jane noted that he had regained little weight since his severe illness a few years prior. Her mother had informed her he'd stopped eating breakfast and often settled for an apple at lunch. It seemed food was no longer a priority in his life.

When not securing new business or encouraging the twins to work faster, he was frequently found at Goldsmiths Hall, gathering the latest gossip and seeking any information that might tarnish the reputation of John Bridge. Rarely did a day pass without a heated conversation at the dinner table about the ongoing travesty. Mr May considered it a disgrace that Bridge still retained the Royal warrant, despite the untimely demise of the original Goldsmiths.

Eventually, dinner was over, and the time for the theatre had arrived. Changing into her finest dress, Jane couldn't help but feel a flutter of anticipation. Tonight promised the rare escape from daily routines and hardships and the chance to immerse herself in a world of make-believe where love stories unfolded on stage and the scenery magically transformed with each act.

The carriage pulled up to their residence, its horses pawing impatiently at the cobblestones. Mr

May extended his hand to assist Mrs May and Jane into the carriage, while Grimes stood guard at the doorway, a reassuring figure in the dim evening light.

A footman in red livery greeted them at the Theatre Royal Drury Lane. He smiled warmly, acknowledging Mr and Mrs May, and nodded respectfully at Jane.

"Good evening, sir, madam. Your box is ready," he said, indicating with an open-handed gesture towards an exclusive staircase to the left.

Such was Russell May's status in society that he could now afford a box at the theatre. Though it was a small box, high up and opposite the Royal box, this was a fact in which Russell May took immense pride. He relished not having to share his theatrical experiences with all and sundry.

They were greeted at the top of the staircase and shown to their seats. Mr and Mrs May graciously accepted glasses of champagne, while Jane respectfully declined.

The play was a rollicking farce that had all three of them doubling over in their seats with laughter. About halfway through the first half, Mrs May suffered a short bout of coughing, which caused her to leave her seat. Jane followed to make sure she was alright. She found her taking a glass of water with one of the staff looking after her.

"I'm quite well, dearest Jane," she said looking at

her daughter's concerned face. "I think the champagne went down the wrong way."

Jane smiled at her with relief and after a moment or two, they returned to their seats. Mr May looked over to his wife to ensure she was well.

During the interval, they enjoyed canapés with those in other boxes. Twice, Jane was delighted to hear people remark that it was a pleasure to see her, as they'd heard so much about the pieces she had created. The young woman glowed with pride. Mr May rubbed his hands together in anticipation of new business.

They settled into their box for the start of the second half. However, the time for the commencement passed and still, the curtain failed to rise on the stage. Rumblings of disquiet started to emerge from the audience. Finally, a gentleman in full evening dress walked onto the stage to make an announcement.

"The leading lady, unfortunately, twisted her ankle during the final scene of the first half and is unable to continue. Instead, the role will be played by her understudy, Miss Violet Rose."

There was an audible groan throughout the theatre. Many people had come specifically to see the leading lady perform. The Mays, too, were disappointed at this news. The leading lady was a firm favourite in the household.

The play resumed, and after a few minutes, the understudy made her appearance.

Violet Rose was young and beautiful and immediately captivated the audience with her charm.

Everyone, that was, apart from Jane.

She stared at the stage in horror as Violet Rose delivered her lines with impeccable precision and had the crowd howling with laughter and joy.

For just one brief moment, the actress looked up towards their box and Jane was convinced she was being stared at directly.

And she knew for certain, in that moment, what she had already feared, that the understudy's real name wasn't Violet Rose at all, but Kate Larkin.

CHAPTER 16

"*T*hat understudy, what was her name? Violet Rose?" Mr May mused aloud, looking across the dining table towards his wife, seeking confirmation of the young actress's name. His face, cast in the warm glow of the evening summer sunlight, held an air of intrigue. His eyes danced as he spoke.

"Yes, dear, it was Violet Rose," Mrs May affirmed, nodding delicately as she cleared her throat. "A truly marvellous talent for one of such tender years."

Mr May turned to their daughter. "What did you think, Jane?" he enquired, a slice of roast chicken still poised on his fork.

Jane hesitated momentarily, wrestling with her own thoughts. She dared not share her true opinion.

"Oh, I agree wholeheartedly. She definitely shows promise for a bright future."

Jane had firmly believed she would never lay eyes on Kate Larkin again. Yet there she was on stage, basking in the applause and admiration of the entire audience. Jane questioned whether her feelings of resentment were too severe. It had all been a long time ago, and Kate Larkin might very well have transformed over the years. But her intuition told her otherwise. The theatre world was known for its cut-throat nature. Jane was certain that Kate Larkin would blend in seamlessly.

Interrupting Jane's thoughts, Mrs May gave a small cough before opining, "It wouldn't surprise me if the girl is headlining her own show within a few months."

"If she does, we should make a point of attending," Mr May concurred heartily, sipping his wine.

Jane merely grunted in response, continuing to tackle her plateful of food. She toyed with the idea of steering the conversation towards John Bridge to divert attention, but she knew all too well that her mother disliked her husband discussing him. It pained her to see her husband become agitated over matters over which he had no control.

In their quiet evening chats, when Mr May was off at his various club meetings, Jane was becoming increasingly aware of her mother's growing anxiety about his obsession with ensuring John Bridge lost the Royal warrant, whilst Russell May Goldsmiths secured it. She worried that it would drive him to do stupid things.

Jane could not help but think back to the special stones. In his quest for wealth and status, Russell May had already done stupid things. Not that she would ever find out about that, of course.

Two days later, Mr May presented Jane with a new project.

It was a small, delicate heart brooch composed of twelve tiny rubies and six slightly larger diamonds. When Jane inquired about the commission, he refused to elaborate. Instead, he simply asked her to complete the piece for him and assured her it would remain their secret.

"More secrets," thought Jane. Had she not hidden enough? Then a thought struck her: it was her mother's birthday at the end of the month. Jane surmised that her father was commissioning the piece for her.

Jane merely smiled and assured him it would be completed within a matter of days.

Later that afternoon, Jane delivered two sets of earrings to the wife of a businessman in a very affluent area of town. It was close to her own house, and so, a week beforehand, Jane had written to Robin, suggesting they meet up afterwards.

Having made sure Jane arrived at her location

safely, Grimes disappeared to stand guard at the door. Thus, it was Robin's smiling face that awaited her when she emerged from the property.

She had been feeling rather despondent for the last few days. Seeing Kate Larkin on the stage, combined with the persistent cough her mother seemed to have developed, had dampened her spirits. She couldn't shake off a nagging suspicion that her mother wasn't well.

However, the sight of Robin's handsome, smiling face lifted her mood. As they walked, she told him about the theatre visit and the haunting encounter with a ghost from her past on the stage.

Robin listened to her story in shock and horror. He clasped Jane's hand and squeezed it gently. "I can only imagine how horrifying that was for you. But please remember, you're a different woman now to the young girl you used to be. Kate Larkin poses no threat to you."

Jane knew Robin made perfect sense. Kate Larkin had nothing to do with her and was not a part of her world. She didn't have to share a dormitory with her. There was no reason for the anxiety that had been plaguing her since encountering her old adversary once more.

"I doubt the woman would even recognise you," Robin said with a laugh. "You've grown into a fine, beautiful woman."

Robin's kind words and the touch of his hand sent a shiver down Jane's spine. She yearned to fall into his arms and for him to tell her that he loved her. But she knew that wasn't going to happen. At least, not today.

"I recognised her," Jane countered.

"What does it matter? More than likely, you'll never see her again."

But Jane did see her again. And much sooner than she expected.

As the carriage clattered to a halt before the grand façade of the Theatre Royal on Drury Lane, a tide of apprehension washed over Jane, making her heart feel heavy and full of dread.

This day should have been one of joyous celebration, for it marked her dear mother's birthday. The previous evening, Mr May had announced over dinner with great enthusiasm that Violet Rose, who had successfully stepped in as an understudy, had been awarded the leading role in a new show created especially for her.

Tickets for the opening night had been swiftly sold out that very morning, with Mr May securing a commodious box. Not only that, as it was Mrs May's birthday, he had already extended invitations to a sizable group of her friends to join them for the evening's performance.

Jane, however, was expected to chat merrily, to

feign delight, and to cheer alongside everyone else at Kate Larkin's performance; an act she found repugnant. Yet even she had to grudgingly admit that her old adversary had turned in a splendid performance. Again, it was a comedy that had their box roaring with laughter, though Jane struggled to join in. All she could remember were the vile deeds this woman had committed against her years ago. The smug, self-satisfied expression on Kate's face when she was chosen as the apprentice over Jane, was etched in her memory. It now seemed that Kate Larkin was set to achieve nationwide fame and fortune. What kind of woman was she, really?

At the end of the performance, Jane stood up along with everyone else in the box to give Kate a standing ovation. The act made her feel sick. Throughout the show, she noticed her mother repeatedly coughing.

"Do you need to see the physician?" Jane whispered to her mother as they sampled the interval canapés.

"It's just a pesky summer cold, dear, it will pass," Mrs May replied dismissively.

Following the performance, the entire party moved to a special dining area that Mr May had reserved in the theatre wings.

"We're marking a special event for a special lady," he said as they feasted on exquisite cuts of beef and pork. It was a fitting meal for such a momentous occasion.

The climax of the meal was the presentation of an enormous chocolate cake, topped with a single candle, placed in front of Mrs May to a chorus of cheers. It warmed Jane's heart to see her mother so happy.

Then, Mr May announced that he had one more surprise.

Jane presumed this would be the unveiling of the beautiful heart-shaped brooch studded with rubies and diamonds that she had meticulously crafted earlier in the month. She had thought it was for her mother and had pictured how stunning it would look against her mother's gorgeous blue dress.

However, instead of revealing a small box containing the elegant piece of jewellery, Mr May stood and left the room briefly, only to return with a woman on his arm. Jane felt her heart plummet once again.

"Ladies and gentlemen, and my dear wife, I present to you Violet Rose, the next great actress of our beloved London," he announced.

Mrs May, along with everyone else, clapped enthusiastically. Violet circulated, exchanging pleasantries with the birthday girl. Jane felt as if she were in a daze. How could this woman infiltrate her life yet again?

"Jane? Jane?" her mother's voice finally pierced through her fog of thoughts. "Come here. I'd like you to meet Violet."

With heavy steps, Jane moved towards Kate Larkin.

"This is my daughter, Jane," Mrs May introduced her, beaming with pride.

Violet extended her hand with a smile. For a brief moment, she seemed to freeze as her gaze met Jane's. Jane instantly recognised that look. She knew perfectly well who Jane was. "Delighted to meet you," Jane managed to force out, extending her own hand in return.

"And you, Jane," Violet responded, her voice steady.

The pair stood there, hands clasped, eyeing each other as if daring one another to bring up their shared, tainted past. Jane recognised that Violet Rose had more at stake in this situation. This was her night of triumph, her premiere as the leading lady at the Theatre Royal on Drury Lane, and she wouldn't want any scandalous revelations, particularly about her workhouse roots, to tarnish her glory. Jane noted that Violet wore a heavy scent, like spices from the East. It was almost nauseating to breathe.

Finally, they broke their clasp, and as Jane's gaze drifted downwards, something captured her attention.

There, nestled on Violet Rose's bosom, glittering under the gaslights was the ruby and diamond heart-shaped brooch. The very same brooch Jane had believed she crafted for her mother.

Jane's heart sank once more as the enormity of what this could mean washed over her.

CHAPTER 17

"he white plague?" Mr May queried in disbelief. "That's a disease of the poor."

"I regret that consumption can affect anyone at any time," Doctor Jenkins said softly.

Jane stood, still as a statue, barely comprehending the harsh reality she was hearing. Her darkest fears had been confirmed. For months, she had persistently nudged her mother to see Doctor Jenkins regarding the nagging cough that had stubbornly lingered. But her pleas fell on deaf ears. Her mother, for reasons Jane couldn't comprehend, had staunchly refused to seek medical assistance. It was as if she was in denial, unwilling to face the gravity of her ailment. As Jane watched her mother's health deteriorate, the weight loss, the pallor, she knew something sinister was afoot.

It was ultimately Mr May who had taken the initiative, mandating a visit from Doctor Jenkins himself.

Now, the doctor was solemnly delivering his diagnosis.

"Will she recover?" Jane finally asked in a soft voice.

"She stands a better chance than most," Doctor Jenkins said, noncommittally yet with a kind undertone.

"Consumption?" Mr May muttered under his breath. "I had no idea people like us could be affected." He paused in the dining room for a moment before murmuring even quieter, "What will they say in Goldsmiths Hall? The shame"

Jane cast him a glance that could cut glass, her eyes shooting daggers.

Her resentment had been simmering since her mother's birthday. Seeing the heart brooch pin adorning the bosom of Kate Larkin was like a stab to the heart. It was a piece that she had crafted lovingly, pouring her whole soul into it, and was meant to be proudly worn by her mother.

But now it was worn by her. The bully. The girl who caused her so much pain and misery.

Over the past few months, Jane had developed various concerns about Mr May and his behaviour. He would venture out more frequently in the evenings, concocting wild excuses about special meetings at his various gentlemen's clubs. But on more than one occasion, when he returned home, Jane was certain she could smell that sickly sweet perfume from the east. She knew in her heart that he'd been with her.

Further mysterious commissions arrived, small pieces, all of them. Jane knew exactly where they were going. And she resented every gem that she delicately placed into the beautifully crafted gold frames.

Mrs May seemed oblivious to it all. More than once, Jane had wanted to broach the subject with her. She attempted to start a conversation, but her mother quickly redirected the topic. It was as though she didn't want to face reality.

Just last night, Jane had decided to broach the subject once more. But her mother cut her off abruptly saying, "One must make the best of every day. Such matters are the way of the world. Men are men."

In that moment, Jane knew full well that her mother was aware of all her husband's transgressions. She probably knew about his past indiscretions with Jennifer in the office. Now that Jane was older, she understood what had been happening in the afternoons when her mother was out with her friends.

The only surprise was that Jennifer hadn't fallen pregnant sooner.

Who knows how many other women Mr May had courted on the side.

How could a man treat a woman so badly? And why wouldn't her mother stand up against such injustice?

She didn't understand. Were all men truly the same? Was Robin? Even now, when he wasn't writing letters or visiting her, was he also making advances towards serving girls? She was confused. Perhaps this was just how life was supposed to be.

But now there was something else mingling with her anger. There was fear.

Despite the doctor's assurances that she had a better chance than most, Jane knew the disease had progressed too far. Her mother had left it too late.

And so it proved to be.

The days turned into weeks, and the weeks into months and her mother's health continued to decline. The once vibrant woman Jane remembered was now almost always confined to her bed, frail and weak. Jane spent every spare moment by her side, offering comfort and solace as best she could.

But still, the commissions kept coming. The Duchess of Norfolk, The Countess of Derby, Lady Shrewsbury and so many wives of wealthy businessmen she lost count. Diamonds, rubies, sapphires, emeralds, opals, amethysts, pearls and garnets all skilfully assembled

Mr May was often absent, his affairs carrying on as though nothing had changed. Jane couldn't hide her contempt. Each time he left, she couldn't help but wonder if he was with her.

She met Robin down by the Thames.

While Robin's embrace offered some comfort, it was tinged with disquiet. It wasn't his fault, of course. It was just that Jane harboured an uneasy suspicion that all men were now the same.

Her mother had insisted that she spend a few hours on a Sunday afternoon meeting her special friend. Jane was initially reluctant, but her mother persisted, claiming that the fresh air would do her good. Mrs Johnson would be there to attend to any of her needs, should they arise. Jane knew perfectly well that her mother would have preferred to say her husband would be there to look after her, but of course, he was not.

He had developed an obsession with Violet Rose, one mirroring his relentless pursuit of a royal warrant.

Jane was pleased she had visited Robin, but she harboured concerns about what he might be up to if she one day became his wife. She realised this worry was illogical. Surely all men were not the same?

"How has she been?" Robin asked softly.

"About the same. No improvement. But no deterioration either."

"That is at least some mercy."

In the early days when Jane shared her worries about her mother's illness, Robin was optimistic. He reassured her that her mother would no doubt improve, that she had access to the best care, and was in the ideal environment in which to heal. Jane believed him, at least to an extent.

Lately, he had stopped making such positive declarations.

It was painfully clear to Jane what was happening.

Her mother was dying.

Slowly, piece by piece, she was fading away. And there wasn't a single thing that Jane could do to prevent it.

One evening, Jane sat and read to her mother until the older woman gently slipped into a blissful, pain-free sleep.

With an abundance of work accumulating, Jane decided she would retreat to the workshop to complete her work on a necklace for a man who owned a shipping company. It could have been for his wife, his daughter, or, more likely, Jane surmised, his mistress.

Garnets and diamonds dazzled as she adjusted the oil lamp to assure a better view.

She became lost in her work. Although she

worried about Mr May's obsession with obtaining the Royal warrant, she too fantasised about what it might be like to craft pieces for the Queen of England herself. For many years, she held onto the conversation about how, when the young princess ascended to the throne and became queen, she would require a new crown for the coronation. St Edward's would be far too heavy for her youthful neck.

What if she could be the one setting the stones in that brand-new crown? For a young girl raised in the workhouse, that would truly be quite something.

As she placed the gemstones into the frame, piece by piece, she lost all sense of time. She worked relentlessly. Finally, the piece was finished. As she looked up, she noticed that the light of dawn was breaking.

Her father had not returned home that evening. Jane had no doubts about where he would be.

Strangely, she didn't feel any fatigue after working through the night.

Mrs Johnson was in the kitchen, hard at work. Suddenly, Jane felt ravenous. She ate bacon, eggs, and fried mushrooms. After that, she wolfed down three slices of toast slathered with butter and sticky, sweet strawberry jam.

Mrs Johnson watched her with a satisfied smile on her face. "It's good to see you eat. At least someone in this house does."

Her mother had clearly eaten little over the past few months. Her condition had caused her to waste away, and she had lost her appetite. Ever since her father's bout of sickness, he never again displayed the same appetite for food. During mealtimes, he would merely play with the food on his plate as he ranted about the injustice of John Bridge holding the Royal warrant.

Mrs Johnson sometimes wondered if her services were required at all.

Suddenly, the door opened, and both Mrs Johnson and Jane were shocked to see Mrs May, resplendent in a fresh nightgown and robe. She had clearly washed and looked surprisingly perky.

"Mother? What on earth are you doing here?" Jane exclaimed, leaping from her seat, concern evident on her face. "You should be in bed."

Mrs May raised her hand to halt her. "Hush, child. This morning, I feel quite well. I'm somewhat hungry." She eyed the remnants of the toast on her daughter's plate. "That looks divine, Mrs Johnson. I shall have toast, please."

She settled down at the kitchen table and managed to eat almost an entire slice of freshly buttered toast. While not a significant amount to any normally active person, it was the most food Mrs May had eaten in at least four months. Both Jane and

Mrs Johnson watched each mouthful disappear with satisfaction.

"Where is Russell?" Mrs May eventually asked after finishing off an accompanying cup of tea.

"I believe he had to go out early this morning. A meeting at Goldsmiths Hall I believe?" Jane lied smoothly.

Mrs May studied her for a moment before nodding her head. "I see."

Jane knew her lie had been seen through instantly. But she didn't want to upset her mother by revealing the truth. The unspoken reality lingered between them.

Over the next few weeks, Jane's mother underwent somewhat of a resurgence. She began to eat more and was often out of bed. She did tire easily, but Jane was overjoyed to see her up and about. Perhaps her worst fears were not about to materialise. Perhaps Robin had been right. Maybe she would recover?

Yet, it seemed that Mr May barely noticed the change. He continued his regular schedule: meeting clients, visiting Goldsmiths Hall, attending his clubs in the evenings, and no doubt, conducting his illicit affair in between. Nothing was spoken on that matter between husband and wife. Mrs May began to join them more frequently at the dinner table in the dining room. Her portions were small, but at least she was there.

Jane yearned for her to challenge her husband on the matter, to question why he wasn't at her bedside while her daughter was. What could he possibly be doing that was more important than attending to his wife's welfare?

She wouldn't. Jane vowed that one day she would stand up for what was right.

Unfortunately, Mrs May's resurgence didn't last long. As the seasons began to turn, so did her health.

The cough worsened once more; her skin took on a sickly, pallid hue and within a week, she was bedridden again.

Jane maintained an almost constant vigil by her side. She watched her mother's breaths become slower and less frequent, each shallow gasp a painful reminder of her condition.

Just minutes before midnight, she made the decision to send Grimes to fetch Dr Jenkins. Usually, it would be Mr May making such decisions. But he was, of course, not at home.

"I've been blessed to have a daughter like you," Mrs May whispered weakly, clutching Jane's hand.

"I'm the blessed one, Mother," Jane replied, her eyes brimming with tears.

"Will you promise me one thing, Jane?" Her

mother asked earnestly, summoning what little strength she had left.

"Of course," Jane responded.

"Look after Russell. He is a good man, despite his faults."

Jane hesitated for the briefest of moments. Russell May should be here at his wife's bedside during her final moments, but he wasn't. He was either pursuing his endless quest of blackening the name of John Bridge, or he was with her. Knowing that her mother needed comfort in these moments, Jane nodded her agreement, "Of course I will."

"This firm will be nothing without you, my dear. Your skills have made it what it is. Remember that."

Her mother then dissolved into a fit of coughing.

"Hush, Mother dear. Rest a while. The doctor will be here soon," Jane reassured her, gently squeezing her hand.

Mrs May managed a smile, even then. Despite her frailty, her mother possessed a radiant beauty.

They sat in silence, Mrs May's eyes gently closing. After a few moments, there was a knock at the door and the doctor walked in.

Jane looked up at him, tears streaming down her cheeks. "You're too late, Doctor. She's gone."

Dr Jenkins did what he had to do, then discreetly left, informing Jane that the undertakers would take care of the rest, depending on how they chose to proceed, of course.

Jane knew that it wasn't for her to decide. She had to wait for Russell May to return home.

Finally, at a little after four in the morning he returned. Grimes met him at the door outside, informing him that he was urgently needed upstairs.

Jane had remained with her mother's body, refusing to leave it. Hearing him stumble up the stairs, cursing as he attempted to hurry, she decided he shouldn't see her mother in such a state.

She emerged onto the landing just as Russell May, bleary-eyed, climbed the final step. "What's going on, Jane?" he asked.

Jane stared at him with contempt. She was no longer afraid of him. "Your wife is dead, sir," she spat out.

"What?" Russell May stared back at her as though he couldn't believe it. As though the obvious decline of Carol May over the past weeks and months had somehow escaped him.

He brushed past Jane, and as he did, she caught a whiff of a sickly-sweet perfume, heavy with Eastern spices.

And, in that moment, Jane vowed revenge.

CHAPTER 18

ne year later

The king was dead.

The gossips had been writing for weeks in the newspapers, and at last, the inevitable happened. The King passed away, his final sigh echoing within the historic walls of Windsor Castle.

Suddenly, the young princess was not a princess anymore. She shed the name Alexandria like an outgrown dress, and the world now knew her simply as Victoria.

Jane couldn't help but wonder what the young woman, the same age as her, was feeling. How do you go about ruling a country at such an age? Who would be there to love and support her? Her mother? Some of the newspapers had said that the two did not get on. Would she have to do it alone? Did she feel the same way as Jane?

The news of the King's death made Russell May bubble with a kind of excitement he hadn't felt since his school days. But this only seemed to fan the flames of Jane's resentment towards him.

All he could see now was the opportunity to obtain the Royal warrant.

The last year without her mother had been difficult. The relationship between herself and Mr May was strained. In front of clients, she still addressed him as father, but in the private depths of her heart, she knew that wasn't the truth. She understood her real standing all too well; she was his apprentice, a tool for getting what he wanted, nothing more, and this arrangement was set to continue until she turned twenty-one. Until then, she was bound by his command.

She could not believe that, when her mother needed him the most, he wasn't there. When she died, he was with her.

The funeral of her mother had felt like a cold hand clutching her heart. She hadn't attended the funeral of her real mother, of course. She was far too young at the time. She had been buried in a pauper's grave somewhere on the grounds of the Southwark Workhouse. Carol May, her new mother, the only mother she had known, was interred in a vault in St

James' Church in Westminster. A fine stone tablet with a brass inscription lay over it. At least Mr May had the decency to pay for something like that for his wife. It gave Jane somewhere to go and grieve.

But that was as far as his decency extended.

Violet Rose, or Kate Larkin as Jane knew her, was the talk of London. The most exciting and beloved young actress on the stage. She was invited to parties and dinners and events. More often than not, she was on the arm of the renowned Goldsmith and recent widower, Russell May.

Jane had already been busy with work prior to the King's demise. She was acutely aware that business would intensify even further as the nobility demanded special pieces for the new Queen's coronation events. Now, with her mother departed, she had taken to spending evenings working too. What else was there to do? She found solace and peace in arranging the gems into works of art. As she did so, a plan began to form in her mind.

In just two years, her apprenticeship would be completed. She was acquainted with countless affluent women across London. Could it be possible for her to establish her own goldsmith's shop? As a woman? If a woman could be Queen of England, then why couldn't a woman become a goldsmith, licensed by Goldsmiths' Hall? Stranger events had surely taken place in this city.

She still saw Robin as often as she could, dreaming that one day they would be together forever. Time and again, visit after visit, she yearned for Robin to confess his feelings for her. He always seemed to be on the brink of doing so, and then stopped, as though something held him back.

She confided her plan to him. He considered it a sound one.

"Time will tell if it works," he said. It was clear to Jane that he had doubts about whether Goldsmiths' Hall would grant her a licence. "But fate always intercedes. What's meant to be will be. Sometimes it can take us down the strangest of paths."

On Sunday, Jane and Robin opted to enjoy a leisurely walk within the lush green of Hyde Park. If they didn't meet by the river, a stroll through one of London's many parks was always the alternative. The new queen had ascended the throne a little over a month ago, and it was a balmy July afternoon.

Seated comfortably near the gentle waters of the Serpentine, they savoured the ginger cake baked by Mrs Johnson. Gone were the days of stealing from the master's kitchen in the workhouse. As they ate, their conversation flowed, touching upon the grand and the trivial, a comfortable discourse between two dear friends. Yet there was a question that had been pressing on Jane's heart, and she finally mustered the courage to ask, "How do you see the future?"

This query had lingered, unspoken, for many months, even years. Jane needed to understand her position in Robin's life.

"The future? An interesting thought. Perhaps carriages that move without horses? Lights that shine without gas?"

"No," Jane countered with a hint of exasperation. "Our future?"

Robin, taken aback for a moment, peered into Jane's earnest eyes. He tilted his head in slight confusion. "Are you implying us... as husband and wife?" Robin asked, needing further clarification.

"Indeed."

"I always presumed that was our unspoken agreement," Robin responded gently. "Is this not your understanding?"

"It is, Robin. It is indeed. Yet, occasionally, a lady, even a workhouse girl yearns for confirmation. She seeks reassurance of her place in the future."

Taken in by her sincerity, Robin hesitated for a brief moment, holding her gaze. Leaning in, he pressed a gentle kiss onto her lips. A thrill of anticipation danced in her stomach, a sensation she wished could last forever. As quickly as it had begun, it was over. "I love you, Jane May," he whispered into the fading daylight, "I always have."

Jane's heart soared at his words. "I love you too, Robin." But then her expression fell.

"What is it?" Robin asked with concern. "Was it the kiss? I apologise if it was inappropriate."

Jane smiled. "No, it wasn't the kiss. I've been waiting for that for years." She closed her eyes for the briefest of moments and savoured it again.

"Then what is it?"

"Jane May... now Mother's gone, I'm not sure I want that name anymore. Do I want the same name as him? I think I might prefer Jane Monday."

"God willing, it won't matter soon. One day you'll be Jane Buckley. I promise you."

Twenty-one still seemed like an age away. A few long years. Then, she could finally do as she wished.

They sat in silence, holding hands, each lost in their thoughts about the future. Then a commotion arose from the nearby gravel road. People were running to the side. In the distance, towards the grand frontage of Buckingham Palace, a dust cloud grew, giving way to horses.

Then they heard people shouting, "The Queen! God save Her Majesty!"

They shared a lingering glance before both rose and ran towards the road. They both wanted to see the young new Queen.

Four horses led the procession, ridden by the Queen's Lifeguards. They were followed by a carriage, drawn by two splendid grey horses, controlled by a carriage driver in flawless red livery, topped with a black top hat. Inside the carriage sat a petite young woman, demurely dressed in beige with a matching bonnet. She waved to the people as the carriage passed by, a man in a black morning suit seated opposite her.

Jane watched, spellbound, as the Queen passed by. Her face was aglow with radiant joy. As the carriage rolled past her, Jane could have sworn that the Queen's eyes met hers, as if singling her out from the crowd.

Once the procession had passed, the crowd dispersed.

"Well, that was the second happening I wasn't expecting today," Jane remarked with a laugh. "Who was the man with her?"

"I fancy it was Lord Melbourne, the Prime Minister," Robin conjectured.

"Did you see how tiny she was? It seems unbelievable that such a woman can rule this country."

"Don't judge her by her size. The Earl and Countess hosted Wellington for dinner last week. He was immensely impressed with her." Robin shared the gossip that had been heard from the junior butlers around the dining table. Nothing was safe from the eager ears of servants in the grand townhouses of London.

Yet Jane knew the Queen's size was an important factor. Mr May was right. The young queen couldn't possibly wear St Edward's crown. Something new would have to be crafted for the coronation.

Upon her return home, she found Mr May waiting for her in the workshop. He was visibly excited. "Where have you been?"

"Out," she replied, evasively. The blind deference she once showed him had vanished.

If this change bothered him, he didn't show it. Despite the fact she was bound to him until she turned twenty-one, she knew she held some power. It was she who crafted the pieces. It was she who was in demand by the rich and well-connected women of society. It was she who could secure a Royal Warrant for the company. Without her, Russell May Goldsmith's had no hope.

He waved a piece of paper in his hand. "We've been summoned," he declared.

A flicker of excitement passed over Jane. Despite her resentment towards Mr May for his actions towards her late mother, she too yearned for the Royal Warrant. She longed to create pieces for the new young Queen, especially now that she had seen her.

"By whom?" she demanded.

"The Countess of Arundel and Surrey."

Jane immediately understood the significance and why Mr May was so thrilled. Four years ago she wouldn't have had a clue who this countess was. But she had made it her business to study her clients and, more importantly, her potential clients. The countess was married to the Earl of Arundel and Surrey. He was the son of the Duke of Norfolk.

The Duke of Norfolk, a divorced man with only one son, held the prestigious title of Earl Marshall of England. It was he who would be responsible for organising Queen Victoria's coronation.

This was the closest commission they could get to the crown without the Royal warrant. It was an opportunity to demonstrate their capabilities to those in power.

Russell May gripped Jane's shoulders and smiled broadly. "This is it. This is our way in, Jane."

She recoiled slightly at his touch. But she too could feel the excitement, followed by a wave of guilt. She felt that enjoying this moment was a betrayal of her mother. She didn't want to partake in Russell May's enthusiasm.

She wanted to create pieces for the Queen, but not for him to take pleasure in it. He didn't deserve it. He was out there, fornicating with that despicable woman while her mother transitioned to the next life. He deserved nothing.

"When do we leave?" Jane asked cooly.

"In the morning. You'll wear your best dress, of course. She has requested your presence. It seems that others have spoken of you, " said Russell May, handing Jane the letter for her to read.

As she read the words penned by the countess, she couldn't help but brim with pride. She knew that pride was a sin, but she couldn't resist. It seemed unbelievable that a girl plucked from the desperation and drudgery of the workhouse was now being summoned to the grand houses of the country's elite.

"I also wanted to show you this," Russell May said, walking towards the workbench at the back of the workshop. He paused to adjust the oil lamp, making it glow brighter.

He unrolled a large piece of paper that had been laid out on the bench. Jane's curiosity was piqued.

She stepped forward and beheld the drawing of a magnificent new crown. Its breathtaking beauty and simple lines made her gasp.

"Its weight will be just half of that of Saint Edward's crown," Russell May explained, watching Jane absorb every detail of the drawing.

There were four tall, thin arches and at the centre of the forehead, a large cross.

"There are 210 gemstones: diamonds, sapphires, emeralds, rubies, and garnets. The cross at the front will be crafted entirely of rubies to symbolise St George's Cross."

He pointed to an alternate view of the crown on the diagram. "At the rear, that there is Saint Edward's

Sapphire. It was taken from the confessors' ring when they re-interred his body in the new abbey. I thought it seemed a fitting addition."

"It's magnificent," Jane gasped as she studied the fine drawing. She could see this sitting perfectly on top of the young queen's head.

"I know," Russell May replied, his voice swelling with arrogant pride at the praise.

"What will you do? Present it to the countess in the hope she shows her father-in-law?"

"No. I'll present it to Goldsmith's Hall. They've already started quietly asking for coronation piece submissions. They haven't gone solely to John Bridge," he said with a smirk. "However, I may take the diagram tomorrow, perhaps show it to the countess, and tell her that you'll be working on the piece if we get the Royal warrant."

Once again, Jane felt a guilty surge of excitement. Might she truly be crafting this crown to be placed upon the Queen of England's head? It seemed incredible. Would she meet the Queen and witness her reaction in person?

She pushed these thoughts aside. There was a vast gap between submitting a drawing to the Goldsmith's Hall and actually securing the commission and the Royal Warrant.

Jane took one last lingering glance at the crown as

Russell May dimmed the oil lamp and carefully rolled up the drawing.

"We will depart at nine-thirty in the morning. A carriage has been booked," Russell May said. "In the meantime, I'm going out for the evening."

Jane harboured no uncertainty about who he would be visiting this evening.

She opened her mouth to utter a word and then promptly sealed it again.

Mr May fixed his attention on her for a moment as if he was deciding whether to say something or not. Finally, he spoke. "I am aware of it all, you know."

"Aware of what?" Jane asked.

"I know who she is. I know about your joint history."

The contempt rose within her, and she went further than she had ever gone before. "And it doesn't bother you? I strongly doubt she told you how she treated people in the workhouse. She was awful. A bully and a brute. The fact she was willing to see you when she knew you were married, tells me she hasn't changed." It was a rant that Jane knew was ill-advised. But she couldn't help herself. "And I'm surprised You show no concern regarding her age. The same age as a woman you introduce to duchesses and countesses as your daughter? But probably her age is the attraction. Is that so?"

Jane detected a flicker of anger ignite in Mr May's eyes. For a brief second, she thought he was going to strike her. She took a small step back in anticipation. As quickly as his anger surfaced, it subsided. "I understand your hurt, but Carol would have wished for my happiness now."

To Jane, it appeared that he could barely muster the strength to utter his deceased wife's name. The woman who had become her new mother.

She yearned to express a thousand thoughts to him. She longed to confront him with her knowledge of how he had impregnated young Jennifer and then turned her and their unborn baby out. She wanted to tell him how sure she was that there were others. She wanted to confront him about his absence at his wife's death. She desired to tell him that, in her eyes, he was the most contemptible man on earth. But she refrained.

"I spoke out of place. Enjoy your evening, sir," she uttered the final word with evident disdain.

She walked past him and went in search of Mrs Johnson to see the preparations for dinner.

"Remember, Jane, the carriage departs at nine-thirty. It's important." Mr May called after her.

She noticed a hint of pleading in his voice. And she knew that he was fully aware that if he ever hoped to get the Royal Warrant, it would be because of Jane. He couldn't afford to alienate her.

Later that evening, after feasting on the chicken and potato pie that Mrs Johnson had lovingly prepared, Jane returned to the workshop.

She managed a mere ten minutes of work before she rose and unrolled the diagrams that Mr May had produced earlier in the day.

Even though she'd seen it before, she gasped once again at the sheer magnificence of the crown. She yearned for the ability to craft such a piece. She imagined the young queen wearing it and a portrait being commissioned to capture the spectacle.

Then she envisaged the master's office in the workhouse. She could see a new portrait of a young queen, wearing the crown that she had created, hanging proudly behind his desk. The master, whomever he might be these days, would have no inkling that an orphan, born within the walls of the workhouse and raised there under harsh conditions, had crafted the piece.

She desired that royal warrant just as fervently as Mr May. However, they needed each other in order to secure it.

She carefully rolled the diagram back up and retired to bed.

Jane slept soundly that night and rose late. The carriage was due to depart at nine-thirty. She rushed to get ready, finishing with just ten minutes to spare. She walked carefully through the attic, its musty boxes filled with who knows what, before descending the attic stairs quickly. Just as she was about to descend the stairs leading to the workshop, she heard Mr May's bedroom door open.

"Don't worry, I'm ready," she said. She paused and turned. But it wasn't Mr May who emerged from the bedroom.

It was Kate Larkin, naked as the day she was born and without an ounce of shame.

CHAPTER 19

*B*uckingham Palace, London, England
"And how have you found the Palace, Your Majesty?" Lord Melbourne inquired, settling into his seat at the Queen's invitation.

The youthful Queen Victoria often sought his counsel; their meetings, intended to be weekly affairs, had become more frequent since her ascension. Melbourne had advised her to vacate Kensington Palace and take up residence at Buckingham Palace.

"I find it a splendid retreat, Prime Minister. I thank you for your recommendation," Victoria replied in a hushed tone.

Impressed by her since her ascension, Melbourne had perceived the insecurity and diffidence typical of her age. However, the Queen was candid about her anxieties, prompting Melbourne to regard her in an almost paternal light.

"So, have we finally settled on a date for the coronation?" Victoria inquired.

He detected a hint of vexation in her voice. They'd been at loggerheads over the issue for some time. Victoria had confessed her concern that the delay might lead the nation to favour a regent until she aged or married.

Yet, that wasn't the crux of the matter. The immense organisational requirements called for careful balancing.

"Yes, significant progress has been made, Ma'am. The cabinet has agreed on the 28th of June next year," Melbourne announced.

"Next year?" the Queen echoed, her disappointment evident.

"We must accommodate the weather, Ma'am. We couldn't possibly conduct a coronation in winter. There will be thousands attending. You will be travelling in an open carriage. We need to create a spectacle."

Victoria nodded, accepting the logic behind Melbourne's explanation.

"The cabinet has also agreed on a budget," Melbourne added, visibly uncomfortable.

Victoria tilted her head, urging him to proceed. "£70,000," he declared.

Victoria paused for a moment. "That seems terribly extravagant, Lord Melbourne."

"It could be considered a compromise, Ma'am. It is more costly than your late uncle's coronation, indeed. Yet, the local businesses dubbed it the 'Half-Crown Coronation', expressing disappointment at its frugality. Such an event is excellent for business," Melbourne said, ensuring the young Queen understood. "However, it is significantly cheaper than your other uncle, George IV's coronation. That was an excessive burden on the Treasury at £240,000."

"I will defer to your judgement on the matter, Prime Minister." Victoria knew that she had little choice in the matter. She may be Queen, but she held little actual power. Her government held that.

"Do you recall our discussions about the crown to be used at the coronation, Ma'am?" Lord Melbourne enquired, changing tack.

"Indeed. You advised that Saint Edward's crown would be highly unsuitable due to its weight, I understand."

Melbourne nodded. "Goldsmiths' Hall has approached a number of reputable goldsmiths for submissions for a new crown, Ma'am. I believe five submissions were made and they have now narrowed the choice down to two. I should like to show them to you if I may."

"Of course," Victoria said, rising from her chair, genuinely interested.

Melbourne slowly rose to his feet and walked over to a table.

"This is the first one, Ma'am. This is submitted by the Royal Goldsmiths themselves, Rundell and Bridge. The drawings depict a magnificent crown with a cross of diamonds above the arches. This one has a number of features, Ma'am. Most notably there, in the cross, is a sapphire. That is Saint Edward's Sapphire, taken from the very ring of the Confessor himself. At the front is the Black Prince's Ruby, worn by Henry V at the Battle of Agincourt. And at the bottom is the Stuart Sapphire. The pearls are said to have belonged to Queen Elizabeth. There are over three thousand gemstones in this piece, Ma'am."

"It is magnificent," Victoria said, fingers tracing over the drawing.

When the queen had finished absorbing every detail, she looked up at Melbourne.

"And this is the second one, Ma'am. This is by Russell and May Goldsmiths, a highly reputable firm. Many of the aristocracy use them to create highly ornate pieces of jewellery. I myself have purchased a piece from them in the past," he said, laying a new drawing on top of the other.

"I appreciate the simplicity," Victoria said, her eyes sparkling. "It is impactful without being garish.

Looking at it, I think this one would be lighter than the other?"

"It would indeed, there are far fewer gemstones. Of course, that isn't the only consideration. Awarding the making of the crown to Russell and May Goldsmiths will mean moving the Royal warrant from Rundell and Bridge."

"Is that problematic?"

"Not at all, Ma'am. It merely brings with it an element of risk, I suppose. Rundell and Bridge have been the Royal Goldsmiths for some time now. They've been trusted with two coronations. If anything were to go awry with a new goldsmith, you can imagine the reaction in the press."

"When will the decision be made?" Victoria asked.

"Within the week, Ma'am. I wanted to show them both to you first, and then pass on any thoughts you might have to the Earl Marshal."

"As always, I trust your guidance, Prime Minister. They both look to be very favourable pieces. I'm certain the right decision will be made."

CHAPTER 20

*L*ate November had draped its cold shroud over London, with the coronation date freshly inked for the 28th of June in the year to come.

Jane was on tenterhooks, awaiting the declaration from Goldsmiths Hall as to who would be given the honour of creating the Queen's crown for the coronation.

The prospect of Russell May Goldsmiths securing such a weighty commission left Jane grappling with how she might contend with the looming surge of work. It seemed she might need an exact double of herself to bear the load. Still, that was a bridge to be crossed if and when they arrived at it. Meanwhile, the who's who of the aristocracy had started to descend upon their goldsmiths, commissioning the most opulent finery for the impending coronation balls.

Her appointment with the Countess of Arundel and Surrey had proceeded well, despite the altercation between Jane and Mr May the evening before and the unfortunate encounter with a naked Kate Larkin just before leaving.

Jane and Mr May had travelled in silence to Norfolk House. She could hardly believe that he had allowed that woman into her home.

Jane had captivated the countess, and Mr May, acting as the dutiful father, was bursting with pride at his daughter's work. They had shown her Mr May's sketches for the crown. The countess had agreed it would be a magnificent piece worthy of the ancient ceremony. They discussed what the countess might like to be created and less than twenty-four hours after the meeting, a detailed commission arrived for a grand necklace, earring, and pendant set, a blend of diamonds and sapphires. Mr May had quoted a handsome price for the work and declared it to be the most expensive piece Russell May Goldsmiths had ever created.

Ever since then, Jane had been tirelessly pouring her skills into the commission. She aimed to conclude it by the year-end, given that a collection of other pieces also demanded her undivided attention.

That's why, even now, as midnight approached, Jane was hard at work in the workshop.

A fragile truce seemed to have taken root between Jane and Mr May. There had been a couple more frosty encounters with Kate Larkin, but Jane was resolute in not letting herself be cowed.

"Kate, I trust you're well," Jane ventured one morning, caught off guard to find her sharing breakfast with Mr May in the dining room in nothing more than a robe.

Mr May stiffened in his chair at her approach.

"It's Violet now, Jane," Kate Larkin retorted, her eyes glinting with defiance. "You know that."

"You're sitting in my mother's place," Jane found herself replying, unable to hold back.

"No, your mother died in the workhouse," Kate responded, her tone icy and matter of fact.

Advancing a step, Jane felt the old anger and resentment swelling within her, like a wave ready to crash on the shore. "Do you remember what else happened in the workhouse, Kate?" She paused for a moment and dropped her voice. "I won't tolerate bullies."

"We aren't children anymore, Jane," Kate replied, buttering a slice of toast.

"Fair enough, I won't tolerate harlots at the breakfast table then."

"Russell," Kate shrieked. "Are you going to let your apprentice speak to me like that?"

Russell, looking tired, was in no mood to be caught between two bickering women.

"Jane," Mr May pleaded. "I understand your resentment towards Violet. But under my roof, you will treat her with respect."

Jane stared at the breakfast table for a moment longer. "For some reason, I've lost my appetite this morning. I'll get on with my work, sir."

These days, she began to use the word 'sir' as a weapon. She would deliberately emphasise it so that he was fully aware of the status she believed she held in the household.

"Is that it? Is that all you're going to say? You're not going to punish her?" Kate Larkin demanded of Russell May as Jane left the room.

"Violet dearest, Jane is very important to the business here…" Russell May began. Jane didn't bother to listen to what else he was going to say. She disappeared down the stairs to the workshop.

She heard Mr May come in at a little after two in the morning. She had two gemstones to insert in this row, and then she would go to bed for a few hours. She needed sleep. Jane felt a shiver down her spine, praying that he didn't have Kate Larkin with him tonight.

"Oh. It's you," Mr May slurred as he materialised under the light of the oil lamp. He was alone and he was drunk.

Jane had probably only seen him drunk once in all of her time here. On that occasion, her mother had pandered to him and put him to bed. But she wasn't here.

"Are you hungry? I'm sure there is some salt beef we could put into a sandwich," Jane asked, in her own attempt to pander to him.

"No. Not hungry," he laughed. "I didn't get it," Mr May said with a rueful smile.

"What?"

"The royal warrant. The crown. The bloody lot. John Bridge got it. Retained his warrant." He walked over and stood over Jane.

Disappointment flooded over Jane.

The truth hung heavily in the air, a cold fact that couldn't be denied; she would not be crafting the stunning crown for the Queen. It would go unmade, a mere figment of imagination, immaterial and unadmired, forever trapped within the drowning.

If the highly coveted royal warrant didn't find its way to Russell May Goldsmiths now, amidst the monumental shift of the monarchy, it likely never would. The business had been passed over, continuity winning out.

Deep within the pain of Jane's disappointment, a sliver of relief peeked out. She had the wisdom to know that the scale of such an undertaking would have overwhelmed her in the constrained timescale. Already the order book was too full.

Additionally, a part of her found odd comfort in the fact that Russell May had been denied his lifelong ambition. There was a taste of poetic justice in the air.

A thousand thoughts shot through her mind. Her plans for the future would remain unchanged. At twenty-one, Jane would marry Robin and no longer be tethered to Mr May as an apprentice. Her wealthy connections spanned society. Even if the Goldsmiths' Guild would not grant her a licence, she was confident in finding gainful employment elsewhere. The spectre of Kate Larkin could fade once again into the recesses of her memory.

"I'm certain John Bridge bribed someone," Russell May grumbled, albeit his tone lacked its usual venom. "His design is downright absurd. A monstrous, overblown ruby, slap bang in the middle of the crown."

"I'm sorry, sir," Jane said, unsure of what else to offer. "But we still have a full order book. Business is thriving."

"John Bridge is going to botch this crown. I just know it," he rumbled ominously, a subtle hint of brewing plans in his voice. "This coronation will go down as the cursed coronation."

A pang of suspicion tugged at Jane, thoughts darting back to the incident of the false diamonds. It seemed Russell May was cooking up a reckless plan.

She stared at him in silence. Knowing that now wasn't the time to speak.

"Do you know who I lay the blame on?" he snapped.

"Who?"

"You. You consume my food. Live in my house. You act as though you are the mistress. You are not my daughter, despite what I tell them. I tolerated the fantasy while Carol was alive. She was just as useless; she could only bring a sick child into this world. Now she is dead, I won't tolerate it anymore. Do you hear me, girl? You have grown ever more insolent by the week " He breathed in her face. The sickly smell of whiskey and smoke hit her. "I do not require your advice. You are here to work. And work only. You will not dine with me anymore, you will take your meals in the kitchen, with the rest of the staff. Do you understand?"

"Yes, sir," Jane replied nervously. But she knew he wasn't finished yet.

"And mind your manners with Violet. No more insolence," he warned. "It will be her who will be mistress of this house."

Jane nodded her head in agreement.

"I'm going to give you something that will remind you of that," he hissed in a low whisper.

And then his hands balled into fists.

And Jane screamed as the blows rained down.

CHAPTER 21

"*J*'ll kill him," Robin declared, abruptly rising to his feet.

"No, sit down, dearest, please," Jane urged, grabbing Robin by the hand and gently pulling him back down.

They were situated on a wooden bench in Hyde Park, nestled under a towering oak tree, but it provided little shelter as its leaves had long fallen. Both of them were bundled up against the biting cold. It had been over three weeks since the incident with Russell May.

Only now were Jane's bruises beginning to fade.

She had deliberately avoided meeting Robin during this time, sending him letters filled with excuses that she was too consumed by work. In truth, she was busy. However, her primary concern was allowing the bruises to disappear. Not out of fear of what Robin might do in his quest for revenge, but because she was concerned that her beauty may have been tarnished, and Robin might no longer find her attractive.

It was just over a week until Christmas and the frost was severe, though the snow had yet to fall.

Jane had just finished relaying the events of the incident to Robin. His emotions, understandably, were still raw.

However, Jane had had ample time to reflect on the matter. While she was hurt and frightened, she remembered what Robin had told her in the work-house all those years ago. *"You have to stand up to these people at some point."*

And that was precisely what Jane intended to do.

However, she planned to do it her own way. There was no chance she would send Robin to confront Mr May. The immediate problem was Grimes, standing guard at the doorway. Robin would be denied access. Even if he managed to get in, Robin could end up on the receiving end of Grimes, and that was a prospect she didn't want to consider.

Mr May had apologised for his actions the following morning. Even he had gasped at the sight of Jane's battered face. He assured everyone that it was a terrible mistake, a result of his drunkenness and despondency. Jane knew all too well that his apology was only because he had come to the stark realisation that the firm's future hinged on her youthful shoulders. The amount of work unrelated to fine jewellery was scant. The plates, chalices and candlesticks for churches and grand houses were few and far between. It was the necklaces and bracelets that generated the firm's wealth, lining Mr May's pockets. If Jane decided to walk out the door and vanish, he would be left with almost nothing.

Mrs Johnson was appalled when she saw the damage inflicted on Jane, even considering resignation. However, Jane talked her out of it. Jane was acutely aware that Mrs Johnson needed the job, and the more allies Jane had around her, the better. Particularly if Mr May's threat about Kate Larkin becoming the mistress of the house turned into a reality.

Slowly she formulated her plans.

Finally, the opportunity arose in February. It was a simple enough commission, a brooch for Lady Wilhelmina Stanhope, daughter of the countess. She had been selected to be a maid of honour to the Queen at the coronation. The countess wanted the brooch for her daughter, as a gift for her to wear at the coronation feast. She had explained to Jane what she wanted, and she said it could be done.

Its intricate design was a miniature masterpiece; a golden rose vine twisted and turned, petals and leaves studded with a constellation of glittering diamonds, each facet catching the candlelight and returning a fiery brilliance. At its heart, a singular, flawless ruby glowed with an inner light, an embodiment of pure luxury.

As she looked at it, she nodded her head. It was perfect. And no one would know until the time was right.

Robin's eyes widened, aghast as he grappled with the enormity of the plan that Jane had just unravelled. "You can't do that!" he protested vehemently, his voice trembling with a blend of alarm and incredulity. It was Sunday, just after noon and they were taking a walk by the Thames.

"Why?" Jane retorted, a mischievous grin playing on her face. "I'm tired of always being told what to do. And to be clear, I've already done the first part."

"Are you certain you won't land in hot water? I couldn't bear it if anything were to happen to you." His face turned pale, and it wasn't due to the snow that now blanketed London with its icy touch.

Jane responded resolutely, a defiant sparkle flashing in her eyes. "Of course not, I'm but a humble apprentice. I do as I'm instructed." She paused for dramatic effect before adding, "And if circumstances warrant, I'll present myself to her and proffer an apology, stating my ignorance. My sincerity will leave no room for disbelief. Remember, she likes me.

My only concern is for the other staff. They will likely end up without work."

Robin still looked concerned. "Well, if there's any way I can help..."

"How funny you should mention that…" Jane said, a thoughtful pause following her words.

In response to Robin's puzzled look, she unfolded her meticulously crafted plan in detail, explaining how his aid would be instrumental. As she anticipated, he agreed without hesitation, his loyalty to his betrothed unwavering.

With Robin as a fellow conspirator, Jane's plan was now set in motion. All that remained was the opportune moment for it to spring into action.

However, an unexpected turn of events necessitated an unforeseen amendment to her scheme.

She was retiring to bed one evening when she overheard the audacious laughter of Kate Larkin emanating from the sitting room.

Curiosity piqued, Jane halted outside the door, concealed by the encompassing darkness, her breath hushed as she strained to overhear the conversation.

The words that filtered through were nothing short of astonishing.

"Just imagine, he couldn't complete his horrendous design because the key element was missing," Mr May exclaimed.

"He is a fool, Russell," Kate Larkin whispered into

his ear, her words slurred, hinting at the influence of the evening's excesses.

"He won't have a clue it was you," Russell cackled in response, clearly in the same condition as Kate. "If it is as easy as you say."

"If I do this for you, what will I receive in return?" Kate asked, her voice suddenly taking a business like tone.

"Anything you want, my love."

"No. I'm serious, Russell. If I do this, it would be the most perilous act anyone could commit in London right now. I will be putting my neck on the line. Literally," she said, her voice now fraught with tension and showing no hint of lack of clarity.

"You could become my wife," he suggested.

"We've trodden this path before, Russell. I shall not be shackled by matrimony," she replied firmly. She paused as though considering. "Three Thousand Pounds, Russell. Cash. And you get what you want. Rundell and Bridge destroyed."

A silence filled the room, the implications of their conversation leaving Jane frozen with apprehension. The outrageous amount of money they mentioned was more than Mr May's exorbitant charge for the countess's necklace. Jane's mind whirred as she pondered, "Could he possibly possess such an astronomical sum? Even if he did, would he give it to

Kate? And what was she actually to do for the money?"

"Agreed," said Mr May suddenly. "But it needs to be done when there is no chance of the piece being altered to accommodate the fact it is missing."

"Excellent," was the succinct response from Kate, a veneer of satisfaction lacing her words. Their plan had been hashed out, their intentions laid bare and now, it seemed, they had reached a consensus.

In the ensuing silence, the room was awash with anticipation, a tension that knotted the air, palpable and electric. It was disrupted by a sound that Jane had not expected to hear: the unmistakable whisper of lips meeting lips and the soft, muffled echo of a passionate kiss exchanged between Mr May and Kate. Jane, still hidden in the shadowy corner, felt a wave of revulsion and unease course through her veins. She sunk back into the darker shadows and without a sound went up the stairs into the attic.

She lay in bed and wondered what the pair were planning. It seemed to her that she would do better to let that matter play out before she went through with her own plan.

When she next encountered Robin, Jane updated him on what she had overheard.

Robin let out a slow whistle. "Sounds like they're planning something foolish."

"It must be linked to the coronation. From what

Mr May hinted at, it seems to be something to do with the new crown that John Bridge is making."

"That makes sense. The crown is the centrepiece of the coronation. Do you think you should inform someone?"

"What is there to report? An overheard drunken conversation between two lovers? It's only hints and rumours at this point. No, we need to wait for them to act. I'll be alert, though."

Robin fell silent for a moment before adding to the conversation. "You are aware quite a few rumours are circulating about Violet Rose throughout the city?"

Jane tilted her head, looking at him, waiting for him to proceed.

"Apparently, she entertains the attention of quite a number of men."

"Do we know if this is true?"

"Let's be fair, actresses have always been the centre of attention for society's elite. The old king lived with one for years; they were practically man and wife. If I recall correctly, his brother did exactly the same thing."

"So her affections aren't solely for Mr May then. I wonder if he's aware?"

"I'm sure he is. If there is one thing Mr May is not, it's naive."

"Do you suppose Kate Larkin is seeing John

Bridge as well? The manner in which she called the man a fool suggested she at least knows him."

"I wouldn't put it past her," said Robin. "This must be some scheme for three thousand pounds. We could live on that happily for the rest of our lives and still have enough to pass down to our children."

Jane stared at Robin for just a moment too long.

"What's wrong?" Robin asked.

She reached out, took his hand, and placed it between her own. Even then, his hand seemed huge against her two delicately small palms.

"Nothing is wrong, Robin. Children? I had never even considered children. Have you got it all planned out?"

He smiled softly back at her. "You don't want children?"

"Oh, I do. It's just that I haven't given it any thought. What you've just said is the most beautiful thing in the world. Our children."

Jane was silent for a moment, imagining what those children might be like.

"I personally imagine two of each," Robin said. "Our girls will be the most beautiful in the world. They'll be little copies of you."

He leaned in and kissed her gently on the lips. Tremors of excitement flooded her body. She couldn't wait until her apprenticeship ended so that she could marry this man, the man who had been so kind and caring to her throughout her life.

They broke their embrace and just stared at each other for a few moments. "So what happens to your plan?" Robin asked.

"I'll wait. See if I can find out more about what these two are hatching. I'm still worried about the other staff. What might happen to them?"

"Those who need to will find other jobs, I'm sure. Grimes would be employed by all manner of people in a heartbeat," Robin said, thinking of the huge, imposing figure of the man.

"It's people like Mrs Johnson that I worry about. There are so many cooks in London town."

"No doubt something will present itself. It always does."

Jane nodded her head. Robin was always optimistic, but Jane was less so.

As much as she wanted her plan to succeed and Mr May to get the payback he deserved, it would mean that Russell May Goldsmiths would be no more.

She didn't want to put good people out on the streets.

CHAPTER 22

"Come along, come along," Jane implored, pulling Robin by the hand towards the throng of people.

He laughed as he went along with her.

It was early April, and the first signs of spring were beginning to bloom across London. They had made it a habit to walk in Hyde Park almost every Sunday.

The reason was simple.

Jane wished to see the Queen.

Most Sundays, Her Majesty would ride out in a carriage, usually accompanied by the Prime Minister, Lord Melbourne. The people of London had almost come to expect it. The crowds seemed to grow week by week.

Jane managed to press her way through to the front, right next to the gravel path.

The clamour of the crowds could be heard from the direction of the palace. The traditional cries of "God save Her Majesty" or "God save the Queen" rang out as the small procession passed by.

For some reason, Jane was mesmerised by all of this.

She was convinced that each time the Queen rode past, she managed to single her out in the crowd. They would lock eyes for just a moment. At least, that is what Jane believed.

Jane yearned to understand what was going on in the monarch's mind. Oh, how she wished she could have been the one crafting the crown for her coronation. But alas, it was not meant to be.

Now, after everything that had happened, Jane's focus had shifted. It was no longer about obtaining the Royal Warrant but rather about seeking vengeance for her mother, and now herself. Russell May Goldsmiths was to be destroyed. They would put him in prison and hopefully throw away the key. It was no more than he deserved.

But she still worried about her co-workers. She didn't want to be the cause of their hardship. However, one of them was no longer her concern.

Hans had vanished the previous week. He had simply not turned up for work. After the second day,

Mr May had instructed Grimes to visit his residence. The man had been renting a room in a rough tenement in the East End. Grimes found it deserted. After a few knocks on doors, he discovered that the man had disappeared over the weekend without paying his last month's rent.

Jane knew she would never see him again.

The twins would surely find work at other Goldsmiths. If indeed they chose to work at all. They were ageing, despite it not being readily apparent in their strange-looking faces. They were becoming slower. Russell had insisted on more than one occasion over the previous twelve months that they work faster. Jane didn't believe they were capable of doing so. Retirement was what they needed.

Jane had been listening in secret. Eavesdropping and straining her ears for any hint as to what Russell May and Kate Larkin were planning.

Skulking in the shadows, she had witnessed events that churned her stomach with revulsion. Russell May couldn't keep his hands off Kate Larkin. The woman, rather than repelling his advances, seemed to revel in them, stoking his desires. The horrifying sounds of their union echoed through the rooms, pervading the very spaces in which she and her dear mother used to sit and talk. She endured the shame, hoping to hear something. Yet there was no mention of the scheme they had jointly devised.

All she could do was bide her time and listen.

The coronation was only months away. They would need to act soon, if at all.

If they failed to act, Jane would simply implement the plan she had previously devised. If they did act and Jane learnt of it, she would try to thwart them.

Robin escorted her home after the Queen had departed. Jane knew that one day, they wouldn't have to part ways at the end of a blissful Sunday afternoon. They would return to their own little house together.

Yet, for now, they were bidding their farewells outside the Goldsmith's door. Suddenly, the door swung open with an air of theatricality, revealing none other than Kate Larkin herself.

A wave of hushed whispers swept through the street as onlookers recognized the famed actress, Violet Rose, making her public appearance. The radiant smiles that graced their faces, the twinkling eyes filled with admiration, all celebrated the spectacle that was Kate Larkin.

Kate instantly fixed her gaze on Jane, intrigued by the young man accompanying her. She sauntered over. The contemptuous sneer on her face only magnified the audacity of her approach.

Her haughty voice cut through the evening air, derision dripping from every word. "A man? You have a man?" Her eyes roved over Robin, judging him with demeaning scrutiny. "Does Russell know about him?"

"It's none of your business, is it, Kate?" Jane retorted. She was sharp and dismissive.

"I could make it my business, though, couldn't I, Jane?" Kate replied, her hungry gaze never wavering from Robin. "He is rather handsome, isn't he? What on earth is he doing with you?"

Jane felt a shiver run down her spine. What if Kate informed Russell about Robin? Would he prevent her from venturing into the city? Was that even possible?

Kate regarded Robin with a predatory look. "If you ever want a proper lady..."

"Madam, I'm with a proper lady," Robin interjected, stepping closer to Jane.

"Whatever you say." Kate scrutinised Robin for another moment. "Don't I know you?" Jane could almost see her mind turning as she considered.

"I would doubt it, madam," Robin replied. He had no intention of revealing his identity. He was certain Jane would prefer it that way.

Jane and Robin could only stare at Kate. Eventually, she grew bored. "I'll be on my way. Remember what I said, young man. I am Violet Rose. You can find me at the Theatre Royal, Drury Lane. I'll be waiting." She softly ran her hand down Robin's chest. Her flirtatious smile and raised eyebrows were the last they saw of her before she disappeared down the street in the direction of Westminster.

Jane was left seething at their interaction, yet she also felt apprehensive. She couldn't help but notice how Robin's eyes had followed Kate as she left.

CHAPTER 23

"*T*omorrow," declared Kate Larkin. "I'm committing to it tomorrow."

"Really? Why then?" inquired Russell.

"Because, before long, he'll be embedding it into the crown. It must be accomplished prior to that. One of his staff members is ill with a fever and isn't permitted to work, save he infects everyone. Another is celebrating a birthday and will be out for the evening. It will only be him and me."

"Is it going to be as easy as you say?"

"He'll be blind drunk," Kate said with a half laugh. "I'll utilise my charm, and I'll be gone before anyone realises anything."

"What about his security? The rumour at Goldsmiths Hall is that it's been increased over the past few months for understandable reasons."

"No one is inside the property. They are all outside. They're accustomed to me coming and going at all times. By the time he discovers it's missing, he won't have a clue who has taken it. It might be days. When he showed me the safe and told me the combination, he was blind drunk. He won't recall doing so."

"But you'll be questioned, surely?"

"Questioned? Possibly. But I won't have it, will I? They'll scrutinise those who work there, those with access to the safe." Kate Larkin studied Russell for a moment. "I need my money."

"You'll get it. I promise."

"Good. And you'll get what you want, Russell."

Jane stood in the dark shadows outside the sitting room, a cold shiver coursing down her spine. It seemed their plan was about to be launched into action.

Jane heard the soft moans of Kate as Russell May kissed her, engaging in who knows what with her. She slipped away and up the stairs to her room, where she would not have to hear anymore.

She would have to consult Robin. She required his advice. The only opportunity would be at lunchtime. She decided to send him a note to meet her down by the river.

It was early May. Only a few minor commissions remained to be completed in time for the coronation. Everything else could wait.

She arrived first and paced up and down. Robin looked pensive when he arrived.

"Are you okay? You said it was urgent? Has Kate Larkin been up to..."

"No. I'm fine," Jane interrupted. "Whatever they're doing, it's happening tonight."

Jane filled Robin in on what she'd overheard the previous evening, deliberately omitting the sordid details of their passionate escapade.

"Should I inform the authorities, do you think?" she asked.

Robin rubbed his chin as he contemplated the situation. "What are you going to tell them? Do you reckon they'll believe that a famous actress named Violet Rose is planning to steal in collaboration with a disgruntled goldsmith, though you're not sure what, from the safe at Rundell and Bridge this evening?"

Jane stared at him, fully grasping his point. Who would believe her? Which authorities would she even inform? She was a nobody, whereas they were notable people in society. She had contacts within society, but whose word would be given credence?

"No, I think you've just got to let it happen. What do you reckon they're planning to steal?" Robin said as Jane considered the situation.

"It must be something intended for the crown." She recalled the illustration she'd seen in the newspaper depicting the design of the new state crown for the coronation. "It must be one of the key gemstones - St Edward's Sapphire, the Stuart Sapphire, or the Black Prince's Ruby. Those have always been the centrepieces."

"The best time to notify the authorities would be after it's been stolen and is in their possession. They can't deny anything then."

"That seems logical," Jane concurred.

Robin was still apprehensive. She could sense it in his demeanour; something was troubling him.

"What's wrong?" she demanded.

"I don't want you involved in any of this. What if their story somehow gets twisted?"

"Twisted? What do you mean?"

"You comprehend the implications. These people are well-known and highly regarded in the community. You're an unknown. What if Mr May and Kate Larkin manage to pin this whole scheme on you?"

"How could that even be possible, Robin? I don't even know John Bridge."

Robin shrugged his shoulders. "I know it sounds preposterous. But what if Kate brings whatever she steals back to Mr May? Then the authorities raid your Goldsmiths based on what you have told them, but they say they know nothing, and it must be you that stole it. I wouldn't put anything past Kate Larkin."

Jane gave him a look that suggested Robin was being fanciful.

Robin gave a shrug of his wide shoulders. "I just have an uneasy feeling about this."

"So, what am I supposed to do? Just let the situation unfold? Ignore the fact that they're stealing something that will impact the Queen's Coronation?" Jane visualised the young Queen journeying in her carriage along the gravel road in Hyde Park. She felt an inexplicable kinship with the woman, perhaps because they were of a similar age. She yearned for the Queen's Coronation to proceed without a hitch.

"Possibly, yes," Robin replied with a hint of resignation in his voice. "I'd much rather that than anything happening to you."

"Nothing will happen to me, Robin," Jane reassured him, reaching out for his hand and giving it a comforting squeeze.

"Just promise me you'll wait until this whole matter plays out. Only if you see them passing a precious gem across the dining room table, then go to the authorities. Agreed?"

Jane let out a quiet sigh, realising that Robin truly had her best interests at heart. "I promise."

They remained silent for a few moments. "I always have my contingency plan, if necessary," Jane said. "You still have the letter?"

"In my desk drawer, ever since the day you gave it to me," Robin confirmed.

"We might need to use it."

CHAPTER 24

*A*s the rain pounded relentlessly down, Robin tried to push himself further against the wall for some semblance of protection.

His efforts were in vain; he was drenched to the bone.

He had now been standing here for over three hours. He arrived half an hour before sunset, in an attempt to find the best vantage point.

Rundell and Bridge appeared to be like any other goldsmiths in this part of London. A proudly emblazoned shopfront bore the firm's name. The only difference other than the name was the royal crest nailed above it. Behind the shop front lay the foundry and all the inner workings of a goldsmith that happened behind the scenes.

Activity seemed minimal. Robin had seen what

appeared to be a housekeeper or maid leave and that was it. He remembered what Jane had told him. Kate Larkin had chosen this evening for her robbery because the place would be quiet.

There was no sign of the security he'd been warned about. Perhaps it wasn't there at all, just a ruse and rumour to put off anyone who had even considered trying to rob the place.

Shortly after sunset, a carriage pulled up in front of the goldsmiths. Two figures alighted. There was a finely dressed young man he'd never seen before, whom he assumed to be John Bridge himself, and the second was Kate Larkin. She was clad in a tight-fitting red dress with a set of furs casually draped over her shoulders. Robin couldn't deny she had blossomed into a striking woman. It was no surprise that her company was coveted by some of the finest names in society. Robin had heard rumours that bankers, merchants, lords and even an Earl or two had been seen in her company.

He watched the couple laugh as they entered the building. The carriage moved off and silence reigned once more.

The rain started about an hour later. Robin regretted his decision to observe what might happen. He had come in the hope that he might extricate Jane from this entire charade. He hoped to never have to present the letter to the countess. He hoped that Jane would never have to report that she saw gems passed across the dining room table at Russell May Goldsmiths.

If he saw Kate Larkin emerge in the darkness, he might be able to apprehend her himself or call for a magistrate or a watchman to assist him.

Truth be told, he hadn't fully thought it through. But now that he was here, he would wait.

Inside, Kate Larkin, or Violet Rose as she was known to John Bridge, was nervous.

She'd had a number of encounters with the impetuous young man but had yet to sleep with him. She knew how to keep the men wanting more.

He was a braggart and a drinker. The combination made him a huge liability. If the authorities at Goldsmiths Hall had dug a little deeper, they likely would not have recommended him for the commission for the crown. The royal warrant would have been revoked and this entire scenario would not be unfolding.

Two encounters prior to this evening, Bridge had been drunk. Whiskey was his favourite, and he had managed to consume almost an entire bottle at the Gentlemen's Club while entertaining Violet Rose. He loved the envious stares of the other men as she flirted with him outrageously.

He persuaded her to return home with him. In a foolish attempt to impress her, he had shown her the jewels that were to be inserted into the crown which were stored securely in the firm's large safe.

He revealed one key from a chain around his neck and unlocked the first lock. He then groped around under the desk in his office and pulled out another key. After turning the second lock and opening the safe, he presented the gems to Violet.

She feigned awe and kissed him passionately as she held the sapphire of Saint Edward in her palm. He managed to have the foresight to lock the safe before they retired upstairs. Violet suggested another drink and filled a glass for him. He raised it and took a slip while stroking her thigh and at that point, John Bridge passed out.

Tonight, Bridge had not drunk nearly as much. His hungry eyes hadn't moved from her body all night. She knew that for her plan to succeed, she would likely have to give him what he craved.

After they returned from their evening out, they sat and they drank. She too opted for whiskey. It would give her courage for what was to come. But whereas she sipped hers with water, John Bridge drank his neat. He drank, and she allowed his hands to explore her.

"I should leave, I have a busy morning ahead," Violet Rose said softly, gently pushing him away. "Rehearsals."

"No," Bridge pleaded. "Stay. I need you."

"I have to be on stage by eight in the morning. The theatre manager will sack me if I'm not there."

"You? Never," Bridge protested. "He wouldn't be such a fool. You are the talk of the town at the moment."

"Am I?" she cooed, stroking his leg.

"Stay," he pressed. "Leave in the morning." He leant forward and kissed her. She allowed herself to be engulfed in his embrace.

After a minute or so, she broke away. "I'll stay. But I must be up with the dawn."

He smiled and his breathing quickened in anticipation.

She topped up his glass one more time, kissed him, and then led him to bed. Just half an hour later, he was snoring like a baby.

She waited for ten minutes and then reached over and gently shook him by the shoulder. He didn't stir.

Violet knew it was time.

She dressed quickly and then gently slipped the key from around his neck, still concealed under his nightshirt. She walked silently down the stairs and into John Bridge's office. The floorboard creaked loudly for one horrifying moment, and she stood still in the darkness.

Nothing stirred. All she could hear was her heart pounding in her chest.

Finally, she moved on. She groped underneath the

desk for the second key. For one heart-stopping moment, she couldn't find it. But then, there it was. The cool metal touching her fingers. She grasped it gratefully and pulled it free. She moved over towards the safe and carefully unlocked both sides like he had shown her previously. The mechanism made a satisfying click as she turned each key. She pulled the door open and felt around on the top shelf where Bridge kept the precious gems.

She found what she came for almost immediately.

The Black Prince's Ruby.

It was huge and irregular in shape. It couldn't be anything else. She swiftly removed it and slipped it into the small bag she was carrying.

She wasted little time.

Her movements were swift and precise. She locked the safe and slid the key back under the desk where she had found it. She pulled out the key and hurried upstairs to deftly place it back around the neck of the sleeping John Bridge.

It was as if the safe had never been opened and the sleeping man hadn't stirred. When he awoke, she prayed he would assume that she had simply left to attend her early morning rehearsal.

There would be others at whom to point a finger.

She took one last glance at John Bridge and then swiftly turned and fled back down the stairs. Slipping her black cloak over her dress, she opted against exiting through the front door. Instead, she navigated the labyrinth of passages leading to the foundry at the rear.

The heat inside the foundry was intense since the fires were never fully extinguished. She paused and with a long iron rod, knocked some of the coals out of one of the fires and onto the floor. She repeated the process after a moment's consideration. Satisfied, she continued on, eventually finding the door she sought and disappearing into the dark London streets.

Back at Russell May Goldsmiths, Jane found sleep elusive. Mr May hadn't been home all evening. He'd announced he was heading to one of his clubs, an alibi in Jane's estimation. If he was out drinking with the great men all night, they would vouch for him if questions were asked.

She tossed and turned. Her ears aware of any possible noise. Would Kate Larkin return here?

It was unbearable, Jane had to know what was happening.

She rose from her bed and dressed. Glancing quickly out of the window, she saw the rain pounding down. She paused, questioning her actions. What was she hoping to see? What could she possibly achieve out there, watching a building?

But her curiosity got the better of her.

She descended the stairs and donned her dark coat before venturing out into the wet night.

It didn't take her long to reach Rundell and Bridge Goldsmiths.

As she neared the building, her pace slowed. After a moment's consideration, she turned into an alley-way. If she'd thought it through, she might have realised her recklessness. Venturing into darkened alleyway was not advisable for a young woman in London, especially at night.

Yet, she emerged at the other end unscathed. She quickly circled to the rear of the building, which was bathed in darkness. The rain found its way down the back of her neck, making her shiver. She felt like a fool. Why had she come?

Then she suddenly stopped and pressed herself against the wall. A figure emerged from the building. Jane couldn't make out who it was, dressed as it was in black, but for some reason, she suspected it was a woman.

Could it be Kate Larkin?

The figure glanced around. Whoever it was did not see Jane and the figure walked quickly on. Jane allowed a few seconds and then followed. The moon wasn't full and there were plenty of clouds in the sky, but Jane took care to walk in the darker shadows close to the buildings.

The figure was poised to re-emerge onto the main

street, pausing as though assessing the situation. Once more, Jane pressed herself as deeply into the building's walls as she could, even holding her breath, though it was impossible that she might be heard.

Then she noticed the figure tilt its head in what seemed like surprise before moving forward again. Over the road, another form came into sight, a head taller than the first, now clearly discernible as the moon commenced its escape from behind the sombre cloud.

It was a man, she was certain of it. Could it possibly be Russell May? Had he left his gentleman's club?

Jane edged forward, seeking a more advantageous viewpoint. The two mysterious figures were embroiled in what seemed like a meaningful exchange.

She moved closer, taking care not to expose her position.

As the moon finally shrugged off its clouded shroud, Jane gasped, barely managing to hold back a shout or reveal herself.

The smaller figure, emerging from the gloom of Rundell and Bridge Goldsmiths, was unmistakably Kate Larkin. But the revelation of the second figure's identity sent tremors of shock through her.

It was Robin. Her beloved Robin.

CHAPTER 25

*I*n the now gentle rain, Jane found herself in a state of disbelieving wonder. Her heart hammered violently against her ribs, seemingly so loudly that she was sure it would reveal her presence.

What was Robin doing there? He was unmistakable, despite the darkness. Her mind went back to that long gaze Robin gave Kate as she walked away from them after their encounter outside her home.

Kate seemed to move closer still to Robin. Was it a trick of her mind, an illusion spun by the tendrils of night's shadow? Or had Kate Larkin just slipped him something that he had put into his pocket?

A surge of audacious bravery tempted her to march across the cobblestones, and unmask Robin's deceit right then and there, but she knew that would be unwise. Then her emotions changed and all she wanted was to run home to her bed and cry. But she found her legs unable to do either. Instead, she watched, transfixed, fearful about what would transpire next.

The moon concealed itself behind a cloud, casting the scene into deeper darkness. The rain fell heavier once again. Kate Larkin turned and walked quickly away from Rundell and Bridge Goldsmiths. Robin melted back into the shadows where he'd been standing.

There was just the sound of the rain, gently hammering on the roof tiles and cobblestones. Time seemed to hold its breath as a general stillness took hold.

Just as Jane mustered the courage to step forward, to interrogate Robin about his presence and involvement in this strange midnight charade, chaos was unleashed.

Figures materialised from the gloom. They were dressed in garbs of darkness, their faces obscured. With an uncanny unity, they descended upon the Goldsmiths. Behind her, she heard the scuffle of hurried footsteps. At least ten individuals, likely more, poured in through the rear entrance. From the front, another wave of intruders charged. Among them, she discerned the smaller silhouettes of children. Was this a street gang? They made no secret of their intrusion, smashing a large window with a hammer and stepping through.

From within the building, muffled shouts echoed out, intermingling with the horrendous sound of crashing and smashing. In less than a minute, the marauders exited, disappearing into the darkness of London as swiftly as they'd emerged. The assault was brief, but it left behind a trail of destruction and terror.

Almost immediately, a man emerged from the shadows, holding a cane. Was this one of the men that was supposed to protect the precious jewels and the crown within the Goldsmiths? Another three also emerged and joined the other. All were armed to varying degrees. But they didn't look like young men. One certainly had a limp, another appeared bent over as though he were plagued by his back. Perhaps they were former army men?

They'd done nothing. They had remained passive spectators to the whole thing.

Although what could they have done, Jane pondered. There were just a handful of men and twenty or possibly even thirty of the thieves who had ransacked the place. If they had tried to intervene, they would have been dead. She wondered what had become of those inside the goldsmiths. Was John Bridge himself inside?

Then she smelt something. It was both familiar

and not. And then she saw it. Flames started to dance and devour the rear of the building. Panic-stricken cries of 'fire' rent the stillness, rousing slumbering neighbours. Men, half-dressed, pulling on shoes came rushing with buckets, attempting to quell the burgeoning inferno.

The guards, or whoever they were, vanished into the Goldsmiths.

Jane was torn between watching the flames rise higher and the darkness where she was certain Robin lurked.

Suddenly, he emerged. He seemed uncertain of what to do. Taking a brief glance around him, he darted off in the direction that Kate Larkin had disappeared. But his flight was abruptly cut short. Two more men materialised from the shadows, closing in on Robin.

"Halt, you're under arrest, sir," the commanding voice of one of the men resonated through the night, as clear as the voice of the deacon delivering his sermon in Saint Paul's on a Sunday morning. Robin tried to run, but they were upon him like a tempest, swiftly bringing him to the ground.

"Get off!" Robin shouted, his voice muffled as his face was forced into the cobblestones.

"No chance, me matey," one of the two replied.

Jane could clearly see now that they were Peelers - the police force that had recently been set up to keep Londoners safe. They wore dark blue uniforms and top hats.

Robin kicked his legs as he tried to resist. One of the two Peelers brought out his heavy wooden truncheon and brought it crashing down on the back of Robin's legs.

He screamed and his legs went limp.

"Stay still, me matey, it will be the best way," the man said. "Save you from getting hurt or anything."

Part of Jane wanted to rush in to help, another part was brimming with anger at what she had seen.

The Peeler started patting Robin down. Any moment, Jane believed that they would draw something out that would incriminate him.

But they found nothing.

"Right, come with us then, me matey," the first Peeler said, dragging Robin to his feet. With that, they set off at a pace, one of the two Peelers on either side, hauling him along between them.

Jane glanced back towards the fire. There were more men there now than ever, and the fire seemed to be somewhat under control.

She heard whistles blow throughout the streets. As she watched, more Peelers appeared, and more men emerged from their beds, assisting with the control of the fire. Before long, it would be extinguished.

Jane followed Robin and the two Peelers at a

distance. They didn't go far. It was just a matter of a few hundred yards before he was dragged into a small police station.

She stood outside, watching for almost an hour. Her mind raced as she contemplated what to do. Finally, she decided the only thing she could do was to return home. Maybe Kate Larkin had returned there, and she could find out what had happened.

Was Robin truly part of this treachery? Her eyes told her so, but her heart told her it could not be.

Somehow, she managed to find her way home. She had no recollection of the journey. She was soaked to the skin. She dragged herself up the stairs to the attic, undressed and dried herself. She pulled a nightshirt over herself and climbed under the covers.

For a few moments, she sat wide-eyed, staring at the ceiling, trying to process what had occurred.

And then the tears came, and she thought they would never stop.

CHAPTER 26

*W*hen Jane finally awoke, it was later than usual. The clock on the bedside table indicated it was a little after eight in the morning. The rain had cleared, the clouds had blown away, and it was a glorious late spring morning. The sunlight flooded in through her small window, bathing everything in a warm glow.

For a few fleeting moments, Jane thought that the events of the previous night were nothing more than a nightmare. Then the stark reality hit her.

Robin was in prison, taken by the Peelers.

What was his role in all of this? Had she been lied to all along?

Reluctantly, she hauled herself out of bed. She had to find Kate Larkin and determine the truth.

She stood, stretching her hands above her head.

Suddenly, a noise at the doorway startled her. She turned to see Mr May staring at her. She abruptly realised that she was wearing her thinnest nightshirt and the sun was pouring in through the window, making it virtually transparent.

She saw his lustful stare and felt nauseous. She remembered those final words from the pregnant maid Jennifer all those years ago, *"Take care little one, he will be inviting you into the office before long."*

She took a step backwards instinctively, covering her body with her arms.

"It's only me, Jane," said Russell May softly. "I thought I would bring you up to date with the news. It seems that Rundell and Bridge was raided by a group of street thieves last night. It appears they set fire to the place as well."

Jane quickly grabbed her robe and pulled it tight around her like armour.

"Really?" She responded, hoping that Mr May wouldn't notice the pile of damp clothes dumped in the corner of the bedroom. "What happened to the crown?"

"Well, apparently the crown wasn't at Rundell and Bridge last night. It had been removed to the palace for a final fitting with the Queen," he said with a slight twang of disappointment in his voice. "At least that is what is being said down at Goldsmiths Hall."

"Nothing was taken?"

"There are rumours," Russell May said, barely containing the sly grin on his face.

"What rumours? What's been taken?"

"They are saying that one or more of the principal stones in the crown have gone missing. They were the final pieces to be added, after the Queen was happy with the fit."

Jane thought back to the drawing she'd seen of it in the newspapers. The principal stones must be the Stuart Sapphire, Saint Edward's Sapphire, and the Black Prince's Ruby.

"The piece will be ruined," Jane said thoughtfully.

"Indeed," Russell May agreed in a cheerful voice. "I just thought you'd like to know."

He walked down the stairs, leaving Jane alone.

She felt uncomfortable. Despite all the years she'd lived here, and all the terrible things that Russell May had done, she had never before felt his gaze like that. It made her feel dirty as though he had already violated her. She shivered.

She knew she had to leave, and quickly.

But first, she had to get to the bottom of Robin's role in all of this.

She thought back to the previous night. Kate Larkin was sneaking out of the back of Rundell and Bridge. It was obvious from their earlier conversations that she had planned to steal something herself.

Jane was fairly certain that it was Kate Larkin

who had taken at least one of these principal stones. But which one?

Jane took her time getting ready. She needed the distraction. The troubling question hovered like a storm cloud over her mind. Should she go to the police station to which Robin had been taken? There, perhaps, she could glean some insight into what was happening. It was evident that when the police searched Robin, they had found no incriminating evidence. It could simply have been a trick of her overactive mind in the darkness, and maybe Kate Larkin had not passed anything to him.

But the more she thought, the more the nagging inconsistencies cropped up. Why would Kate approach Robin, having just stolen one of the precious gems that were about to be used in the crown for the new young queen? She should rather have been making a swift exit. Why interact with him at all? The mystery compounded further when she pondered why Robin was present there in the first instance.

These questions swirled in her head as she contemplated the possible scenarios, but each seemed more baffling than the last.

By the time she finished dressing, she had made up her mind. She had to find Kate Larkin. If that meant going to the theatre on Drury Lane, then so be it.

As she descended the stairs, Russell May was preparing to leave. He cloaked himself in his coat, adjusted his top hat, and turned to her. "I'm going back to Goldsmiths Hall," he declared, glancing at Jane with an inscrutable gaze.

"You were there rather early this morning, sir," Jane quipped, a deliberate hint of naivety cloaked her words. "How did you know something had happened?"

Jane knew all too well how he knew. It was all part of his plan. But she couldn't resist the tantalising prospect of making him squirm.

However, he remained unmoved, offering no tell-tale signs of discomfort at her pointed question. "I'm surprised you didn't hear the commotion last night. The place was raided. There were policemen and people everywhere. I ventured out to see what the fuss was about. It seemed natural that everybody in the business would converge on Goldsmiths Hall afterwards."

"I heard nothing up there in the attic," Jane replied. She realised how fortunate she'd been. She'd managed to get home and to bed before Russell had left to see the outcome of his plan. "Well, I hope you find the answers that you seek."

He nodded in acknowledgement and exited.

As Jane reached out for her coat, her stomach rumbled with an insistent hunger. The nocturnal exploits had whittled away at her energy. She navigated her way to the kitchen, where Mrs Johnson quickly rustled up some toast which she savoured with generous slathers of butter and damson jam.

"What would you do if you didn't work here, Mrs Johnson?" Jane asked.

Mrs Johnson shrugged her robust shoulders. "Oh, I'm sure I'd find work somewhere. It's always been my dream to serve in one of the grand mansions. To cater for the aristocrats. I'd love to create meals for some of the finest in society."

Mrs Johnson studied Jane for a moment. "Why do you ask?"

Jane's gaze remained steady. "Just with news of the raid at Rundell and Bridge. Who knows the repercussions? I'm certain their business will suffer, what if such misfortune befell us? We might all find ourselves turned out onto the streets."

"What will be, will be," Mrs Johnson said, noncommittally.

With renewed determination, Jane decided on her course of action. She'd venture past Rundell and Bridge, past the police station where they held Robin, and if she found nothing of interest at either of those two locations, she'd go to the Theatre Royal on Drury Lane to confront Kate Larkin.

However, before she could put on her coat, Grimes opened the door and in walked Kate Larkin.

"Have you come for the rest of your money?" Jane challenged. "He's gone to Goldsmiths Hall."

"I know, Grimes told me. I shall wait," Kate declared with a prideful arrogance that grated on Jane's nerves. "But what do you mean, the rest of my money?"

Jane took a threatening step forward and saw a fear flicker in Kate Larkin's eyes. No doubt she held a bitter memory of their past confrontation in the workhouse.

"I overheard you and Russell in hushed whispers," Jane retorted. "Three thousand pounds was the agreed price for the foul deed you carried out last night."

"I don't know what you're blathering about, little Jane," Kate Larkin shot back with a forced chuckle, but her eyes belied the fear etched onto her face.

"Of course, you don't," Jane replied, her words dripping with sarcasm. She advanced another step, causing Kate to recoil. "I was there."

"Where?"

"At the rear of Rundell and Bridge. I watched you slink away. I followed you. And then I saw you meet Robin Buckley. What exchange took place? What did you give him?" Now, it was Jane's voice that faltered, the mere mention of Robin's name enough to send a jolt through her heart.

The change didn't escape Kate Larkin, who slowly

grinned, her teeth gleaming ominously. "What if I did give him something? The word of an apprentice against me?" Kate took a bold step forward, their faces so close Jane could feel her warm breath. She lowered her voice to a sinister whisper. "Robin has been a part of it all. The final piece in the intricate jigsaw I've been assembling. You thought I didn't recognise him the other day. But of course I remember him from our workhouse days. He was your little ally then, your only one, from what I recall. But that isn't where I recognised him from. He knew me and I knew him. We just played the perfect theatre."

Confusion washed over Jane. "What do you mean?" she asked, her voice trembling.

"There was no need for him to come running to me at the Theatre Royal. He knows where to find me. He has done for years. You see, little Jane, me and your man have always been lovers."

CHAPTER 27

uckingham Palace, London
"Good morning, Prime Minister," the Queen greeted, her voice carrying through the grandeur of the room as Lord Melbourne responded with a respectful bow.

The solemn countenance on the prime minister's face told her something was wrong. It was a stark contrast to the usual smile that had greeted her since her accession to the throne.

"Your Majesty," Melbourne commenced, a strain evident in his usually steadfast voice. "I'm afraid I bear distressing news."

Attempting to diffuse the tension that had suddenly gripped the room, the Queen mustered a feeble smile. "What might it be? Surely nothing insurmountable? Will you take tea, sir?"

She delicately gestured towards a plush chair, its upholstery exuding an air of regal grandeur. She took her own seat first, as was the custom. Melbourne then took his. Protocol dictated that if the Queen stood, so did everybody else in the room.

"A cup of tea would be most welcome, Ma'am," Melbourne responded, his fingers drumming an uneasy rhythm on the rich mahogany of the chair's armrest.

The Queen rang a small silver bell and a footman appeared with a low bow.

"Tea, please," she said. The footman responded with a further bow and retreated from the room, not once turning his back on the Queen.

Summoning her courage, the Queen urged Melbourne, "Please, enlighten me on the nature of this unfortunate predicament."

Swallowing hard, the Prime Minister relayed the disturbing events of the previous night at the Royal Goldsmiths, Rundell and Bridge. "Regrettably, a number of minor items were pilfered, Ma'am. But I'm afraid to say so was the Black Prince's Ruby."

Victoria gasped audibly, her azure eyes darting involuntarily towards the far corner of the room where her grand new crown stood upon a velvet cushion. The slot that should have held the stunning, blood-red centrepiece was horrifyingly vacant.

"Just the Black Prince's Ruby?" she asked, her

voice a mere whisper. Her eyes flicked between the other empty slots for the gems.

"Indeed, Ma'am," Melbourne confirmed. "It seems oddly specific, given the other gems remain securely within the safe."

Victoria pressed for more information. "What have we discovered so far? Who were the thieves?"

"Certain perplexing details have emerged, Your Majesty. The safe required two keys for access. One was forcibly taken from Mr Bridge, at the threat of a blade to his throat. The second key was ingeniously concealed beneath his desk. Despite no evidence of its disturbance, we believe it may have been used and replaced. Bridge's key was found still in the lock. It is the only plausible explanation at present."

"Nothing else?"

"We have a suspect in custody, Ma'am. An employee of the Earl of Stanhope. He was loitering outside the premises for several hours prior to the burglary. The property, as you know, is under constant surveillance, but there were likely twenty to thirty infiltrators, they could do nothing. The Home Secretary is personally handling the situation. I received a report before departing Downing Street; the suspect is denying any knowledge and surprisingly, implicates an actress."

"An actress? Who might she be?" Victoria asked,

fully aware of the association her dead uncle had with actresses.

"A certain Miss Violet Rose, Ma'am. She's recently gained considerable acclaim at the Theatre Royal."

"And how does this actress connect with the crime?"

With visible discomfort, Melbourne ventured into the delicate matter. "The accused, one Mr Buckley, insists that Miss Rose is romantically entangled with another goldsmith, a Mr Russell May. If you recall, Ma'am, it was May whose design was rejected for the crown's commission. You seemed to prefer his design, but the advice from Goldsmith's Hall favoured Rundell and Bridge."

The Queen remembered the design well. Of the two drawings she reviewed, she had favoured that one. Yet, she had to concede that the completed crown, crafted by Rundell and Bridge, was a remarkable work of art. Yet, without the Black Prince's Ruby in its rightful place, it would need changes. And quickly.

"The allegation suggests a form of revenge against Rundell and Bridge," Melbourne explained.

"And what of the actress? Has she been located?"

"The Home Secretary is pursuing the matter, Ma'am. Whilst we cannot dismiss Mr Buckley's allegations outright, they seem rather calculated to divert our attention away from the true culprits."

"What could possibly motivate the thieves to steal the gem? Surely, they understand it's not sellable, given its renown."

"As I said, Ma'am, the investigation is still in the early stages. It is my view that they likely intend to ransom the gem."

"Why wasn't the gem better safeguarded at the goldsmith's?" The Queen's voice carried an edge of frustration. "Should it fail to be recovered, what becomes of the crown?" Her gaze lingered on the vacant spot in the crown. "And what of my coronation?"

Lord Melbourne paused, contemplating the Queen's question. "Ma'am, I truly do not know. I am prepared to tender my resignation if you deem it necessary."

The Queen looked at him in stunned silence. "Such action is unwarranted, Lord Melbourne. I have no desire for your resignation. This incident is not of your making, and I refuse to disrupt the stability of my government over this matter." She lowered her voice. "I value your advice, Sir. I should not wish you to leave your post."

Lord Melbourne nodded, appreciative of the Queen's vote of confidence. "There is still ample time, Ma'am. I have full faith in the Home Secretary. He will get to the bottom of this matter, and the gem will be recovered."

"Do we intend to disclose this to the public?"

"No, Ma'am. We will only disclose to the press that a small number of items were taken and that the crown was already here at the palace. As far as the newspapers are concerned, they have no inkling of the significant loss. and we aim to keep it that way."

A knock came on the door. "Enter," the Queen said formally. A butler entered with a tray bearing a China teapot and associated accompaniments.

Victoria stood up and walked over to where the butler had laid out the tea on the table. Melbourne immediately followed suit. "Very well, we need to keep up appearances. We shall proceed with our usual ride through the park, Lord Melbourne. After tea, of course."

"Certainly, Ma'am," Melbourne agreed, relief evident in his voice as he acknowledged the Queen's strength in the face of such a crisis. There was not yet an event that had occurred to which the Queen had not risen to the occasion.

CHAPTER 28

*J*ane sat in tears by the banks of the Thames at Westminster Bridge.

She was consumed by confusion. Despite her most valiant attempts in the past hour, she couldn't make any sense of it all. To her, there was no logical explanation.

It had taken all her restraint not to punch Kate Larkin in the nose, just like she had done in the workhouse all those years ago. She merely glared into the face of her rival before pushing past her onto the bustling London streets. She could still hear Kate Larkin's incessant cackle echoing behind her.

Could it be true? Had she and Robin really been lovers?

Usually, Jane would have given such a comment little weight. After all, Kate Larkin had a notorious history of being vindictive, and to Jane, she would be more malicious than to others.

However, two things troubled her. First, why had Robin been outside Rundell and Bridge last night? Second was the lingering look Robin had cast at Kate as she walked away after their encounter.

She knew she needed to confront Robin and hear his side of the story. But at present, that would be impossible. He was in prison. If they truly believed he was involved in part in the theft of the Black Prince's Ruby, he could hang. The thought brought a shudder down her spine. She had to get to the bottom of the matter, she couldn't see him die.

Suddenly, a newspaper seller was shouting while crossing Westminster Bridge. Jane sprang up and bought a copy.

As expected, the incident at the Goldsmiths was the top story. Interestingly though, the article suggested that the crown had been safely tucked away at Buckingham Palace the previous night. This seemed to align with what Russell May had told her that morning. It said a man was being held in custody. Nothing more. Robin wasn't named. It didn't say he was being charged with an offence.

There was no mention of the theft of the Black Prince's Ruby.

She began to wonder if this was a deliberate omission, designed not to raise public concern about the upcoming coronation. Perhaps they were attempting to recover the jewel first?

She cast her mind back to her strange conversation with Russell May that morning. In all the years she had lived in his house, he had never ascended the stairs to her bedroom while she was in it. Not once. So why start now?

Then she remembered something. When she awoke that morning, she had heard a rustling noise, a commotion outside her bedroom. Up until this point, she had dismissed it, attributing it to her dreams. In fact, she had forgotten it as soon as she had arisen. Could it have been Russell May rummaging through his storage boxes? Over the years, she had rarely seen new additions placed in the attic boxes.

She remembered one of the first conversations she'd had with her mother: "Don't worry about the boxes, dear. That's where my husband stores various items," she had reassured Jane.

It seemed peculiar that he would be sifting through those boxes on this very morning. Could it be that Kate Larkin had met Russell May and handed over what she had stolen, and he had stashed it away up there? If so, that was a perilous move. Would he really keep such incriminating evidence on his own property? But then again, why not? He believed the perfect crime had been committed. Why would people be searching at

Russell May Goldsmith's for the Black Prince's Ruby?

As Jane stared down into the waters of the Thames from the centre of Westminster Bridge, she realised she was standing on that very spot where, all those years ago, she had tossed all of Mr May's fake diamonds into the river. In disposing of the stones, she allowed his secrets to sink to the river's bottom, never to be found again.

Of course, that wasn't strictly true.

Something strange had happened that evening, just before she was about to walk out onto Westminster Bridge. A thought nagged at her. She found herself reaching into the velvet bag and pulling out four of the imitation diamonds. They sparkled in the gas lights, looking beautiful even if they were fake. Even today, she couldn't quite explain why she did it. But something told her that one day she might need leverage against Russell May. She held onto the four fake diamonds, placing them in her left hand as she hurled the velvet bag containing the rest of the incriminating stones into the river below.

She had kept those four counterfeit diamonds hidden over the years. There was a loose floorboard in her bedroom where she kept certain precious items. That was where she'd slipped the stones. And that was where she retrieved them from just a few weeks ago when she decided to place them into the brooch that she was creating for Countess Stanhope's daughter, Lady Wilhelmina.

That was what was in the letter that Jane had carefully written, and Robin had placed in his desk drawer. It was a letter from Jane to the Countess, expressing her concern about a number of the gemstones which Russell May had instructed her to place in the piece she had created. Jane suggested they should be taken to Rundell and Bridge or some other reputable goldsmith to have them examine the gemstones.

In the letter, Jane had apologised profusely, stating that as an apprentice she had little say in the actual gemstones that were used in the pieces. Her fears were that she had placed fakes in the piece at her master's insistence. The matter had been nagging at her mind, resulting in her correspondence.

At a time to be agreed between them, Robin was to present the letter to the countess, claiming it had been delivered anonymously. He was to feign ignorance of its contents.

Of course, with Robin now under arrest, and either in the police station or Newgate Prison, he had no possible way to execute the plan.

She stared into the deep black waters of the Thames, formulating her next steps.

Russell May had to be incriminated, one way or the other. Her mother needed vengeance for all those years of betrayal. She needed vengeance for the way he had used her to con countless clients and for that horrible night on which he had beaten her.

She would return to Russell May Goldsmiths and search through the boxes in the attic.

If she was unable to find what she was seeking, she would approach Countess Stanhope and personally tell her what she'd written in the letter.

One way or the other, she knew Russell May had to be arrested. If she found the stolen gem, all well and good. If not, at least he would be behind bars, charged with a crime. A crime of which Jane could prove his guilt. If he was apprehended for that, then he might indeed confess to being behind the theft of the Black Prince's Ruby. It could be the only way to secure Robin's release.

In her heart, she didn't believe what Kate Larkin had said. Could she and Robin have been lovers for years? It simply wasn't conceivable. Her heart affirmed this to her.

Larkin, of course, was a skilled actress; she should always remember that. When she asked Robin the question outright and he answered her, she would be certain. He would not be able to hide behind lies. She would know in his eyes.

As it stood, she chose to believe in his innocence. It was the only way she could possibly react. It could be up to her to save his life.

She took a deep breath, steadied her resolve, cast a final glance at the Thames, and headed back to Russell May Goldsmiths.

Just as she was about to turn onto Cockspur Road, she paused. She contemplated the situation once more. Was she being stupid and naive here? Was she walking into a trap? Kate Larkin was now aware that she knew something. What would happen if she conveyed this to Mr May? He would not want her telling her thoughts to all and sundry.

But she knew she had to search through those boxes.

She decided not to enter the property through the front entrance. Just in case. She would slip in through the back, using the passages she'd seen Jennifer utilise as a means to visit men in the city all those years before.

Then, she would sneak up the stairs and swiftly rummage through the boxes.

She walked briskly, her heart pounding. She slipped past the gate, past the foundry where she heard the voices of the twins curiously grunting at each other. She entered via the pantry, navigated her way through the kitchen, and then suddenly felt a hand on her shoulder. She nearly screamed in shock, but another hand pressed over her mouth. She was spun around, and there she met the gaze of Mrs Johnson.

"Hush," the cook whispered. "The Master returned and he is furious. He wants to know when you get back. Grimes is to detain you."

Jane's breathing slowed a little, recognising who it was. "Will you tell him I'm here?"

"No, Miss Jane, I won't. But I've never seen the man so angry. My suggestion is that you pack your bags and leave. Slip out the back way again. No one will know you've been here."

"Where is he? Is he here now?" Jane asked, her voice laced with panic.

"No, he left for an important meeting at Goldsmiths Hall, I believe. Grimes is on the front door."

"What about her? Violet Rose?"

"No, she isn't here either. She came and she left," Mrs Johnson said. "Please, Jane, pack your things and leave. Quickly. I dread to think what might happen to you if you don't."

"Thank you, Mrs Johnson. For everything." Jane felt like she might cry at this moment. But she felt the firm hand of the cook gently guiding her towards the stairs.

"Go, be quick."

With that, Jane silently darted up the stairs and then took the next flight to the attic.

Her heart sank with disappointment as she stood in the room next to her bedroom. She'd been thwarted. Four boxes had been pulled from their neat stacks onto the floor. It was clear that someone had come to hastily grab whatever they wanted.

Her suspicions, she was sure, had been correct. Mr May had hidden the Black Prince's Ruby in one of these boxes earlier that morning. He was forced to speak to her, to pretend that he had come to tell her what had happened, otherwise she would have seen him and wondered what he was doing. Now he knew that Jane was fully aware of his involvement in the scheme, he had been forced to move it again, in case she told the authorities.

She quickly rummaged through the boxes that had been pulled to the floor. Unsurprisingly, she found nothing of interest.

She kicked the floor in frustration, cursing her foolishness. If only she had thought first thing in the morning, she could've had the Black Prince's Ruby in her possession and handed it over to the relevant authorities. As it stood, Russell May had been granted another opportunity to hide it.

She stood silently for a few moments, assessing the situation, then dashed into her bedroom. As Mrs Johnson had recommended, she needed to escape.

She quickly packed her personal belongings into a carpet bag. It didn't take long. Apart from her clothes, she had few personal effects. She did, however, rush to the corner of the room where she pried open the floorboards and retrieved a small bag of coins that she'd saved over the years, along with two sheets of parchment neatly folded in half. She also picked up the four real diamonds that she had not placed in the piece for Lady Wilhelmina. She paused for a moment, thinking about this final step. It was theft, the only time she had stolen from Mr May over the years. But considering everything he had done, it was some recompense. She quickly overcame her guilt and carefully placed them in the bag.

She took one final look around her attic room and knew that she would never return. Whatever transpired from this moment on, her future lay away from Cockspur Street and Russell May Goldsmiths.

"What do you think you are doing?" a voice came from the darkness of the attic room. "Are you going somewhere?"

Jane looked up and saw Kate Larkin emerging from the gloom.

CHAPTER 29

*T*ension filled the small attic space. Jane regarded the expression on Kate Larkin's face, seeing only the spiteful girl who had first struck her on their initial encounter at the Southwark workhouse.

"Surprised to see me?" Kate Larkin asked with a haughty chuckle, a cruel glint lighting her eyes.

Jane clearly remembered the triumphant stare in the master's office when Kate had been selected for the apprenticeship at the Theatre Royal. That same arrogance was etched on Kate's features, even more potently now.

Jane understood the dangerous game they were both playing; she couldn't afford to betray a hint of apprehension. For if she did, Kate would greedily devour that fear. Kate would simply feed off it and grow into an even bigger monster.

The words of Robin in the yard all those years ago came back to her. "You have to stand up to these people at some point."

"Step aside, Kate," Jane commanded, her voice betraying nothing but nonchalance. She tried to act like her presence was nothing.

"I don't think you're going anywhere, little Jane," Kate sneered back, brazenly widening her stance and leaning in, an intimidating gesture.

"Do you really want to do this, Kate? It ended badly for you last time."

Jane's words were met with a brief flash of uncertainty in Kate Larkin's eyes. No doubt, Kate was also dragged back to the memory of the workhouse where Jane had sprung upon her unexpectedly that evening, changing everything between them.

"Don't for a moment imagine that because we are now women and not children, it will prevent me from striking you," Jane warned, an icy edge to her tone. Her voice felt unfamiliar as it laced threats, a departure from her normal parlance. Yet, there was something about Kate's very presence that ignited a flame of rage within her. "Step aside and let me pass. If you have any sense, you'll follow me out the door. You'll take your money, head to the coast, and board the next available ship out of England. Go to France. Because before this day is over, they'll be looking for you, and they won't stop until they find you. When they do, they'll take you to a prison cell and make you confess everything, and then you'll hang."

A look of confusion washed over Kate's face as she attempted to decipher the ominous prediction.

"Russell will say nothing about me. He loves me," Kate insisted.

"He'll say anything to save his own skin, and you know it," Jane retorted, taking a step forward. "And even now, Robin will be implicating you as the orchestrator of last night's theft."

"He loves me as well," Kate spat back defiantly.

"Oh, he doesn't. You haven't been lovers for years. In fact, you have never been lovers and never will. The first time he saw you in years was the other day when we saw you outside. He knows a lot about you, though. Did you know about the stories about Violet Rose that circulate around the servants' quarters in high society? Is there a gentleman's bed you haven't slept in?" Jane taunted, her own vindictiveness surfacing. "How many other men have you slept with as their wives died? You'll be remembered, for sure. But not for your exploits on the stage."

Kate Larkin's body seemed to go limp, and a look of resignation crossed her face.

At that moment, Jane knew that Kate's allegations about Robin had been a lie. She suddenly recalled the apparent surprise in Kate Larkin's body language when she Robin standing outside Rundell and Bridge the night before. She hadn't been expecting him at all. It was a chance encounter. Robin was probably there to see if he could discover something himself.

This realisation emboldened her. Jane moved yet another step closer, and Kate Larkin receded another step.

"I'll offer this counsel to you one final time, Kate. Flee now, with your ill-gotten wealth, if you hope to preserve your life." Jane wondered why she was extending this olive branch. This was Kate Larkin, her lifelong nemesis, the embodiment of her trials and tribulations. She wished to witness her downfall almost as much as she yearned for Russell May to meet his comeuppance. "Heed my advice, Kate. Step aside, let me pass, and then follow me and flee. They will come for you. "

A tense stillness enveloped the pair as they continued to measure one another, a moment seemingly frozen in time. Jane remained vigilant, anticipating Kate might launch herself with the same volatile unpredictability she had exhibited years ago. But she didn't. Defeat was painted clearly across her face, her once formidable posture now slouched, and with a resigned sigh, she stepped aside. "Go."

Without wasting another precious moment, Jane seized the opportunity and bolted down the attic stairs. Deep down, she knew she would never cross paths with Kate Larkin again.

She longed to find Mrs Johnson and offer her thanks. But she knew there wasn't time. If Kate Larkin had appeared suddenly, the house could soon host Mr May or possibly Grimes, lurking in the corridors. She had to escape, and fast.

She retraced her entry path, darting through the kitchen where Mrs Johnson had conveniently made herself scarce to feign ignorance in the face of her master. Through the pantry, past the foundry, and finally through the creaky gate that stood as the final barrier to freedom.

She sprinted as far from Cockspur Street as her weary legs would allow.

Eventually, she slowed to a halt, panting heavily. She had what she needed. She took a few minutes to gather her thoughts and came to the conclusion that her next destination had to be the Countess of Stanhope.

As she walked towards Mahon House, a thought niggled at her. There was another place, forgotten in the flurry of the past weeks, where she must venture before proceeding to see the countess.

A place she hadn't been to in a number of weeks,

distracted by her work on pieces for the coronation and deeply engrossed in the unfolding events.

She went to pay her respects to the woman she still considered her mother. Carol May.

St James' church provided an immediate sense of tranquillity. It was as though serenity itself had found a home here. The Sunday morning service had run its course leaving the church bells long silent, and it would be several more hours before the faithful would gather again for evensong. She was alone.

With careful steps, she moved up the nave, her soles barely making a noise on the tiles. Pausing briefly, she genuflected before the high altar and then made her way to the right, towards the peaceful solitude of the Lady Chapel. Here, she eased herself onto the cold, unforgiving floor next to the stone vault that cradled her mother.

Her hand reached out, fingers gently tracing the engraved inscription. Oh, how she yearned to feel the warm clasp of her mother's hand in this moment. She needed that comforting touch, that surge of courage that was so needed now.

"I'll get your revenge. You deserve it. You were treated so poorly," she murmured softly, though she knew Carol May wouldn't have been the slightest bit interested in revenge. Carol May had been blinded by her love for her husband, prepared to overlook all his infidelities and indiscretions. But that was no way to live a life. Just because her mother had been overly willing to dismiss Russell May's weaknesses, Jane was not. Russell May had now overstepped all boundaries. She felt the sting of his fists raining down on her even now.

She thought of the Queen's coronation hanging by a thread. If the Black Prince's Ruby couldn't be found, how would they alter the design of the crown on such short notice? And what of Robin? She knew that without someone else to blame, he would be the one to suffer. She needed to ensure Russell May was arrested, and then hope that he would confess to where the ruby was hidden.

She took a few moments, the silence around her a comforting blanket, before promising her mother she would be back. She then rose from the stone floor and slowly moved towards the wooden door and the bustling city beyond.

The visit had given her the courage she needed. Admitting to the countess that one of the pieces she had created contained counterfeit diamonds was something she dreaded, but it had to be done.

As she neared the church's entrance, she halted abruptly.

She suddenly realised something. There were fresh flowers in the brass vase adorning her mother's tomb. Since her passing, nobody else had placed flowers there apart from Jane. Now, suddenly, the vase was full?

A chilling thought struck her. She let her carpet bag thud to the ground as she darted back to the vault.

The vase held a selection of early summer roses in pinks, reds, and whites. They were not from her. The last time she had placed flowers was probably two months prior. She studied the shape of the vase. Could it be? The vase was attached to the vault, making theft impossible. Other than that, the vault was of a very simple design. Russell May clearly hadn't wanted to spend much on it. While many other wealthy businessmen would have commissioned elaborate tombs, he had not.

Who would put those flowers there? Only one person came to mind - Russell May. But why would he do that?

As far as she knew, Russell May hadn't so much as visited his wife's grave since it was sealed.

She swiftly snatched the roses, careful not to prick her fingers on the thorns, and laid them gently on the ground. She reached into the vase and her fingers brushed against a velvet bag, typically used for storing gems. She lifted it out, and it felt weighty in her hands.

With hands trembling in anticipation, she gently opened the bag. To her shock and awe, she beheld the magnificent Black Prince's Ruby. An ancient part of the crown jewels, given to the son of Edward III and worn with pride by Henry V on the battlefield at Agincourt. Now, it was in the hands of a little workhouse orphan girl.

In her hands, she held a piece of history and the power to shape her future.

CHAPTER 30

$\mathcal{J}$ane stood outside the imposing edifice of Mahon House, contemplating her next move.

She had decided that the best course of action was to visit the Countess of Stanhope, a woman who knew and trusted her, and present her with the Black Prince's Ruby. The countess, well-entrenched in high society, would surely have the contacts necessary to deliver this priceless jewel back into the hands of its rightful possessor - Queen Victoria herself.

She would recount everything that happened, how Russell May had plotted to steal the ruby simply to make Rundell and Bridge Goldsmiths look like fools, and hopefully cause the removal of the Royal Warrant. She would also reveal to her that counterfeit diamonds had been placed in the brooch for her daughter and give her the pieces of paper that she had taken from under the floorboards in her room. Jane expected subsequent interrogations by the police, but she had the truth on her side.

However, the countess wasn't home.

The footman Jane encountered was unfamiliar with her and ignorant of her past visits. He politely, but firmly declined her request to wait inside without an appointment. For all Jane knew, the countess might be at one of her country estates with her husband, the Earl. She might not return for days or even weeks.

Jane knew she had to act promptly. Robin was languishing in a prison cell, being threatened with who knows what.

She had to get him out.

Then she realised that it was Sunday, and a daring plan started forming in her mind.

But it was crazy and rash and had a high probability of failure.

She made the decision; it had to be done. Jane bolted towards Hyde Park, her steps fast and determined, her heart pounding like a drum.

The frenzied events of the day had disrupted her perception of time. She might have already lost her chance. She said a silent prayer, pleading for her timely arrival.

She heard the cheers in the distance as she drew closer, fuelling her need to run faster.

"God save the Queen," they cried.

Relief flooded her as she realised she had not missed the opportunity. She sprinted towards the end of the gravel path, aware from previous experience that the crowds tended to be thinner there. Jostling her way to the front, the spectacle of the Queen's carriage ride with her prime minister unravelled just a stone's throw away.

"I have it, I have it!" Jane shouted, clutching the velvet bag containing the ruby in her hand. But her breathlessness reduced her proclamation to a mere whisper.

The Four lifeguards at the head of the procession trotted by, their golden helmets glistening in the sunlight, short lances poised at the ready.

"Your Majesty, Your Majesty, I have it!" Jane hollered, jumping up and down in desperation.

For a moment, it all seemed absurd. She was hailing the Queen of England, trying to tell her that she had recovered the stolen gem that should be in her crown.

Then the grey horses pulling the Queen's carriage came into view. As the carriage drew level with her, she cried out once again, "Your Majesty, I have it. The ruby."

For a fleeting moment, Jane thought she saw the

Queen's eyes meet hers. But, to her dismay, there was no response. No wave, no directive to the coachman to halt.

In a final act of desperation, Jane tossed the velvet bag into the carriage. "Your Majesty!" The words tore from her throat as the bag soared through the air and landed in the centre of the carriage

Lord Melbourne, ever vigilant, immediately lunged forward, grabbing the velvet bag. He seemed to shield the Queen with his own body, as though the incoming object were a possible threat. Melbourne reached into the bag and drew out the Black Prince's Ruby. His eyes widened in astonishment, mirroring those of the young queen. Jane watched the hurried exchange of whispered words between the two before Melbourne ordered the coachman to halt.

The cavalry soldiers, trailing the royal carriage, pivoted their steeds, their gaze following Melbourne's pointed finger. "Her, the woman in blue, the young one with the carpet bag. Stop her. Detain her."

Jane had no intention of fleeing. She needed to explain her story. As the soldiers dismounted their horses to detain her, she assured them that she would cooperate entirely.

What happened over the next three or four hours was nothing short of remarkable.

CHAPTER 31

he cavalry soldiers marched her up the gravel path towards Buckingham Palace, carpet bag in hand. She was keenly aware of the stares of the crowd that had gathered to watch. There were some boos and jeers, even though they had no idea of what had transpired.

She was taken to a side gate and placed in the guard room. Two cavalry soldiers stood next to the door. She was made to sit on a bare wooden chair and told to wait.

Around half an hour later, the Captain of the Lifeguards appeared. He was firm and stern. He questioned her. She explained who she was and relayed the entire story of how Russell May was so desperate to obtain the Royal Warrant that he would do anything to discredit the firm of Rundell and Bridge.

So much so that he conspired with an actress called Violet Rose, who had become his lover even as his wife was dying, and agreed to pay her the sum of three thousand pounds to steal the Black Prince's Ruby, thus preventing the completion of the crown in time for the queen's coronation.

She explained how she'd overheard plans for a theft of some sort and watched Violet Rose sneak out the back of Rundell and Bridge just before the fire and the raid by the gang. She offered her own viewpoint that Violet Rose had been the one to organise the chaos in an effort to disguise her own role in the theft. Jane stressed that this was her own theory, and she had no evidence of this. She told the captain that she understood that they had taken a man named Robin Buckley into custody. He, too, had been watching the premises in an attempt to catch Violet Rose in the act. She had no idea if this was the truth behind Robin's role in the matter, but it was her best guess.

She described to the captain how Russell May had been acting strangely that very morning. When she realised what he was doing and went to search for the missing gem, he'd already moved it. She found it on the grave of her mother in a place where no one else would find it, but from which Russell May could easily retrieve it.

She also revealed to the captain who was now

wide-eyed in wonder at the story how, for many years, Russell May had used special stones which she now knew to be counterfeit diamonds in many of the pieces he had supplied to wealthy clients throughout society. She explained that the final piece she was aware of that contained these counterfeit stones was one that had been produced for the daughter of the Countess of Stanhope, Lady Wilhelmina, who Jane knew would play a key role in the forthcoming coronation.

The captain of the Lifeguards seemed somewhat stunned by the conversation. But he listened to every single word that Jane uttered, and after a few clarifications, he left, leaving the guards on the door.

Around twenty minutes later, a message was sent back down to the guard room and Jane was moved into the palace. It was a rather austere-looking room, not something that one might consider as being part of a grand palace in which the Queen lived. It resembled more an office, furnished as it was with a simple table and a scattering of chairs. The two cavalry soldiers still stood guard by the door. This time, she was interviewed by a thin gentleman in a black morning suit, who informed her that he was the Clerk of the Green Cloth. He explained his role in the Royal household, but she couldn't quite comprehend where he fitted in. She ended up recounting her entire story to him as well. The clerk took notes as she spoke. And after she finished her story, he bustled out, taking his papers with him.

The next thing she knew, she was being moved again, up a flight of stairs, this time into a grander-looking office. This was painted a delicate shade of blue, with portraits of people she didn't reconsider hanging on the walls. The furniture was clearly of a finer quality.

An old gentleman with a white beard peered at her over the desk. For some reason, she thought of the master at Southwark workhouse. But this man wasn't overweight. He was neatly proportioned and wore a peculiar set of spectacles that sat on the end of his nose.

Yet again, she repeated the entire conversation she had just had with the Clerk of the Green Cloth.

The Lord Steward fired off a few questions, which she answered with a warm and honest smile. He soon bustled off, and again the guards stood at the door.

Half an hour later, she was moved again.

This time she was brought into the presence of the Lord Chamberlain, the most senior member of the royal household. "I've been told the most astonishing tale," the Lord Chamberlain said.

"All of it is true, sir. If they have relayed it as I said it."

"Why don't you tell me in your own words?"

Once again, Jane was compelled to recite the entire story. She was growing weary. All she wanted was to ensure that Robin was released from prison. She felt, at this stage, that she had done her duty. She wanted to be reunited with the man she loved and to know he was all right.

The Lord Chamberlain left the office. But he returned a quarter of an hour later with another stern-looking man. "Jane, this is the Home Secretary, Lord Russell."

"Let me guess, you wish me to tell the story?" Jane retorted, now not in the least bit surprised by these visitations from powerful men.

The Home Secretary listened to every word, nodding his head. "You have done well, young Jane. Tell me, what is your story?"

"I was raised in the Southwark Workhouse. It was all I knew; I was taken there when I was just hours old. My mother died shortly afterwards. I was raised an orphan, as I never knew my father." Jane spoke as though she were talking to Grimes and not a man with the power of life and death over Robin. "It was there that I met Violet Rose, of course I knew her as Kate Larkin then, and I know her as that to this day. She was a vindictive, spiteful soul, and in all honesty, I don't believe she's changed at all."

"I've seen Violet Rose on the stage of the Theatre Royal," the Home Secretary said to the Lord Chamberlain. "She put in a fine performance; my wife was most impressed."

"She's a villain, nothing better than a petty pickpocket on the streets."

The two powerful men studied her, considering the points she had made. Both nodded their heads.

"I was then apprenticed by Mr Russell May. He wanted me because of my delicate fingers. He was unable to craft the pieces that I could. It was his belief that a young woman would retain the skill, unlike a young boy, whose fingers would grow large and clumsy as they grew." She paused and scratched her head, thinking of what else she could add. "That is my story, Sirs. I am betrothed to be married to Robin Buckley, who I believe you have in custody over suspicion regarding this crime. I don't know what he's told you, but I'm sure he was outside the goldsmith's that day in an attempt to apprehend Kate Larkin, sorry, Violet Rose as you know her after she committed the crime. I have known him all my life, he too was in the workhouse until he was apprenticed. He would not be a party to a crime."

The Home Secretary studied Jane for a few moments. "We do indeed have a Mr Buckley in custody. From what I am told, he tells much the same story as you."

"He tells the same story because it is true, sir."

The Home Secretary and the Lord Chamberlain exchanged murmurs with each other.

"Wait here," the Lord Chamberlain said.

"Sir? Might I be permitted water? I am very thirsty," Jane almost pleaded.

"I shall have some sent in," he said with a nod of his head.

Ten minutes later, a footman dressed in red opened the door. He had a golden tray in his hand which had upon it a jug of water, a pot of tea, a plate of sandwiches, and small squares of cake. "With the compliments of the Lord Chamberlain, Ma'am." He gave Jane a small bow as he left.

Ma'am, thought Jane. After four recitals of her story, it seemed she had gone up in the world.

CHAPTER 32

Once the footman had excused himself from the chamber, Jane rose, poured herself a glass of water and a cup of tea, and set about devouring the dainty sandwiches assembled on the fine porcelain plate before her.

Strangely, she found herself thinking of Mrs Bird, the old matron at the workhouse. If only she could see Jane now. Here she was at Buckingham Palace, the residence of the Queen of England, being served sandwiches and tea by a footman as if she herself was nobility. The events of this extraordinary day had taken a turn that could only be described as bizarre.

Yet, unbeknown to Jane, they were about to become far more out of the ordinary.

Just as she'd finished savouring the delightful

squares of spicy ginger cake, the Lord Chamberlain returned.

With an air of authority that had been earned through years of royal service, he promptly dismissed the guards, dispatching them back to the guardroom with a curt nod.

"Jane, will you come with me, please?" he asked in a formal tone.

Jane stood, gathered her carpet bag, and obediently followed the Lord Chamberlain. "Am I in trouble, sir?"

"No, Jane," he said, his stern features softening into a reassuring smile, "quite the opposite."

Jane followed him up another grand flight of stairs and along a corridor, its floor lined with a carpet of the deepest red. As they passed by numerous rooms, she found herself marvelling at their grandeur. The ornate walls were adorned with enormous portraits, the gazes of long-deceased royals following her. The elegant statues stood in silent judgement, surrounded by an array of exquisite furniture that whispered tales of opulence. Porcelain vases, delicate yet brimming with history, adorned the tables and mantelpieces.

The Lord Chamberlain stopped outside a door. "I believe you know the lady inside," he said, knocking gently before stepping in.

Jane was stunned to see the Countess of Stanhope seated in the centre of the room. By her side was a young woman, whose striking resemblance to the countess led Jane to assume this must be Lady Wilhelmina.

"I will leave you for now. I will return in roughly fifteen minutes, Lady Stanhope," he said.

"Thank you, Lord Chamberlain. Jane, please come in."

Jane stepped slowly into the room, her gaze immediately drawn to the magnificently painted ceiling, depicting semi-naked men and women who Jane assumed were meant to be celestial figures.

"It's magnificent, isn't it?" the countess asked, following Jane's awe-struck gaze to the painted heavens above. "Jane, this is my daughter, Lady Wilhelmina."

"It's a pleasure to meet you, Lady Wilhelmina," Jane greeted, her voice barely above a whisper as she tore her eyes away from the breathtaking ceiling.

Suddenly she was consumed with guilt. It had been her idea to insert the counterfeit diamonds into this innocent girl's new brooch for the coronation. It was, however, a necessary evil to finally bring about Mr May's downfall.

"I am terribly sorry about your brooch, my lady." Jane's face flushed. "I'm always given the gems to insert into various pieces by Mr May. I've had my suspicions for some time, but due to my position, I was unable to say anything." It was the only lie she had uttered today.

"I completely understand, Jane," Wilhelmina responded. "My mother tells me you've crafted some exceptional pieces for us in the past."

"Please, have a seat," the countess said kindly. "I've been told about your recent adventures. You've shown great courage."

"Thank you," Jane replied, again finding her face turning crimson. She always found it hard to accept compliments. " Can I ask why are you here at the Palace, Lady Stanhope? I actually went to your house earlier today but was told you were absent. I intended then to tell you about my suspicions."

"The maids who will attend to Her Majesty during the coronation had a rehearsal planned this afternoon, and I accompanied my daughter. We've been informed about the situation. So, you believe there are fake diamonds in this brooch?" Lady Stanhope held out the small piece in her hand.

"It seems I was fortunate that you were here, so I can explain. Yes, I'm afraid I suspect four diamonds to be counterfeit. If you take the piece to a reputable goldsmith, I'm sure they'll be able to identify the false stones for you."

"And previous pieces?" the countess queried, her gaze firm on Jane.

"To the best of my knowledge, there are none in the others," Jane responded. "Mr May would give me what he would refer to as special stones. When he first started I was none the wiser, but over the years as I understood more, the deeper my fears grew." Her face suddenly lit up, remembering two sheets of parchment. "I have something here. I should've given these to one of the gentlemen earlier to help validate my story."

She reached into her carpet bag and extracted the two sheets she'd been keeping under her attic bedroom floorboards. These two sheets of parchment held the power to validate her tale and implicate Mr May.

Over many months as she plotted Mr May's downfall, she'd sneak into his office while he was out. She remembered many of the pieces she'd created into which Mr May presented her with 'special' stones to be inserted. She'd simply referred to Mr May's thick, black, leather ledgers where he kept his accounts, and jotted down the names of the pieces, the clients, and the prices charged. Though she had little doubt that she may have missed a few, here she had an incriminating list of at least 35 pieces belonging to various high-profile individuals within

London. She knew when a goldsmith checked the gems, he would find the fakes.

She handed over the list to the countess. She was sure it would be enough to ensure that Mr May would be imprisoned for a considerable time.

"I find myself puzzled, Jane," the countess began. "Initially, you identified yourself as the jeweller who worked on my first piece, but as I've gotten to know you, I've come to understand that you're actually Russell May's daughter? But I understand from your story today, you are actually his apprentice."

"It was quite a complicated circumstance, Lady Stanhope," Jane replied.

She swiftly recounted her story of becoming an apprentice at the Southwark Workhouse. She explained how she had quickly discerned that Russell and Carol May were each pursuing different objectives. "Carol really pined for a daughter's presence, and not having a mother of my own, I naturally grew close to her. She insisted I call her mother which I did willingly. He, however, only decided to call me his daughter when it suited him. He did not wish to introduce an apprentice from the workhouse to clients such as yourself, Lady Stanhope. So it suited him to call me daughter in front of clients. He felt that people would accept a woman working on their pieces if she was family and, without sons, people would have believed I was his heir." She paused for a moment to gather her thoughts. "Outside of those meetings, he rarely called me daughter, I think I can but recall one occasion. Unfortunately, the crimes that you already know of are not his only fault. It distressed me deeply to witness the anguish Mr May inflicted on my mother over those final years. I won't delve into the specifics - the tale is too sordid."

Lady Stanhope nodded gently, casting a glance towards her daughter. Jane surmised she was about the same age as her, though undoubtedly not as worldly. Jane anticipated that the countess would not relish the telling of tales in front of her daughter of clandestine meetings between Russell May and Violet Rose in the drawing room of the Goldsmiths and how he had made the young maid with child.

"And what of your future after all this commotion settles?" Lady Stanhope enquired, her gaze steady on Jane.

"In terms of employment, I'm not entirely certain. I hope to earn a goldsmith's licence from Goldsmiths Hall someday. But if that is possible, I am not sure. Perhaps you aren't fully aware, Lady Stanhope, but I am betrothed to Robin Buckley, your assistant comptroller. I grew up with him in the workhouse and encountered him again after I began delivering the pieces to you."

"I've heard some whispers," the countess admitted, smiling slightly. "I am pleased for you."

"I do hope that Robin will be released from custody soon, and that he will retain his position with you?" Jane looked at the countess expectantly.

"If Robin has committed no wrongs, then rest assured he will keep his position, Jane," the countess replied kindly.

There was a sudden rap at the door which opened to reveal the Lord Chamberlain. "She is ready, Countess."

The countess nodded briskly. "I must bid you farewell, Jane. I appreciate your efforts in bringing this matter to my attention. Please know that I hold no blame against you whatsoever. Should you ever require a reference, don't hesitate to ask."

"Come, Jane. She awaits," the Lord Chamberlain interjected.

Jane's confusion must have been evident on her face.

The countess reached out to her, giving her knee a comforting pat, a rare gesture of affection from the aristocracy. "Just be yourself, Jane. You'll do splendidly. She's a delight, truly."

In truth, the words only deepened Jane's confusion. She had no idea what the Lord Chamberlain meant. Nonetheless, she picked up her carpet bag and followed him out of the room after casting a respectful curtsy to the countess and her daughter.

The Lord Chamberlain ushered her through a

grand pair of double doors at the end of the corridor. "Leave your bag there, please, Jane," he instructed, pointing to a table and chair. "Remember, address her as 'Your Majesty' the first time, and then 'Ma'am'. Curtsy when you enter. Only speak when spoken to. The Prime Minister is also present; address him as 'Sir'. Do you understand?"

Suddenly, the realisation struck her. She was about to meet Queen Victoria, the woman she had watched ride in her carriage every Sunday for the past few weeks. The woman for whom she had just saved the coronation.

"But I'm merely an orphan from the workhouse," Jane stammered, a hint of panic bleeding into her voice as her hands frantically attempted to iron out the creases in her dress.

"Don't worry, Jane. As the countess said, just be yourself. You have performed admirably today. The Queen will not be harsh. She wishes to meet you personally and thank you. She knows the full story, as does the Prime Minister," the Lord Chamberlain reassured her.

Jane took a deep breath and nodded.

"Are you ready?"

"Yes," Jane replied with as much confidence as she could muster.

Following the Lord Chamberlain, she walked

across the spacious room towards another set of doors. There, he knocked respectfully.

A faint "Enter" wafted from within in a delicate female voice laced with unmistakable authority. The Lord Chamberlain pushed the doors open, and Jane found herself stepping into the regal presence of Queen Victoria.

CHAPTER 33

*T*he Lord Chamberlain had escorted her inside before closing the door behind them. He stood at the door and gently pushed her a few steps forward. The Queen and the Prime Minister were standing in anticipation of her arrival.

"Jane," Queen Victoria greeted, her voice rich with warmth as if they were old companions. "I'm so glad you could join us."

"The heroine of the hour," Melbourne chimed in, a slight chuckle tinting his words.

It was at this point that Jane remembered what the Lord Chamberlain had said and quickly curtsied.

She kept her eyes cast downward until she rose. Only then did she address the Queen.

"Good afternoon, Your Majesty," Jane managed to say hesitantly as she rose from her curtsy.

"Good afternoon, sir," she directed her greeting towards Lord Melbourne.

What struck her as quite remarkable was the Queen's diminutive stature. She stood probably no taller than five feet, if Jane were to get any closer, she would tower over her. Melbourne appeared as a giant next to the petite monarch.

She had heard tales of the Queen's small stature. It was why she required a new crown. Only now, seeing the Queen in person, did Jane fully comprehend these tales.

"Please take a seat with us, Jane," the Queen invited, gesturing towards an empty chair.

Jane stared at the Queen for just a moment longer. It was almost as if she were back in the master's office in the workhouse, staring up at the portrait of the latest monarch. But this time, the monarch was not confined to a gilded frame. Jane felt as if her legs were leaden. While the Queen had made her feel welcome, Jane still found herself in an unbelievable situation for a workhouse orphan.

She was about to converse with the Queen of England and the Prime Minister.

The Queen gracefully took her seat, her silken skirts pooling around her, followed by Lord Melbourne, and finally, Jane settled down.

She adhered to the Lord Chamberlain's instructions, keeping quiet, mindful not to speak unless spoken to.

"I believe I owe you a great deal of thanks," the Queen declared softly, her voice barely above a whisper, yet resounding in the quiet room.

"I'm sure I did what any good Englishwoman would do," Jane responded, her voice uncertain, struggling to process the enormity of the Queen's gratitude.

"Don't diminish your bravery, young Jane," Lord Melbourne admonished gently, nodding thoughtfully. "It takes great courage to do what you undertook. You unveiled a great conspiracy, and now, thankfully, the coronation can proceed as planned."

"I am sorry for the worry it must have caused you," Jane said. "I was glad to retrieve it."

"I believe I have seen you before in Hyde Park, Jane?" the queen asked, tilting her head to one side as though studying Jane.

Jane felt a warm glow inside her chest. She knew in her heart that she hadn't been imagining those occasions where their eyes had met and locked for just a brief second. She felt privileged, almost singled out, that the Queen had remembered. The Queen must see thousands of subjects in a week, yet she had remembered Jane. "Yes, Ma'am. My betrothed, Robin and I often stroll in the park on Sundays. I always insist that we wait until your carriage passes."

"Your name has been spoken much in these corridors this afternoon, Jane, The Countess of Stanhope holds you in very high regard and I believe you have completed pieces for many of the members of the court," the Queen said.

A blush of pride tinged Jane's cheeks, "She is very kind, Ma'am. Yes, I think there will be quite a display of my jewellery at Westminster Abbey," Jane smiled. She swallowed down the disappointment before adding, "I was only sorry that I could not work on a crown for you. Although Russell May did not deserve your patronage, I can't deny that it would have been quite a claim to have worked on your crown."

"I am certain that what you would have created would have been remarkable," Victoria said, acknowledging her disappointment.

"The Home Secretary tells me that we have apprehended Russell May," Melbourne said. "We are, however, still in pursuit of the actress."

Relief washed over Jane. She was about to get real justice for her mother. "I'm glad you have him." She wondered if Kate Larkin had taken her advice and fled. Although she probably had a hundred places to go to seek refuge in the city. No doubt she would turn up. "Will I need to testify in court against him?" Jane asked. It had been something that had played on her mind.

"Time will tell," replied Melbourne mysteriously.

"And what of my betrothed, Robin Buckley? He works for the countess, and he was apprehended outside Rundell and Bridge. He will be set free, I pray?"

"I believe the Home Secretary has already had him released," said Melbourne. "You can go home tonight, safe in the knowledge that you have done your Queen and country a great service."

She nodded, but her heart sank a little. "I don't believe I have a home now that Mr May is likely to go to prison."

For the first time, there was an air of tension and discomfort in the room. The Queen sat in silence as though thinking of a reply.

Jane's eyes flicked around the room and suddenly she gasped. "Is that the new crown?" she asked, forgetting completely the instructions not to speak unless spoken to. She stared at it with professional wonder. Even without the principal stones, it was magnificent.

"It is," replied the Queen. "Would you like to examine it?"

"It would indeed be an honour," Jane replied, awestruck.

The Queen rose, and Melbourne and Jane followed suit. The Queen moved towards the crown with regal grace, indicating with a flick of her wrist that Jane should join her. The Prime Minister followed a few steps behind, maintaining a respectful distance.

Jane was captivated by the intricate detail of the crown; she feared even this would be too large for the Queen's head. The quality of the work was superb. The various crosses and fleur-de-liss shone with the magic of a thousand diamonds.

"I am fond of the pearls," Victoria commented. "They say they once belonged to Queen Elizabeth, possibly from the necklace her mother wore with the 'B' pendant."

Jane nodded, although she didn't quite understand. She knew Queen Elizabeth's mother was Anne Boleyn, who had met a grisly end at the Tower. However, she couldn't recall ever seeing a depiction of her.

The Black Prince's Ruby lay next to the crown. Jane leaned in to examine the setting for the ruby. Its irregular shape must have posed a great challenge to the craftsman. For a fleeting moment, Jane forgot her surroundings and the dignitaries present. She reached out and picked up the ruby, assessing the setting one final time. With a deft touch, she slotted the ruby into its place.

A gasp escaped Jane's lips as she realised what she had done. She expected to be admonished, or worse. But Melbourne chuckled, "We've been trying to do that all afternoon. John Bridge was on his way. It seems his services are no longer required."

The Queen smiled, "Thank you, Jane, it looks wonderful now." Victoria paused for a second. "You can now truthfully say you worked on the crown for the coronation."

Jane offered her a little smile, and she felt tears in her eyes. She fought them back.

"Well, I thank you one more time for your bravery in this matter, Jane. My thanks will never be enough for the service you have shown me," the Queen offered. "If there is anything that I can ever do to repay you?"

Jane let the silence fall for a few seconds. The expected response would be to demur and offer humble words about doing it all again. But empty words wouldn't put food on the table or improve her situation. She decided to be bold.

"I do have something in mind, Your Majesty."

CHAPTER 34

 hursday 28*th* June 1838

JANE KNEW PERFECTLY well she ought to be bleary-eyed. The guns had been firing in the Royal Park since four in the morning. However, she was anything but. She was wide-eyed with excitement.

"It's not yet seven o'clock, and there are so many people," Robin remarked, almost disbelievingly.

"It's amazing," Jane agreed as they tried to navigate through the throngs of people towards the abbey. "The newspapers reported that the railways were bringing in hundreds of thousands from outside the city. Some estimates suggest that there could be a million people lining the route. Imagine that; a million people watching the Queen." Jane couldn't resist speaking of her as though she were a personal acquaintance.

So much had transpired in the short time since that odd meeting with the Queen and the Prime Minister.

Upon her dismissal from the palace, she found Robin waiting outside the gates for her. They fell into each other's arms.

"Why were you even there?" Jane finally asked, the first words that escaped her lips.

"I'm not sure. I was hoping to intervene, keep you out of it somehow. Then suddenly she emerged from the darkness, confronting me. She said the most dreadful things. She claimed that Grimes was holding you a prisoner in your own bedroom and that you would be accused of the theft after the coronation. Then she whispered that there were men watching and that they would seize me if I attempted to follow her or go back to help you. She patted my arm in the most disconcerting manner, as if I were a puppy," Robin recounted.

Jane shuddered at the revelation. It was that pat in the darkness that had led her to believe that Kate Larkin had passed Robin a package.

"I hesitated for a moment, deciding what to do," Robin continued "Then all those men appeared. By the time they had no doubt ransacked the place and run away, I resolved to go back to try to rescue you from Grimes. It was then that another man appeared from nowhere and grabbed me. I kept telling the police what had happened, but initially, they didn't believe me. As time passed, however, they received messages from somewhere."

"I guess that was my story. I have a tale to tell. You won't believe what just happened."

After buying some bread and cheese, they settled down by the river, waiting until the daylight almost gave way to darkness, and caught up on the day's event. Robin whistled with shock as Jane told how she was taken to see the Queen herself.

Jane told Robin about Kate claiming that she and Robin were lovers. Robin repeatedly insisted that it was not true. It was merely a spiteful lie. Jane already knew this from the look in Kate Larkin's eyes the last time they met. Had that really only been this morning? Nonetheless, it was reassuring to hear it from Robin in person.

"So, what happens now?" Robin asked. "You need somewhere to live, surely?"

Caught up in her predicament and her excitement about the request she had made to the queen, Jane hadn't considered her immediate circumstances.

"Why don't you ask the countess?" Robin suggested, "Given the circumstances, I'm sure she would offer you a bed in the servants' quarters for a while."

The countess was delighted to see her and Robin that evening. She assured Robin that he still had his position and Jane put forward her request after explaining the circumstance. Jane also presented her with the pristine diamonds that should have adorned her daughter's brooch. Jane hastily and rather vaguely explained that she'd found them at the gold-smiths and assumed they were the original pieces intended for the brooch before Russell May had decided to substitute his fakes. It was yet another small lie, but she felt better returning the diamonds to their rightful owner.

In the following days, Rundell and Bridge identi-fied the fakes and provided evidence to the police that would help convict Russell May. They also replaced the fakes with the original diamonds. The countess's daughter would now be able to wear the piece with pride.

Such was the countess's gratitude that she did indeed provide Jane with accommodation, but it wasn't in the servants' quarters, it was in the visi-tors' wing. Jane could scarcely believe her good fortune.

But that wasn't all. Two days later, the countess invited her for tea in the afternoon and presented her with a large envelope.

"Open it," the countess urged, a smile playing on her lips.

Jane complied and pulled out two red cards emblazoned with the royal coat of arms.

It was an invitation to the coronation for both her and Robin, signed by the Earl Marshall himself.

She would be in the abbey to witness the crown being placed on young Queen Victoria's head. The very crown, she fondly remembered, that the Queen had said she had helped create.

And so it was that Jane and Robin found themselves hurrying through the streets, jostling through crowds to reach the abbey. Given the large number of people expected to attend and observe the ceremony, they were due to arrive by eight in the morning, a full three-and-a-half hours before the Queen was set to appear in person.

The countess had shown Jane great favour by lending her a dress that belonged to her own daughter, Lady Wilhelmina. Although the countess had offered to arrange a carriage ride to the abbey, they chose to walk, eager to experience the atmosphere in the same way as the ordinary people around them.

Once the coronation was over, Jane planned to visit one of the Royal Parks to enjoy the lavish entertainment sure to be on display there.

This was a day that would be long remembered, and Jane was going to enjoy it.

Six hours later, the climax of the coronation service was playing out inside the Abbey.

The Archbishop of Canterbury held the new crown high in the air before gently setting it on Queen Victoria's head. Embedded in the crown was the Black Prince's Ruby, the very gem that Jane had set in the crown.

"God save the Queen," the Archbishop proclaimed.

The entire Abbey, filled with thousands of peers, knights of the realm, politicians, leading figures in society and two former workhouse orphans at the very back echoed his words.

"God save the Queen!"

EPILOGUE

1

0 February 1540
St James Palace, London.

JANE HAD NEVER SEEN the Queen look more beautiful.

She wore a dress of white satin adorned with trims of orange flower blossoms. The veil would be the final piece for her wedding day, it was made of Honiton lace. Over two hundred people worked on the veil alone.

"Are you sure you're okay, Jane?" the Queen whispered softly in her ear.

"I'm quite well, Your Majesty," Jane said. "I still have almost three months until my due date. I'm sure the babe won't come before then."

Jane married Robin Buckley just three months after the coronation. She was free from her apprenticeship with Russell May, who was now a convicted fraudster. Interestingly, he was never charged with the theft of the Black Prince's Ruby. The theft was never mentioned in the press. It was clear the authorities did not want to let it be known how close the coronation had come to disaster. There was no need for Jane to testify at the trial because Russell May had pleaded guilty.

She and Robin agreed that a deal must have been struck. He would accept the charges regarding the fraud with the illicit diamonds, and no mention would be made of the Black Prince's Ruby. This would allow Russell May to escape with his life. That's exactly what happened. He was transported to Australia for a minimum of eight years.

The wedding of Jane and Robin was a simple affair. It was held at the church of St. James's in Westminster, close to the tomb of Carol May, the woman Jane considered her mother. Jane proudly wore a small pink brooch, a personal gift from the Queen herself.

Jane imagined that Mrs Johnson would be revelling in today's events. She would be in the kitchens at Buckingham Palace, helping to prepare the wedding day feast. The service would take place in the Chapel

Royal, one of the most ancient royal palaces in London, but the celebrations would continue at the Queen's home in Buckingham Palace. Employing Mrs Johnson was one of the requests Jane had put forward to Her Majesty. Mrs Wilson was also employed somewhere in the Royal household, but she had chosen to work at Windsor Castle, so Jane rarely saw her. The twins, as she suspected, had retired from goldsmithing. Grimes, no doubt, was eking out a living somewhere.

Kate Larkin, the actress known as Violet Rose, had never been found. It seemed to Jane that Kate Larkin had taken her advice. She hoped that one day the woman would become a better person because of all that had happened.

Jane made one request to the Queen for herself: that the Goldsmiths' Hall grant her a license to become a goldsmith in her own right. Unfortunately, it was a request that not even the Queen of England could grant. Jane had not completed her apprenticeship, and the fact that she was a woman was something the senior members of Goldsmiths' Hall simply could not fathom.

Instead, the Queen made Jane a personal offer.

She created the position of Maid of the Queen's Jewels. Essentially, Jane would be responsible for everything related to the Queen's personal collection, from maintaining the pieces to helping dress the Queen.

Jane immediately said yes.

After her marriage to Robin, they had moved into the married servants' quarters in the palace mews. Six months ago, Robin had joined the Royal household himself. The Countess of Stanhope was upset at losing him but fully understood his need to be close to his wife. He became an assistant to the Clerk of the Green Cloth.

Now Jane was pregnant with their first child. When she told the Queen, Victoria was thrilled and had been doting on Jane ever since.

They had been discussing which jewels the Queen should wear for months leading up to the wedding. Jane was amazed at her vast collection. Ultimately, they decided on the Turkish diamonds, a personal gift to the Queen from the Sultan of Turkey.

On the night before the wedding, Prince Albert, soon to become the Queen's husband, presented his betrothed with a sapphire brooch. It was a last-minute addition to the Queen's attire, but she insisted on wearing it.

Jane delicately placed the Turkish diamonds around the Queen's neck, making a few adjustments until she was satisfied. The Queen glanced at herself in the mirror and nodded her head.

"Thank you, Jane. Please go and rest now," the Queen said.

Jane curtsied. "Good luck, Your Majesty."

Victoria smiled. "If Albert and I are as happy as you and young Robin, I will consider myself truly blessed."

ALSO BY ROSIE DARLING

The Ghosts of Winter Orphans

A workhouse orphan, a handsome man with an inheritance and a dangerous dream that brings their world crashing down.

Ada knew that dreams and aspirations were dangerous. She knew that the wolves were waiting to come to the door.

When her husband's reckless dreams failed and the wolves came, they were driven into the slums of Whitechapel. Ada steals to survive and build a new future for her family without fear.

When ghosts of her past visit Ada, she is forced to reassess everything she knows to be true.

Memories of the horrific workhouse come flooding back, and Ada will do anything to avoid a return.

But her ghosts know what will happen if she continues. Will she heed the warnings in time to save herself?

As the lines between reality and fiction blur and the stakes grow higher, will Ada have the courage to chase her own dreams, or will fear consume her?

DOWNLOAD NOW

WHAT HAPPENED TO KATE LARKIN?

Get a free short story now

The Redemption of Kate Larkin

Thrust into exile after a bold and reckless crime; Kate Larkin abandons England with her sights set on New York City. Her goal? To carve out a new existence using her adept skills at beguiling men.

However, a surprise encounter and turn of events on the ship that took her across the ocean changed everything for Kate.

Suddenly, young Flora is thrust into her world, triggering a sense of responsibility Kate had never planned for. But then realises that she cannot become saddled with another woman's child.

Kate resolves to ensure the proper care is given to the girl on their arrival in New York.

But Kate finds she can't escape the memories of her past as easily as she can escape the shore of England.

Will Kate find the life she is seeking? Or does redemption lie in a direction she never anticipated, one that veers away from her plotted course?

DOWNLOAD NOW

Printed in Great Britain
by Amazon